Little Star of Bela Lua

Little Star of Bela Lua

Luana Monteiro

DELPHINIUM BOOKS

Harrison, New York • Encino, California

FIRST EDITION

Designed by Jonathan D. Lippincott

Library of Congress Catoging-in-Publication Data
is available upon
request.

Library of Congress Control Number: 2005924879

ISBN 1883285267

Thanks to Walasse Ting for permission to use his beautiful painting for our cover.

Para
Josefa Gomes da Silva

Contents

Little Star of Bela Lua

A NOVELLA

A Fish in the Desert

(SATURNINO SERTANEJO)

No one remembers exactly when or how the fish, that bizarre and calamitous creature, with its strange smile and fins of foreign colors, arrived in Jatobá. No one except Otália Ermerentino, whose life it changed forever. It came unannounced, like a gust of rain or an apparition of the Virgin Mary. But unlike the Virgin, whose manifestations, according to local lore, occurred exclusively under lambent midday skies, the fish appeared in the cool hours of dawn, at the small adobe hut Otália shared with her husband, Justino, on the outskirts of town. Why it chose the old couple as opposed to, say, Padre Miguel Inácio, or Don Armando, or even the pious widow Gertrudes, remained as much of a mystery to the people of Jatobá as its origins. Otália knew, however, that the fish had been an answer to her endless pleas, a gift from the Virgin or God himself, who, instead of quickening an old, infertile womb—imagine the scandal among the neighbors (not that God was incapable of such marvels, but she was no Sarah, and Justino certainly no Abraham)—offered her something that, in a region where oceans and rivers exist only in the fevered imaginations and dreams of its citizens, was nothing short of a miracle. Saturnino, the name Otália tenderly gave the creature, became known throughout the backlands of Pernambuco as the fish of cursed blessings.

1

She discovered him one Wednesday in January, the hottest and driest month of the year. On the previous evening, after the customary dinner of fried eggs and yucca, Otália and her husband sat outside, on chairs Justino had crafted from straw and wood, and drank their coffee while the night cast its slow net of shadows over the parched land. The chapel bells pealed six times, prompting Otália and Justino to cross themselves. A few neighbors wandered by: Eusébio with his stench of *cana* liquor; Manuel and his two skinny cows, which he swore were inherited from a distant relative; Abigália and her eighth belly, no doubt another boy, for her husband only made males; Gertrudes wearing the black veils of her widowhood. "*Boa noite, Dona Talinha, boa noite, Seu Justino,*" they called out upon passing, and the couple raised their aluminum cups in response, "*Boa noite.*" The man and woman exchanged no words. Forty years of marriage had taught them an unspoken language.

When the diamond of the first star shone that night, Otália repeated her wish of forty years: "Mary Virgin, mother of God, grant me a child so that I may give him the sweetest love of all, the love only a mother can give. In return I will teach him your rosary as soon as he learns his first words; will send him to church every Sunday; will baptize, commune, and confirm him; will teach him all the prayers for all the saints, yours above all, that he may adore you and praise you, amen." She said it now more out of habit than hope, with eyes shut, fists tight, brows creased, lips moving soundlessly. Justino too had a wish, but he kept it a secret even from his wife, for such are the wishes of men; sometimes they remain locked inside until the moment of death, when delirium tricks the brain and the mouth utters: "I wish I had seen the ocean."

Otália opened her eyes.

"Justino, look at that." She pointed toward the horizon, where a dim yellow moon slowly waxed.

"Yes, the moon."

"No, above it. Don't you see? There, next to the star——"

Justino stood, shading his eyes as if protecting them from the sun. He saw the incredible but unmistakable sight before him and said, *"Vixe Maria,* a cloud, a dark cloud, filled with rain!"

"May God hear you, *homi.* Quick, I'll get the pots, you feed the donkey, and let's pray that after nine months without a drop, Santo Antonio has taken pity on us!"

She ran inside, cursing the two chickens for being perpetually underfoot, and rushed out with a pile of pots, pans, and bowls that she distributed around the small yard to collect the water from heaven. Before joining her, Justino, with his old limp, relieved himself in the roofless outhouse, a hole he had dug and surrounded with a lattice of wood, zinc, and clay. The money Justino earned from working in the fields barely bought the daily bread; years ago, when Don Armando's sons were still children, Otália had brought home a small salary from tending the boys. But boys soon become men, and such are the contradictions of life that the rich are never as fertile as common folk, so the extra income was short-lived. How they had managed to survive all these years, only God knew. They witnessed the miracle of the multiplying loaves each night at the dinner table.

Lulled by the sound of his own urine, Justino heard the shouts of Pascoal, a self-proclaimed philosopher and messenger of truth who predicted the death of the sun, cosmic collisions, knights on dark horses, worms that never die, the advent of the angel, beasts from the sea. "Seven beasts, and so near I can smell them," he would proclaim, his eyes alight with apocalyptic fervor. Justino thought it unlikely that Pascoal could smell anything over the stench of liquor that exuded from his skin.

That evening, the rain cloud near, the last sound Justino

heard before entering the house were the echoes of Pascoal's sermon, "Jatobá is found, he's coming, my friends, be ready, he's
coming, he's found us. . . ."

Idiot, Justino thought. Not even the end of the world would
find this place.

Otália swept the living room and kitchen. She blew the dust
from the picture on the wall, the only one of the couple together,
taken on the day of their wedding after hours of travel to the sole
photographer in the region. In it the handsome young man, a
thin sculpted mustache defining his upper lip, grips the girl's
hands as if afraid the camera may steal her away. She wears an
innocent smile, already unveiling the dignity of a woman familiar with suffering. Now her face resembled the land—brown,
burned, carved by lines like deep, empty riverbeds.

"Calm down, *muié*, you'll wear yourself out like that."
Justino removed his shirt, exposing a broad scarred back, and lay
on the straw mattress, the one on which his wife surrendered her
virginity years ago. But Otália, immersed in thought, did not hear
him. She lit the kerosene lamp beneath the image of *Padim* Ciço,
patron saint of the Sertão. Above the lamp's nozzle, a crescent of
light flickered, then shrank into a dense pebble of fire. Otália sat
on a chair by the window, untangling the knots of her long blue-
black tresses, not a trace of white in them, with a green plastic
comb. The smell of impending rain filled her with hope. The
entire firmament was one great cloud, certainly a reflection of
everyone's collective prayers, proof that, as the saying goes, the
cloud is provided according to the thirst. She thought of her own
pleas. If she could have chosen between blessings, a deeper thirst
would have been quenched, even if it meant another nine dry,
infernal months.

She felt selfish, ashamed. Her throat tightened, and her eyes
welled with frustration. Her heart (she opened both hands on her
chest) pounded blindly, a stubborn drum. She looked over at her

husband to make sure he didn't see her in this state, afraid of having to answer if he asked her, "What's wrong, woman? Why do you cry when we've been blessed?" for her anguish originated in a faraway place, devoid of reason. Once assured that Justino had fallen asleep, poor man, worn out from so much work, Otália started to cry, and not even a minute passed before it started to rain.

2

"Wake up, Talinha, wake up!"

Otália heard her name echoing from afar. She opened her eyes and saw her husband. She straightened her back on the chair, picked up the comb which had slipped from her hand, and glanced outside at the rain no longer there. Dawn seeped through the wall's cracks. "If I hadn't seen it with my own eyes," she mumbled in a sleepy voice, "I wouldn't have believed that it rained last night."

"Yes, you would," Justino said, smiling, "because the bowls are filled with water. Look."

She saw that he had already collected them and was in the process of filling the main bucket. "But I didn't even hear you get up!"

"I tried to call you, but you were smiling in your sleep and didn't budge. Here, I made you some coffee."

"And you?"

"I've had mine," he lied, for there had been enough for barely one cup.

She sipped her coffee, placed the cup in the sink, and headed for the outhouse, barefoot. Once inside she pulled up her dress and squatted over the hole, but a sound like boiling water stopped her short. The latrine was brimming with the previous night's rain. She crossed herself and stepped back, her eyes riveted on the glowing creature that swam in the murky liquid. An intense brilliance emanated from its scales: radiant colors, like sunlight through stained glass. A shout of fright escaped her.

A fish. Oh my God, a fish!

Justino, shaving in front of a cracked mirror, heard her scream. He followed the sound to the outhouse and saw Otália, one hand still holding the thin white dress above her knees, the other pointing at the latrine. He calmly shook his head from side to side, wiping the traces of soap from his face with his sleeve.

"Poor thing," he said. "What misfortune to end up in this end of the world."

"But . . . but Justino, how could it possibly have gotten here?"

"The rain, *muié*! The rain, of course! What other way?" He scratched his head and inspected his fingernails.

"Justino, have you ever seen one of those things before?"

"What you mean? Of course!"

"But here, Justino?"

"Well."

"Okay then, since you always have an explanation for everything, Mister, will you please explain this strange light?"

Justino examined the air. "Otália, what in the world are you talking about?"

"Don't you see it? The air is full of colors!" She waved her hands.

"I don't see anything," he said abruptly. "The light is from the sun, the same light of every morning right after sunrise, and speaking of which, I have to go. Untie the donkey. I have to finish getting ready."

"But what the hell will I do with this fish, Justino?" she asked, her voice frantic.

"Nothing. What can you do? Leave it there. . . . it's half dead already. Just put some earth over the thing later, so that it won't stink the place up more than it already does." He glanced at it one more time. "Damn, it's ugly!" he said, and withdrew toward the house.

No. She was certain it didn't belong to the Sertão. And Justino was wrong. It wasn't half dead, and it wasn't ugly. She crouched over the hole and studied the fish more closely—the plumpness of its gleaming body, the vigor of its circular, agitated swimming, its sad smile. Poor thing, she thought, you're a long way from the ocean, then considered that it could well have been a freshwater fish. Who knew? Maybe beneath the sand and rock, deep, deep down, a clean blue river bore fat shiny fish. God's odd sense of humor was known even in Jatobá, where faith and hope were the only riches one possessed, except for those few who owned a cow or two.

The longer she stared, the closer she felt to the beautiful orphaned creature. What sorrowful eyes. If it had a voice, she thought, it would say, "I'm here, take me." Then she remembered her husband, and hurried out to untie the donkey, whispering from the doorway, "I'll be right back."

Outside, a typical Wednesday morning despite the rain of the previous night: some men on their way to work; others, less fortunate, already on their way to the local *venda* to drown their frustrations in shots of *cana*. This was the day of the week when Padre Miguel Inácio visited Jatobá for confessional, and already a group of women in Wednesday dress strutted by, clutching rosaries in belated attempts to compensate for a week of neglected penance. Among them, a rumor circulated that Padre Miguel Ignacio went about naked beneath his robe. All day they would kneel by the pulpit of the chapel under the five sacred wounds of a crucified Christ, lighting votive candles and intoning with competitive passion countless Ave Marias and Pai-Nossos, until the handsome priest arrived to redeem them. A few round-bellied children, clad in dirty underwear, played nearby with a flat bicycle tire and a switch. Otália kissed her husband on the cheek and watched man and donkey—the latter's bushy tail never relieved from the task of repelling horseflies—meander up the road leading out of town. Once sure that no one watched her, she rushed inside and filled the largest clay bowl in the house with the previous night's precious rain. Precisely, like a chemist, she anointed the water with a dab of salt, certain that the fish was from the ocean. She carried the bowl to the outhouse and carefully transferred the animal from one water to the other, enjoying for a moment the touch of the slick, writhing body between her fingers. She didn't care about the filth it left on her hands.

Otália stepped out into the yard with her prize. Her body trembled; a cold finger of sweat descended her spine, as her vision darkened and her legs quaked. She fell to her knees, and as the bowl slipped to the ground, she felt a violent wrenching in her stomach and felt the world's weight on her bladder. Before she could stop it, a warm torrent gushed down her legs. "*Virgem Santa*, what's happening to me?" she murmured. And the truth descended on her. She was living what Mary went through with Jesus, Abigália with her seven boys, and all of womankind since the beginning of creation, the pain she had secretly prayed for every day of her life. She glanced over at the bowl, whispered a faint "Saturnino." The last thing she saw was two slow, yellow tears rolling from its eyes.

3

The person who found her was Clemilda—black, stocky, and blind in one eye, a woman who had grown up on the same street as Otália. The townspeople said that any rumor that reached Clemilda spread instantly to the rest of the world, that Clemilda knew events before God himself. They called her *Radio de Deus*,

Radio of God. No detail escaped her good eye. She could give an omniscient account of everyone's possessions, lovers, habits, likes, and dislikes, so it was perfectly natural that she be the one to find Otália and thus relate the story of the fish's first miracle. The heat had already set in, the relentless, solid heat of that January. Clemilda hesitantly shook the unconscious woman by the leg.

"Otália! Otália!"

Otália opened her eyes and crawled to the bowl. She hugged it in an attempt to hide her treasure, but Clemilda was already questioning in her bird voice: "Goodness, what happened to you? Where the hell did you find this fish? What are you gonna do with it? It looks poisonous."

Otália stumbled to her feet, struggling to regain her composure.

"Get away from it, Clemilda, this doesn't concern you!" Her voice took on a harder edge. "And I would appreciate it if you kept this between us, if for no other reason than the memory of our mothers' friendship."

"Come on, Talinha, what can you hide from me after all these years?"

Otália pressed the bowl to her chest, embracing it with both arms, and said: "Excuse me, I must pass."

"Wait! Something happened to you. Are you all right? I don't think you're well, Otália!" She blocked Otália's path. Otália tried to push her aside, but Clemilda grabbed Otália by the shoulders. "You need help! Look! You peed all over yourself!"

"Let go!" Otália pulled away from her grip. Water from the bowl splashed her dress, a few drops sprinkling Clemilda. "There's a limit to everything!" Then, as though she had pronounced an incantation, Clemilda fell to the ground like a severed rope, one hand over each eye.

"I can see!" Her first shout conveyed disbelief, but her skepticism soon evaporated. "I can see! I can see out of both eyes!" She embraced Otália; more water spilled from the bowl. "Oh my *Jesusinho*, a miracle!" She knelt on the ground, both hands raised toward heaven. "Jesus, Mary, Virgin Mother of the Seven Sorrows, *Santa Aparecida*, and Our Lady of Conception, I thank you with all my heart!"

Otália wanted to disappear inside her house. From the street she heard voices coming closer, drawn by Clemilda's manic litany of saints, angels, and archangels. She remained mute as, one by one, people drifted into the yard, crowding around the two women. She could feel the fish thrashing through the clay and thought that never had she held anything so alive. Her neighbor's faces blended before her, confused, hot, ghastly, terribly animated. She made her way through them and walked toward the house, the bowl in her arms.

She barred the door and staggered into the room. She placed the bowl on top of the bed and slumped beside it, both hands clasped on her lap, musing at length on the strange sparkling light—the light only she saw—her expression weary, skeptical, fascinated. "Whatever happened out there, I know it was you," she said. The fish, now appeased and calm, might as well have been floating in midair, because seen from above, it was impossible to distinguish the fine, evanescent line between air and water.

Finally, she thought, I can pay my promise to the Virgin. It wasn't exactly what she had prayed for, but a miracle nonetheless, and given the scarcity of miracles these days . . . Otália wrapped the rosary between her hands and knelt by the bed. At that moment the light from the bowl was so strong that even with eyes shut Otália saw it pulsate; where before there had been only darkness between her closed eyelids, a moonless night, now a constellation of exploding stars lit the corners of her mind.

"Thanks be to you, *Virgem Santa*, Mother of God, for giving me what I could not have on my own, and for not letting me die without feeling a mother's love." She tried to block out the awed murmurs of the crowd and the continuing ravings of Clemilda, which still reached her from the yard. Otália knew that it was only a matter of time before all of Jatobá heard what had occurred. She hoped that the people would not associate Clemilda's healing with the bowl, for if indeed they realized the origin of that miracle, never again would there be peace for her and Justino. Not to mention Saturnino, poor thing, who would have to cure all kinds of infirmities, abundant in the Sertão. She could see it already: The curious would journey from all over the country to witness his miracles; priests and bishops would come to assure that he was no spawn of the devil; criminals would plot to steal him and then sell him to a circus or a scientist; powerful men would try to take him from her, would bring papers ordering it, so that in the name of evolution they could open his body to dissect his soul. These unpleasant thoughts infused her Holy Marys, Credos, and Our Fathers. She wrapped the rosary around the bowl, promising to continue later, and peeked through the window. Clemilda was marching in the direction of the chapel, followed by a noisy throng of men, women, children, dogs, and chickens.

The afternoon shadows already stretched past the house. Soon Justino would return.

4

He had already heard it from three people on his way home. As soon as he walked into the hut, he demanded, "What's all this fuss about a miracle in our yard?" Justino cherished his reputation as a hard worker and a private, pious man, and was quick to address any hint of defamation to his character. (A long time ago a rumor went around that he chronically spilled his seed and thereby diminished his virility. But Justino was such an exemplary Catholic—rigorously attending Sunday mass and all major masses of the year, unimpeachable during Lent, never swearing, never raising a *cana* bottle, always pulling out the crucifix from under his shirt and kissing it when passing the chapel or the priest—that the gossip never really caught on, the gossipers grudgingly forced to admit the unlikelihood of his committing such a venal sin.)

Otália, clean, combed, perfumed, and prepared for this predictable reaction, said, "Come in and sit down. I'll explain everything."

The house smelled of yucca and toasted bread. On the hearth a pot of *cuzcuz* was simmering, and two empty glasses sat on the table. She made his plate, mixing together the yucca, the *cuzcuz*, and two fried eggs just the way he liked; filled both glasses with cheap brandy given them by Don Armando as a Christmas present. With a pair of tongs she plucked a live coal from the fire and lit the kerosene lamp. Tamed by the intoxicating aroma of his wife's cooking, Justino almost forgot his concern altogether. In a much softer tone, he asked her the reason for the drinks.

"Well, I was boiling water for coffee, but when I opened the can there was nothing left. And you know how dangerous it is to eat *cuzcuz* with nothing to wash it down."

"Whatever happened to water?" He took a sip from the cup.

"*Ai, homi!* Water, wine, what's the difference? All I know is that today we must celebrate."

And she proceeded to tell him the whole story, from the time he had left for work until right before he had come home, when the fish, so adorable, so endearing, ate a handful of *cuzcuz* and a piece of yucca.

"Shit, Otália! Have you gone completely crazy?" He spoke through a mouthful of food. "That's all we need, a fish that eats like a man, and worse yet, Clemilda with *two* good eyes! Imagine what's gonna happen now! She'll be seeing through walls!"

Otália stared at her husband for a moment, stupefied. "Have you heard a word of what I said, Justino?"

"Yes, Otália, I have. And now I can die. You know why? Because now I can say that I've heard it all!"

Otália quickly averted her face so as not to burden Justino with her tears, but he sensed them, and was overcome with something closer to awe than pity, for in their whole life together, only four times had he witnessed this event, infinitely more rare than rain. The first time was on their wedding night, her tears a subtle elixir of fear and joy; then, at the wake of her beloved *painho*, an old-fashioned man whose love of the world, and particularly of Otália, was as fierce as the sun of the Sertão. She also cried in Pernambuco, at the doctor's clinic, where her insistence on getting a second, third, fourth, and final opinion had led them. The last tears Justino saw from her were shed four years later, with the passing of her beatific mother, Juana, aptly named after the blind saint of Santiago.

He stood and squatted by her side of the table, drawing her close to him. "Don't cry, Talinha, don't cry."

"Justino, can't you see we've been blessed?"

"What if the thing is a curse?"

In a feeble voice, she corrected him. "Saturnino."

"What?"

"I said he has a name—Saturnino."

"Ah, for God's sake!" Justino knew from experience that he was helpless before his wife's intransigence. He held his head between his hands, fingers plunged into the thatch of white hair as if clinging to his thoughts or, on the contrary, trying to stop them altogether—a snake, a fish, a temptation. Otália felt his frustration and shared it. How could she ever explain to him the complexities of a mother's heart, the simplicity of a mother's love, when not even she understood? She might as well have been describing the sky to a blind man who has never seen it—*It is blue*, she would say. *What does blue look like*, he would ask. *It has a sun. What is a sun? I don't know, I have never looked directly at it. Why not? Because if I look, I'll become blind like you. Then what is the use of having eyes, if you look but do not see?* "Love," a word so short, so simple, had absolutely no definition, for the sublime can never be described by the tongue, by a name, by a label, like Otália, orphan of her own child. All her life she had felt that love haunting her, but no one had ever come to claim it. Until now. On the surface it seemed ridiculous, insane even, that she should feel this way about a fish. Not sure of what else to say, she let out three faint words: "But the miracle—"

"*Miracle?* Otália, a miracle is what happens in this house every evening when we sit at this table to eat. You yourself have said it hundreds of times." He tapped her fork, smeared with a dollop of cold *cuzcuz*. "This is a miracle. Whatever happened today, whatever that was, shouldn't have happened. If indeed it was that animal—"

"Saturnino!"

"As I was saying—" his tone assumed a rare gravity—"you can't get in the way of God's plans. Nothing on this earth comes without a price, you know that. Even Jesus had to pay for his miracles."

"How do you know this wasn't God's plan?"

"How do I know? Because no sane God would give Clemilda another eye, that's why!"

She couldn't contain a small smile. "Yes, but when have you seen a fish like this around here? Can't you see? And what was I to do? Leave the poor thing in the latrine? Animals are also children of God, you know."

Dourly, with a resigned hopelessness, Justino told her, "Do whatever you want." He could only pray for her to be careful. He stood, rubbed his bad leg, and retreated to the outhouse. The evening sky had shifted from blue to the somber shades of night.

Otália could see two lights in the house, that of the red moon outside her window, and the aura from the bowl nestled on the bed, flickering yet constant, like a sun that hides behind the leafy canopy of a tree. She removed the bowl from the bed, making sure Saturnino was still inside, and placed it under the image of *Padim* Ciço. When Justino returned, she pretended to be fully engrossed in her actions. She cleared the table, putting away the pots, clean ones on one pile, dirty ones on another. After washing them, she unwrapped the rosary from the bowl and mouthed her evening prayer.

Otália had been kneeling only for scant minutes when she heard a faint grunt. She opened her eyes and saw her husband sprawled on his left side, stroking his cramped, swollen leg. She rose and searched for the tube of liniment prescribed for the donkey, who had recently acquired a mysterious growth on one of its shanks. After positioning Justino's leg over her lap, she massaged it with the ointment, first his hip, then his thigh, until he gradually succumbed to the balm of sleep, facing the wall so as to hide the shame felt by men when at the mercy of women.

As he snored, she gently moved his leg to the side and got up. She dipped her cupped hands into Saturnino's bowl, in the same way one does when drinking from a stream, and released the water over Justino's leg, following with a fierce rub. Then she lay beside him.

5

Justino arose before the rooster's second crow. Otália watched him through drowsy, half-closed lids. He put on his pants, opened the window, yawned, and walked outside with a brimming bucket of water for the donkey. She made an intense effort to hide the joy that came over her, quelled the impulse to run, hug him, and say,

You're healed, *querido*! Look, your leg is the same as before the accident, you will suffer no more!" But when he stepped back inside she pretended to be asleep. She felt his fingertips run over her cheek, felt a soft kiss there, and thought, Jesus, he still hasn't noticed.

"*Bom dia,* Talinha." They still greeted each other with words of affection after forty years.

"*Bom dia,*" she replied, and faced him. All the familiar traces of pain were gone from his eyes. "How's your leg?" she asked.

"My leg?"

"Yes, your leg. How is it?"

Justino rested a questioning hand there. He looked at his wife, frightened, puzzled. He walked in a circle, lifted his knees, jumped, and sat down again, covering his open mouth.

"*Meu Deus*, it's fine! My leg is fine. It doesn't hurt!" He saw the bowl, his wife biting her lips.

"Otália, you didn't—"

"Do you believe me now?" She held his arm, but he yanked it away.

"You—you had no right to do this, Otália. That pain was rightfully given to me by God, and now, now that thing took it away!" He pointed a condemning finger at the bowl. Then he put on a shirt, the same one as the day before, and picked up his hat. "You can't just go on changing the order of things. From now on I don't want to hear about this animal anymore. I want nothing to do with it, you hear? Nothing!"

"You ingrate!" she shouted as he stormed out. She stood at the porch, until his outline merged with the donkey's, then with the dust. She shut the door and commenced her morning rituals, a little differently today, since instead of eating with her husband she ate alone with the fish.

An hour or two later, Abigália appeared in the window, breathless. "*Cumade*, I need a word with you. I'm sorry I'm here so early." Her round, red face was oily with sweat. Otália gestured for her to come in and fetched a chair from the table for the panting woman, who held her immense stomach with both hands, trying to regain her breath. Otália brought her some water.

"It's all right, I've been up for a long time. Tell me."

"You know I'm due any time now." Otália nodded, placing an absent hand on the woman's belly. "I heard what happened with Clemilda yesterday. She walked by my house throwing a scandal, saying a miracle had happened, 'Thank you, *fulano*, thank you, *cicrano*, I can see. . . .' People are saying it happened in your yard, and that you have something to do with it. That's why I came, *cumade*." She grabbed Otália's hands and brought them to her lips. "You don't know what a burden it's been to raise seven boys. All these years I've been praying for a girl, but when the time comes and Jurema lifts up the new baby, what's the first thing I see? Two big, purple balls. I love my boys, may God bless each one of them, but they grow up, become men, learn to drink, and that's it, end of story. With a girl it'd be different, I know it."

"But *cumade*, you never know, this may be the girl you've been praying for."

"No, it's a boy." She leaned over, whispering, "Last night, when me and my husband were in bed, you know, talking, I heard him cry. The same cry as all the other ones, the cry of a *macho*! Then it was me who began to cry, the little ones woke up crying; it was a big mess. I knew you were my only hope. I didn't even wait for the sun to rise—I left without telling anyone and came straight here. And I was outside when Justino left, Otália." She crossed herself, and Otália at once understood what Abigália noticed but dared not say: the absence of a limp in Justino's walk. "Please help me, *cumade*. If I see another set of those swollen purple things, I'll die instantly." Abigália clutched the old woman's hands, nervous, hopeful, as when one clasps the hands of a priest or a doctor.

Otália thought of her husband's words, about changing the order of things, but found no sense in them whatsoever. When had there ever been a time when order was present in the world? She regarded the shining bowl under *Padim* Ciço. Poor creature, it barely arrives in this world, and already so much burden on its shoulders. She, like Saturnino, had no choice in this. And anyway, how could anyone walk away from such suffering, such hope? "Lift up your dress," she said, picking up the bowl.

Abigália hoisted the dress to her breasts, exposing the rotund dark skin, tattooed with stretch marks, tight as a tambourine's hide, and beautiful, more beautiful to Otália than the infamous red moon of the Sertão. Otália instructed her to close her eyes, cupped her hands and released the water over Abigália's womb.

Abigália kissed Otália's hands. Before leaving she asked would Otália be her daughter's godmother. The old woman, doubtful as to whether the water would perform this third miracle (although the bowl shone with more intensity than ever), said, "Let's wait and see, Abigália, God writes straight through crooked lines," something she had heard from her mother many times but had not fully understood until this week. Her body felt drained, torpid; her legs trembled. Later she would go to the store for coffee, *cuzcuz*, matches, and a few other things that she'd pay for on credit with Justino's forthcoming salary, for this month's had already been used up. For now, she only wanted to rest. She lay on the right side of the mattress, propped on her elbows, gazing at the serene Saturnino. His eyes, wide open, stared with the same absent expression as always, and she wondered, Do fish sleep? She examined the patterns of his scales meticulously, as if tracing them with her fingertips, and was reminded of a time when, as a little girl, in one of the rare trips with *painho* to Campina Grande, a gypsy had read her palm. She could not recall the woman's fortune, but that ageless face, and the firm trail of the woman's red nail against a curved line in her small palm never left her memory. Now she imagined that she had the palm of God in a clay bowl, and that she read there the lines of all creation, lines that crossed, narrowed, were interrupted, became tangled. Those two spots on its spine were like eyes.

She crooned a lullaby, one she had often used to put Don Armando's two sons to sleep when they were children, still innocent of the world and of the relationship between masters and servants:

> *Sleep little babe,*
> *The Cuca is coming nigh.*
> *Daddy is with the coffee,*
> *And mama with the rye.*

Otália had fallen asleep, she realized when she awoke, startled, to a sparrow's chirping at her window. The afternoon sun warmed her feet. She got out of bed, smoothed the wrinkles on her dress with her hand, loosened her smooth raven hair and then tightened it again, this time rolling it up on the nape of her neck with two twists held by a barrette. She placed the fish in the usual location, its assigned shrine, and locked the windows and the door behind her, a precaution she had never observed before. One never knows, she thought. *É melhor prevenir que remediar* (It is better to prevent than to remedy).

The street was sleepy and deserted, except for a few kids playing soccer with a flat ball and a single goal marked by empty food cans. Their steps kicked up dust, and it seemed they glided in a gilded cloud. In that landscape, so empty, so dry, the sun played at illusions, everything appeared to be something else. Outlines trembled, undefined; the floor shifted like solid waves, and the sand moved like water. The scene resembled a child's drawing: a road, a house, a sun, a bird, a lonely old woman, perhaps the child's grandmother, beneath a barren blue sky.

From the store's front door, Otália spotted *Seu* Mané behind the counter talking heatedly to two men on the opposite side, one fat and one skinny, separated by a bottle of *aguardente* and two full glasses. They exchanged words with exaggerated flourishes, passionate gestures, brash and strident voices. Above the men, combs of different colors dangled on a single rope, and an old Luis Gonzaga song crackled from the phonograph. The men stopped talking when she entered, their toothpicks paused in their mouths. At the counter, she greeted *Seu* Mané and, pretending not to notice the sudden silence or conspicuous eyes, asked for a pack of Café Petinho, a kilo of *cuzcuz*, a box of matches, and a bar of yellow soap. "Please put it on the tab, *Seu* Mané."

"Otália, may I have a little word with you?"

Otália recognized that tone, the same one used by Abigália early that morning, and knew what would follow. She wanted to tell him she couldn't, but she owed *Seu* Mané many favors. If it weren't for his courtesy of *fiado*, the tab he let them run, she and Justino wouldn't be able to survive, God forbid.

"Yes, *Seu* Mané?"

He led her into the storage room, stocked to the ceiling with sacks of beans, rice, countless bottles of liquor, and *cana*. The smell of coffee permeated the small space. He offered her a glass of water, which she accepted and drank in one gulp. When he spoke, an unbearable stench of onion filled the air.

"Is it true that *cumpade* Justino's leg is healed?"

She hesitated and nodded.

"That's what I thought. He's telling everyone that it is because of some cream you rubbed on his leg—the donkey's cream. But no one believes him, especially after what happened to Clemilda. And there's more, Otália."

This time he furtively checked outside the room for anyone who might be listening. "I found out that Abigália is having a girl. Now *that's* some miracle, *cumade*."

"*What!*" She feigned surprise. "How can you know?"

"My wife said so. Abigália came over to buy milk for her boys, all happy, smiley, and then she got to talking with Jurema. Within two minutes they were both in here, Jurema with her ear against Abigália's belly, stroking it, saying that the way she carried the baby—" he formed a semicircle with his hands, from one side of his back to the other "—all round and disproportionate, like this, was the mark of a *fêmea.*"

"Ah, *Seu* Mané, how can Jurema be so sure?"

"*Cumade!* My wife's delivered just about every baby in this city, and you know how it is, women always know these things." He stroked his thick mustache, his stubbled chin. "Otália, I know about the fish."

A deep stillness fell between them. Otália could have retorted that even if Abigália were to have a girl, who was to say that it wasn't the will of the Lord, that it had nothing to do with her or the fish she had found in her latrine, that Justino's healed leg was indeed the liniment's work, and Clemilda's eyesight the work of her own prayers. God or the devil, it doesn't matter. In such cases, *cumpade*, one can never tell the difference, she would have said. But he would know she'd be lying.

"I'm not asking for much. In fact, I'll make you a deal. If you accept, Otália, I'll eliminate the debt you and your husband have with the *venda.* What's more, I'll let you take whatever you need for an entire year. Whatever you need, *cumade*, in exchange for what I'll ask of you."

He cupped her ear with his hands and told her about his affliction. It descended upon him one night like a curse, without any warning symptoms. He had tried all the popular recipes for such a malady: pigeon eggs, fried peanuts; he had even managed to order oysters from an island in Bahia, to no avail. He was afraid that Jurema wouldn't be able to stay faithful forever, with him in this condition. He couldn't risk the reputation of a horned *corno.*

"She's a very healthy woman," he said, "and I a healthy man. What has happened to us is a horribly humiliating blunder of fate. Just imagine, *cumade*, what that would do to a man."

Otália blushed. This was going further than she had imagined. How could she help *Seu* Mané? She would never dare to put her hands *there*. No, she had to be resolute. Here is where she would draw the line.

"I'm sorry, *Seu* Mané, you've been good to us, but—"

"Please, Otália, have pity on this old sinner. You just tell me what to do, I'll take care of it myself. If it doesn't work, I'll still honor my end of the bargain." He stared at her with deep pain in his face, placing a supplicant's hand on her shoulder. "*Cumade*, I beg you, don't let me down. Look. Just think about it. Tomorrow I'll stop by before noon. The groceries are on me. Take whatever you want."

6

In the days that followed, Abigália had her first girl, and *Seu* Mané did not open the store for a whole week, much to the chagrin of the town drunks. By the third day two men appeared on Otália's doorstep carrying their allotted water cans, pleading for her to turn their water into *cana*. "Why not?" they argued; "Jesus did it, and *cana* is cheaper than wine." She ignored them, but the fame of the wondrous fish had already spread throughout the Sertão. Everyone knew that a saint in the form of a fish was actively miracling in Otália and Justino's house. It seemed to Otália as if the whole world had an unfathomable problem, some type of misfortune, an illness, a heartache, the evil eye. At first they came during evening hours, usually after the sun cooled down. They brought small presents for Otália and water or salt for Saturnino's bowl, which she now had to refill daily. Please, *cumade*, God bless you, you're a saint, they would say. But lately they showed up at every hour, unabashed, as if the fish belonged to all, a redeemer of their calamities, forcing Justino to withdraw more and more into himself with each passing day.

Padre Miguel Inácio also visited Otália, and after a long, solemn examination of the fish, declared for all to hear that the animal was a blessing from the heavens, for fish had always been a symbol of the Lord Jesus Christ. After that clerical pronouncement the curious crowds kept an endless vigil, setting up camp outside the house. Crushed by the throng, vendors elbowed their way through and cried out their merchandise—*"Rapadura, rapadura, man, dudu*, peanuts, roasted cashews, popcorn, cotton candy, *picoleeee!"* Invalids of the body and mind pleaded for health: *Dona* Gertrudes with the paralysis of her right hand, a man from Camaragibe who could scarcely walk, convinced that roots were growing from his feet; a crippled Catalonian nun from the Confraternity of Our Lady of Sorrows carried by her fellow brides of Christ; an ex–*Pai-de-Santo* who, having sold his soul to God in a rare moment of shame, was condemned to a life of goodness and could no longer drink without throwing up, dance without tripping, or imagine a naked woman without guilt.

Some asked for love; these were the only ones whom Otália allowed to drink the water. Most, however, came in search of fame, success, wealth, revenge. After a while she stopped asking about their problems; she wasn't the doer, after all. It was best not to know, for she had no energy left to argue, as with the young woman who wished harm on her husband's mistress, or the gamblers wanting to bless their dice. "What you need is a *santeira*, a mother-of-saints," she would say. But now, resigned to her fate, her only question was the source of the complaint, so that she could sprinkle the water there, and send them away. The fish was the only one who remained oblivious to his own acts.

7

One April morning, before leaving for work, Justino announced that he was not returning.

"This is not my house anymore. It belongs to the fish."

He paused at the door, giving Otália just enough time to say that she was sorry, that she never dreamed things would get so out of hand, that her life without him was unimaginable, that she would rid them of the fish, but instead she chose to remain silent, daunted by the presence of a small group of supplicants already lined up before the door. He picked up his hat, brushed the back of his hand against her hair and cheek, and kissed her forehead. Otália always wondered how the touch of such hard hands could feel so soft upon her skin. She lowered her head. Later that night, alone on the mattress for the first time, she would think that she should have wept, should have said everything with tears. Justino would have understood; together they could find a solution. But she had only asked where he was going. He replied that he was going to Pesqueira to work with his brother, Altamiro, that he would send her money, unaware that the food, gifts, and occasional money people insisted on donating in exchange for Saturnino's services were more than enough for her survival. Otalia had hidden these offerings from him since the beginning, for she knew that despite their necessity, he would never have approved. The image of Justino putting on his hat before leaving, the light of the bowl reflected in his eyes, would flicker in Otália's memory until the day she died.

8

Two weeks after Justino left, Saturnino fell sick. One Wednesday, Otália woke up and knew instinctively that something was wrong.

The glimmer from the bowl no longer polished the air. She found Saturnino floating on his left side, one fin treading water, his smile sadder than ever. She warmed a piece of yucca from the previous night, held it close to his mouth, brushed it over his lips. Nothing. She then added fresh water and sprinkled a dab of salt, immersing her hands in the bowl and gently turning his body to its natural position, only to see it flop sideways as soon as she let go. "Saturnino, for the love of God, what's wrong with you!" She knelt by the bowl, sobbing, and intoned a chain of prayers, one for Saint Lazarus, patron saint of the wounded, another for Our Lady of Perpetual Succor, in case Saint Lazarus needed help, another for Our Lady of Sorrows, for sorrow was what she now felt, clutching her heart, and finally, when she arrived at Our Lady of Holy Remedies, since remedies always come last, it dawned on her, in a flash of epiphany, that Saturnino had still not been baptized. She left at once, the bowl held tight between her arms and covered by a blanket, quietly so as not to arouse the sea of dormant supplicants who besieged her home, the ground littered with burned-out candles and empty bottles. The sky was still dark, and a cool breeze greeted her. As she walked down the silent roads, Otália hoped that Padre Miguel Inácio would arrive early.

At the back door of the Capela da Santíssima Consagração, Otália waited, seated on a large stone. She saw the star that had granted her wish, burning as it retreated. The sight of Saturnino, his lithe body collapsed to one side, stung her heart with a worry she had never known. She closed her eyes for a prayer and slid into a dream. She must have slept for a long time, for when she heard Padre Miguel Inácio's voice, he was already inside the church. She looked through the side window and saw the chapel already full, with the regulars by the pulpit on their knees, one following the priest to the confessional.

"Padre Miguel!" She burst through the back door and ran to the confessional, opening his side of the booth. The hushed litanies stopped in mid-verse, and each eye in the church, perhaps even that of the crucified Christ, stared at the disheveled old woman with the clay bowl in her arms.

The priest stood. "Yes, Otália?"

"I'm sorry, Padre, but I need you. It's a matter of life and death." The walls of the chapel echoed her desperate plea.

"Otália, please sit and wait a minute. I'm in the middle of something important," he whispered and shut the door quietly.

Otália opened it once more. "Padre, it can't wait. It concerns Saturnino. Look, he's sick." She lowered the bowl to the level of his eyes.

"Otália, you need a veterinarian, not a priest."

"But Padre, he needs to be baptized!"

Perpétua, the penitent on the other side of the booth, slid the curtain aside. "Otália," she said, "you better run to your house, *querida*. Or haven't you heard? Clemilda woke up deaf this morning, saying it is your fault; the whole town is looking for you." Otália heard a stifled giggle behind her. She walked down the aisle to the gleeful titters of the women present. For them, Otália was a senile hag, abandoned by her husband, obsessed by a fish; after all, they were young, radiant, bodies like silk, nails glossed, eyebrows plucked, legs shaved, thighs taut—what could be more important? They did not need miracles, except maybe that of seducing Padre Miguel Inácio into their beds. She exited the chapel, her head high, resisting an urge to collapse under the weight of all her years.

"Don't worry, Saturnino, you'll soon be baptized. My *santinhos* have never failed me; why would they now, after all these years?" She raised her eyes to the pitiless sky and saw a buzzard hovering overhead, adrift from its sisters. "Poor creature, no one cares about you. God bless you, bird," she murmured. She looked at Saturnino, back at the buzzard, and shuddered as if scales had suddenly grown on her back. When the buzzard vanished, she found herself alone in a wilderness as vast as the sky, alone with the knowledge that the Holy Mary was equal to Jezebel, Jesus to Judas, herself to those women in the church, and then she said, "The world is one."

Otália did not return to her home by the accustomed route. Rather, heeding Perpétua's warning and her own intuition, as well as the growing clamor at the edge of town, she crested a small hill just outside Jatobá, where she paused and witnessed the spectacle from afar. Otália saw that Clemilda held both her ears, and she did not need to hear to know that threats of hell and damnation spewed from the woman's mouth and the mouths of the furious multitude. They were all there: Abigália with two of her boys supporting the inert form of her eldest son, whose arrival in this world Otália had witnessed eighteen years ago; *Seu* Mané, whose recovered stamina had caused him to close his store for five days, now shielding his face in shame, an unyielding, obscene bulk bulging from his pants, and all the others, kneeling, lying, crying, waiting for the old lady and the fish who were culpable for their cursed blessings. Some men clutched *peixeiras* in their hands, the knives' blades shining in the sun, sharp enough to cut Saturnino's body with one slash. If there is a hell, Otália thought, this is it. She turned around, wrapped her head in the blanket she had used to protect Saturnino, and searched for a secluded spot where she could sit and wait for night. She was hungry, tired, numb with regret, but never had her heart felt such determination as now.

She would wait until late, when there would be a moon and stars to show her the way. She had heard stories of men who traveled entire seas guided by them, and the desert was no different.

9

"Okay, *senhora*, this it. Good luck."

Otália glanced out the truck's window and saw a small road just like the ones in Jatobá, except here the dirt was white. She nudged open the door and planted her feet on the ground. The smell in the air reminded her of the brine that had gushed down her legs on the day Saturnino arrived.

"Thank you, *seu moço*. God bless you."

With the clay bowl held tightly between her exhausted arms, Otália took the final steps of her pilgrimage. The road faded into a row of dunes. She heard the mournful cries of seabirds calling out like lost children, and underneath their cries a muffled roar like the breath of a sleeping lion. For the first time since she left Jatobá, Otália was afraid. She sat down, hugging the bowl to her stomach, and thought of Justino.

She thought of how close they had been to the ocean all their lives, without even knowing it, and she thought of the world without him. She thought of the beautiful old man on the day he left, his face limned by the light of the bowl. She remembered his words: "Nothing on this earth comes without a price, you know that. Even Jesus had to pay for his miracles." What a selfish old woman I've been! And it was at that moment, right before grief swelled over her, that Saturnino, his body back to its natural position, moved impatiently, splashing water over her dirty white dress. The bowl had recovered its light.

10

She summoned her tenuous energy and ran. Before her the ocean, in all its glory. Dear God, so much water, and so many dying of thirst! The glare of sunlight on its surface reminded her of fire.

Otália paused at the edge of that enormous body, paused, then moved into it, her callused feet disappearing into the wet, clutching sand. The sun was melting into the horizon; as she struggled to maintain her balance against the surf, her skirt plastered to her thighs like a second skin, Otália licked her hand and tasted that salty water.

Go with God, Saturnino. You are now baptized.

The fish trembled with the imminence of freedom. Otália turned the bowl upside down and released him. The entire sea glowed, a liquid desert of many colors. As she watched Saturnino swim away, a sudden wrenching twisted her gut. She placed both hands on her womb. But what Otália did not see, on the sand beneath the waves, was the hard bowl losing its shape, becoming, once again, raw clay.

Little Star of Bela Lua

The other day this television woman in São Paulo stuck a microphone in my face and asked me, "What about your boyfriend, your husband—he lets you live this life, singing all around like this?"

"Look here, lady," I told her. "No one is born tied together. They can be twins, but they still come out one at a time. The world is filled with frigid, adulterous housewives, not female troubadours, you hear?" I have little patience for reporters and their impertinent questions. There's one thing I'm certain of in this life and one thing only: nothing will ever prevent me from traveling, singing the beauties of this world, the fortunes and misfortunes of the destitute, the meanderings of the heart.

Not that I had a choice. Many times I've wanted to break this damned guitar in half, throw it against a wall, walk away from it after a *repente* duel, forget it ever existed. But I can't, I just can't. It's a curse, runs in my blood. What can I do? It's as though God decided to punish me for some great sin from another life, and instead of filling me with the desire for a husband, a house, for children, like most women—especially women in this forsaken desert, the Sertão—he gave me these rhymes that won't leave me in peace, won't let my feet rest in one place. I haven't stopped moving around since that first *burro* carried me away from my family in Bela Lua and down the stony path of the *repente*, littered with endless rhymes and guitar showdowns, territory of *cabra machos*—real men, the kind that would rather be caught dead than crying or smelling a flower. Whoever heard of a woman rhymester, a female *repentista?* Especially in those days, when I started. Although I was only a child, my name already graced the tip of everyone's tongue: "Senhor Batista's youngest, Valquíria, turned out a rhymester, poor man. A lost girl."

They might as well have called me a *puta*. But now I've traveled by airplane, across oceans, over continents. I'm sure *painho*, my dear father, would love to see the way men tremble when I stroll into a salon, guitar slung across my shoulder, how they lower their hats over their eyes and whisper to one another. How their faces whiten when I challenge them to a duel and they look at their watches and suddenly have to run home for dinner, pick up a child from school, attend a doctor's appointment, make a bedside visit to a dying mother. Oh yes, were he still alive, my father would be proud of the rhymester I've become. After all, he steered me in this direction—and each time I strike a chord I still see the same sad smile with which he handed me my first guitar, just a week before my thirteenth birthday.

At that age I'd only witnessed two duels, both in the main square of Bela Lua and on the same hot Saint John's night: one Pinto Zarazua versus Cartolinha, the other Chico Azevedo versus Gonzaga do Agreste. I don't know who, if anyone, won. I just remember strong silence inside me, my organs shutting down, blood, brain, heart. I marched home, gathered all my dolls into a potato sack, and pushed them at the girl next door.

When Father asked what I would like for my birthday, I didn't hesitate. My brother, that sanctimonious skinflint, fought him all the way: "Don't give it to her, Father; it will be the death of our name."

But *painho* peered into my eyes and said, "Is this what you truly want, daughter? A guitar?"

And I said yes. So he put on his hat and went out to track down this guitar.

My brother said, "Father is crazy, he's going to buy a guitar, and the girl has never written a verse in her life."

My mother, from her purgatorial place at the stove, joined him: "This Batista really *is* crazy."

But before nightfall Father appeared at the doorway with the guitar: "Here, Valquíria." Unstrung, it filled the house with the dense, dark scent of rosewood.

I wrapped it in a blanket, hid it on the top shelf of the closet, and the next day father said, "Now I'm going to call the young man to sing with you at your birthday party." He saddled the *burro* and rode to confer with Aparecido Fernandes, a rhymester who lived in Maurá, a dusty, three-hour ride through the desert. The two men arranged the day and time. My father bought Bela Lua's entire stock of fireworks so that everyone would know the exact moment when the rhymester arrived.

Four days later the sky lit up with a huge *pra-prum-pum-bum*, and my mother said, "Listen, my girl, that's the car with your *repentista*, hear?" I stood in my blue dress, gazing out the window. I stepped outside and saw more people than I'd witnessed in my short life: folks from our village, from the neighboring towns. Some I knew, most I'd never met. People sitting cross-legged on the benches father had built, leaning over fences, on horses, bicycles, rooftops. Kids, old-timers, teachers, merchants, even the mayor, even Padre Miguel Inácio was there, just before he vanished into the jungle, never to return.

Then I saw him. Dark, tall. Impeccable in his white linen suit, the fabric rippling over his back and chest as he walked. On one shoulder the strap of his guitar case, a woman hanging on to the other, a woman like no other seen in those regions, blonde, high heels, dark glasses, nails bright red, her dress matching his suit. He waved to everybody, his smile smooth, self-assured. He patted me on the head, turned to my oldest sister, and said, "Is this the one who's going to sing?"

Father said, "No, it's this one."

The man pointed at me. "Oh, this child?"

"This very one."

I opened my mouth for the first time that night. "Let's not waste time, because the hour is advancing. Here are the strings my father bought. I know I can't play yet, but I want the guitar ready so I can lean on it," I told him. He expertly strung the guitar, tuned it, strummed a few chords.

Then this rhymester perched on the stool next to mine, crossed his long legs, and after adjusting his guitar between his thighs, calmly rolled a cigarette—the first of many he would light and wedge between the strings at the head of the instrument. "What styles don't you want to sing?" he asked.

"Head-Twister and Hammer-Gallop, all else is fair game," I answered, as if I'd been singing for all thirteen years of my life. And that was that. He threw the first rhyme at me and I answered, my voice shaky, uncertain, especially since the guitar was tuned low, in a range comfortable for a man:

> *All of you who now are present*
> *Listen well to what I say*
> *You may think I'm just a child*
> *With no wisdom to convey*
> *But I've been here long before you*
> *I've been singing since the day*
> *Eve was tempted by the serpent*
> *No—since God made flesh from clay.*

Dead silence, and then the whistles, laughter, clapping of the crowd. I challenged all his verses with verses of my own, which sprouted from God knew what seed inside me, for there had never been a *repentista* in the family. The themes revolved around birth, death, the hardships and blessings of the Sertão, God, the devil. Love, of course, though I had not yet become acquainted with that particular devil.

Extraordinary images bloomed in my head—the white sails of a ship on the horizon, a grinning skull with teeth of gold, a very old man with enormous wings, a rain of frogs. While he hunted for the last bit of his verse, the punch line meant to inhibit me, my riposte would be ready. I saw the end of my verse before I saw the beginning, which is how I still compose today. In *repente*, as in war, if you don't think fast you're dead.

So the knot he tied with his hands I untied with my feet, and if anyone stopped the duel it was him, shaking his head, scratching his chin, switching rhyme schemes. He tested me, all right: *Alagoan-Hammer*, in which the first line rhymes with the third and the fifth; *Mourão*, a six-line form in which the *repentistas* share two lines within the same verse; *décimo*, in which the first singer chooses the tenth sentence, that will close the verse of both competitors; *Mourão Voltado*, with its thirteen verses of seven syllables, the singers alternating lines until their voices join in the eighth to say: *"Isso é que é Mourão voltado,/Isso é que é voltar Mourão!"*

We started when the moon had barely risen and ended when the sun gilded the mountain. When it was all said and done, this *repentista* squeezed my father's shoulder and told him, "Look here, Mr. Batista, this girl's a star, she's universal. If there are no obstacles, no barriers in her path, this girl will never stop."

But of course a sea of obstacles awaited me, starting in my own home. Earlier that day, before the rhymester had arrived, my brother, ashamed, closed his leather shop and fled from town. Nothing can be more embarrassing than having a *repentista* for a sister. Even now, after I've wandered this world from one end to another, after I've recorded the first CD by a woman troubadour, I still have to endure the prejudices of men—and the prejudices of women too, who say that *repente* is a man's thing; playing guitar is for men; hitting the road is for men; women who don't have children are an aberration in the eyes of God. Well, I say that when two people need to sign a paper to make any kind of deal, it's a sign something's gone wrong, twisted. I have no need for licenses.

That's not to say that I didn't come close to marrying once. Until this day I thank God for having that *desgraçado* disappear on me, or instead of dedicating my life to what I love most, I might have wasted it washing diapers, cooking *feijão com arroz*, crying over soap operas on the *televisão*.

Our fates collided not long after I left home. By that time my parents' house was a co-op for troubadours. The whole state of Pernambuco now knew me as Estrelinha, Little Star of Bela Lua. Men from all parts traversed the badlands to sing with the young girl; many of these so-called *repentistas* used my novelty to burnish their own stars. One rhymester would knock in the morning, another in the afternoon. At dinnertime a couple more would arrive and stay for a meal of *cuzcuz* and yucca, bean soup, fried eggs, sweetbread. After two years my mother decided she'd had enough. She grew tired of bumping into these men while sweeping the floors, tired of serving them the coffee, hearing their guitars, the singing, the duels. They often brought their own bottles of *cana*, too, and the harder they drank the worse they behaved. What's more, she missed my brother, her favorite. So her ultimatum was no surprise to me: "Listen, Valquíria, either you stop with this *cantoria*," she said. "Finish school, get a regular job, or you leave. I want this place to go back to being a decent household."

I had just turned fifteen. Father didn't have much say; he'd

come down with a strange affliction that struck him one afternoon, rendering him blinder and quieter each day. By the end of
the year he was completely mute and, four years later, when he
died in his hammock, completely blind. I'm convinced he sick-
ened from vying so long with my mother, a woman without a lick
of poetry in her soul.

I didn't think twice. I wrapped up my few pieces of clothing,
tucked my guitar under my arm, kissed my father and two sisters
good-bye, and rode a borrowed *burro* out of Bela Lua to Juazeiro,
where I hoped to meet Zé do Cangaço. Not a day went by that I
didn't hear his name exalted; he'd been the only one who had
never challenged me, so I determined to challenge *him*.

Everyone in Juazeiro knew Zé; I had no trouble finding his
house, painted an ugly green, like an avocado. Zé himself
answered the door, smelling of old man's cologne, a perfect part
in the middle of his lustrous white hair. He was shorter than I,
which bolstered my confidence. I drew myself up to my full five
feet five inches.

"You may have heard my name," I said. "I'm Valquíria
Batista of Bela Lua. Better known as Estrelinha."

"Oh, they never said you were so pretty! Can I offer you a
cafezinho?"

"Sir, I did not come all this way for coffee. I came here to
challenge you in a *repente*. You're the only one in this entire state
I've yet to defeat. So let's get it over with."

He smiled and motioned for me to enter. He pointed to a
couch covered in clear plastic, and sat on a rocking chair before
me. Above his head hung a portrait of Jesus, and next to it, the
faded photograph of a handsome, stern woman. As I tuned my
guitar he rocked back and forth, hands laced across his stomach.
His easy silence made my palms sweat.

"Well, sir? Your guitar?"

"Go ahead, child."

I threw out an opening I had perfected on the two-hour ride from Bela Lua, a verse I was sure would stump anyone. The cadence of his rocking never flagged, and I could tell, from the first line of his riposte, that Zé do Cangaço possessed a talent and authority far greater than any I'd encountered. But it wasn't until the tenth verse or so that he revealed the depth of his genius. To this very day I've only been able to approximate it. The beginning of his coup de grace went something like this:

> *Now that I've made your acquaintance*
> *had the pleasure of your pride*
> *listen closely, Estrelinha*
> *I've got something to confide*
> *I've been singing with the brain*
> *that maneuvers my left side*
> *but the truth is I'm left-handed,*
> *so in my peculiar mind,*
> *left is right and right is left,*
> *what is left is always right*
> *like that gringo John Paul Jones*
> *"I've not yet begun to fight."*

From that point on he cast an intricate web of words that slowly ensnared me. I lost miserably, but in my defeat I was elated. I had found my teacher.

My apprenticeship lasted about four years. The man was like a grandfather to me: proud to have me under his wing, and afraid that as I grew up and started seeing men with a woman's eyes I'd deviate from the *repente*. Toward the end of my stay, he devised a plan to prevent what he considered a potential tragedy.

Thanks to that plan I met the man I almost married—the only one I've ever loved until today.

He was an astrologer, the kind who devoted more time to

numbers than people, who saw in scorpions and fishes and crabs and virgins and mules with human heads in the sky, and prophesized about the day the Sertão would be ocean and the ocean Sertão. He was the only man I'd seen who wore his hair long, like a woman's. It tumbled down to his shoulders in yellow locks that matched his mustache and beard, making him look older and wiser than his age. Years later, on a tour through Europe, I'd visit Amsterdam, that chaotic city of his mother; but as a girl, all I knew was that the accents of his Portuguese held a song at once strange and familiar. So this astrologer told me to be careful, to not waste time with men, that there were a lot of good-for-nothing, predatory *machos* out there. "You're to stay right here for now. Your life is in this." He pointed to my guitar. "Your life is in the music, the rhymes." Then he told me about Uranus in my house of travels; he said that at first I'd journey by horse, bus, truck, but that later it would be limos, helicopters, airplanes, north, south, east and west, singing my rhymes and dueling against famous *repentistas*, that I would confront even the big cities' future version of rhymesters. "Who will call themselves M.C.'s," he said, "after astrology's *Medium Coeli*, midheaven, and sing in a style they'll call hippie-hoppie, which for you will be no challenge at all."

"Hippie what?" I asked.

"Hoppie. Hippie-hoppie," he said, jumping from one foot to the other. He made me laugh, that *cabra*. So much I'd forget myself. He saw many more things in my future—money, prizes, records, revealing all of it enthusiastically, because that's how he was, full of energy, always speaking in that agitated voice of his, waving his arms about and staring at the world with green, limpid eyes that looked as if they'd just opened from a decade of dreaming. We both sat in the little patio behind Zé do Cangaço's house, across from each other at the stone table, where he had scattered the tools of his trade: papers, notebooks, colored pencils, ruler, compass. He drew a map of all the planets, and the sun and the moon, their paths, their cycles. He told me about comets, supernovas, and their effect on people's destinies. After much research and philosophizing, he had formulated a theory all on his own that explained the strange cases in which people vanished into thin air, never to be heard from again. He proceeded to draw graphs, parabolas, and hyperbolas to prove the inevitability of such occurrences.

"This happens, Valquíria, due to a rare phenomenon which I have dubbed *Nulus Planetarius*. That's when one of someone's lunar nodes conjuncts a black hole at zero degrees, resulting in an astrological vacuum. At that point their existence in the physical plane is nullified, and they're literally catapulted into the astral realms."

I swear that's how he talked. I listened to all his ramblings without uttering a word, almost without breathing, staring into his eyes, careful not to miss the slightest inflection of his voice. All I know is that I put down the guitar when he began speaking and only picked it up again hours after he'd left, to compose a slow, whimsical *xote*.

Every now and then I still stare up at the sky and grow nostalgic, and wonder whether that *cabra* didn't get sucked into one of the black holes he loved so much. I can't help it. But then I remember how the whole rigamarole was a farce, and my nostalgia evaporates instantly.

I found out about his deal with Zé do Cangaço six months later. We'd been meeting every night by the water well. He waited until the new moon—according to him, the best time for new endeavors—and begged me to run away with him to Recife.

"What are you saying?" I asked. "I thought your stars told me to stay put."

Then he confessed how Zé had hired him to counsel me, instructed him on what to say, bit by bit, no matter what he saw in my stars; how while some of the things he told me were true, others were "slightly manipulated." He'd left out, for instance, the great convergence of our combined maps. "Trust me, Valquíria," he said, "it's unprecedented. Something I've never witnessed in all the thousands of charts I've studied. With your music and my science, nothing can contain us."

So I asked him to read my map again. "Seriously this time," I demanded. He broke a small stick from a tree and sketched it right there, on the sand by the well, circling the indelible knot formed by our woven destinies.

"This is bigger than us, Valquíria. It's all over the stars, don't you see?"

Then he asked me to marry him. We were to meet in a fortnight, when the moon was at its fullest.

I ran home, my feet barely touching the ground. That same evening, I grabbed a long skirt, two blouses, a *camisão* against the cold desert nights, and stuffed them in my guitar's hard case—a gift from Zé do Cangaço for my eighteenth birthday. Those two weeks I wrote no verses. Every halfhearted note I plucked served only to mark the time. I ate very little, and slept even less. But finally the day came when I wrote Zé a note of farewell, thanking him for everything he had done for me. In it I promised that, as his pupil, I would keep the glory of his name alive.

At the appointed time I waited by the well. By dawn I'd lost all hope, and the fire in my heart turned to ashes. From that moment on I didn't need astrologers or seers or priests or *mães-de-santos* to tell me I would never fall for a man again.

Around that same time I received word of my father's passing. Zé do Cangaço accompanied me home for the funeral. There was my brother, whom I hadn't seen in almost six years. The star of his destiny had not fallen down a black hole. He had moved to Caruaru, reopened his business, and now had a wife, a son, a daughter. He conspired with my mother, as always. They bluntly accused me of my father's death. "If you hadn't gone out in the world like a lost girl, if you hadn't given him so much worry, Valquíria, he might still have been here today," he said.

"That's right," my mother piped in. "If you'd only stayed here and helped take care of him like your sisters and put away that guitar and married a nice man and devoted yourself to a decent occupation." Then the two of them bickered, one blaming the other for not prohibiting Father from giving me the guitar. "You were his wife, he was your responsibility!" my brother shouted.

"You were his firstborn, his only son, he listened to you better than me!" yelled my mother. All this in front of my father's fresh corpse. As I looked at him amid the yellow gladioli in his casket I felt an infinite pity for the man. Like me, he'd been assigned to the wrong family. To assure him a final moment of peace, I said what I knew would shut them up.

"All right, you two. You want me to get married, to leave the life of rhymery? That's just what I'll do, then."

They gaped at me, stupefied, and in unison mouthed, "What?"

"On one condition," I said. And before I realized it, I was telling them that I would marry the first man who beat me in a *repente* duel. They knew better than to quibble; this was their sole chance to marry me off.

A week after the funeral my brother set up a stage in front of the house, a replica of the one Father had built long ago; only now, along with the two stools, there were two microphones and three oversize speakers in the center. My mother began cooking days in advance. She bought enough drinks to irrigate a couple of sugarcane plantations. I heard Zé do Cangaço trying to persuade my mother to renounce the whole idea, telling her it was a waste of time and money, that the man did not exist who could defeat me in the *repente*. "Of course you would say that, Senhor Zé," she said. "She is your pupil. But God does amazing things. My prayer is infallible. So is my faith. You'll see."

The word quickly reached all *repente* circles in the Northeast. Pamphlets, posters, leaflets circulated like bad currency; I couldn't walk to the corner *venda* without someone accosting me, to wish me luck, to offer advice, news, prayer. I even heard an announcement on the radio a week before the event: It said that rhymesters from as far away as São Paulo were promising to attend and "capture a little star." I couldn't fathom why so many men would go through so much trouble. My looks were nothing extraordinary. Not that I was exactly throwaway material—my legs were long and sturdy, my body strong. But my skin was always dry from the sun, and already some crows'-feet marked the corners of my eyes. I never cared for lotions, lipstick, blush, tweezers. My eyebrows met in the middle. The shadow of a mustache darkened my upper lip.

Nevertheless, on that inevitable day, the men appeared in droves. They signed up on a list organized and secured by my brother. Each had the right to three chances, but I selected the style and meter of the songs. There was no need for judges. One of *repente*'s beauties is that winner and loser are clear-cut, not just to the rhymesters, but also to the audience.

Turned out that what on my part was meant as a joke, a stunt of sorts, was taken very seriously by most people. Now I felt scared, especially when I saw the men lining up, some ugly *cabras*, the kind that hurt the eyes. Hard-looking *machos*, scars, limps, missing teeth, most of them—since young folk even back then already considered *repente* a thing of the past—with one foot in the grave. Here and there I saw one or two who could have been five, maybe ten years older than I. But absolutely none who disturbed the compass of my heart.

The first contestant, Ananias Adalberto, was an old friend of my father's, a man who at one time had carried me in his arms.

My God, was I shocked. I chose Mourão, a simple, smooth style to compose in, just to give him an inch of hope. Also to save the more involved ones for later, in case I needed them.

I started playing, my guitar tuned way down as usual: By then I already had a callused voice that could sing in any octave. He threw the first rhyme at me:

> *If you're looking for a husband,*
> *Don't look further than your side.*

He hesitated and I jumped in:

> *I don't like perverted men*
> *shameless, ancient and cross-eyed*
> *When the one for me arrives,*
> *I will gladly be his bride,*
> *But I won't waste precious time*
> *with one so undignified.*
> *All your fingers would be broken*
> *were my father still alive.*

The crowd hollered. He stood, amid a wave of catcalls and jeers, and extended his middle finger to everyone. He didn't bother with a second verse.

The next contestant I'd never seen before. Another old, toothless man who, by the gold chains on his bald chest—his shirt unbuttoned all the way to his stomach—must have fancied himself a Roberto Carlos type. When he opened his mouth, his high, nasal voice emulated that of the trendy singer's:

> *God made woman from a man*
> *said, "Eva, this is your hubby"*
> *don't forget, even Tarzan,*

> *had a Jane to be beside him*
> *to cook, clean, care for his children*
> *and let him go out on Fridays.*

The verse was so bad, I almost stumbled in my reply from pent-up laughter:

> *If God made women from men,*
> *he wanted to take his time*
> *he made Eva, said "Amen,*
> *now this creature is sublime."*
> *I say get up, take your gold*
> *because while I'm at my prime*
> *your teeth have already fallen*
> *and your rhymes don't even rhyme.*

By the third rhymester I was no longer afraid. Despite the heaviness in my heart for my dear father, I felt pleasure seeing my mother's and brother's distraught faces whenever a contestant stood, humiliated, put away his guitar, and exited the circle— although I did feel sorry for some of the men, like O Gaguinho, whose verses, even with his stuttering handicap, I greatly admired.

Around four in the morning I glanced up and saw my mother storm toward the house, her eyes filled with tears. I felt sorry for her, as I always did when she cried.

If it weren't for my treacherous mind, burdened by my father's death, my mother's tears—if I hadn't thought about that damned astrologer at the worst possible moment, I would never have lost to Caruso dos Sertões—an immense, intelligent man so named for his smooth tenor voice and cryptic verses.

We had been going for a good hour, back and forth, way past the three allotted songs. I finally let him choose a theme. I had run out of them. A well-read man, Caruso tossed out a verse about

Greek mythology. It was then that the image of that son-of-a-bitch astrologer, who had taught me all I knew about Pluto, Mercury, Aquarius, invaded my mind and diluted my focus—and in the split second I hesitated, Caruso dos Sertões came in for the kill. I'll never forget that complicated verse for as long as I live. It left me completely tongue-tied:

> *Minerva, Diana, Juno,*
> *Anfítrite, Androcéia,*
> *Vênus, Climene, Amaltéia,*
> *Plutão, Mercúrio, Teseu,*
> *Júpiter, Zoilo, Perseu,*
> *Apolo, Ceres, Pandora,*
> *Little Star, I'll pay to see*
> *you untie this great Camorra!*

I stared at him in absolute surprise, a mixture of admiration and betrayal swirling inside my stomach, my heart in the soles of my sandals. He smiled mischievously and winked at me, but I didn't understand. I searched for Zé do Cangaço's face in the crowd, the only person besides my father who had ever shown me real support, and received the biggest shock of the entire evening: instead of the sympathy I expected to see from him, the man was also smiling.

It seemed that I *was* to marry, after all, contrary to the instinct in the bottom of my stomach that I would be a perpetual spinster. Unlike my mother, I held back my tears.

My brother ran home to impart the news to Mother. I wanted to die imagining her exuberant face, her glorious victor's attitude. But she looked very serious, grim almost, as she emerged from the house and made her way toward us. She asked me if it was true. I nodded. She asked if I meant to keep my word. "Of course," I said. Once I offer my word, I never take it back.

"Very well then, the wedding will be tomorrow." She turned to the crowd and announced, almost in a whisper, "Everyone is invited."

The next day I, along with my mother, my brother, the local priest, and four hundred guests, waited in vain for the groom to arrive and make a respectable woman of me. The collective shifting, sighing, and fanning grew with the heat. Even the saints sweated in their alcoves, their pious grins mocking us. Finally I said, "People, we might as well go back to the house and eat before the flies get to all that food." My mother shot me a black look, as though I had engineered the charade. I shrugged, wondering if this new suitor had encountered the same fate as my astrologer.

Only recently did I learn the truth about Caruso dos Sertões.

I encountered him once again in São Paulo, at the bar of the Teatro Municipal, which hosted the First Brazilian Championship of Repentistas Against M.C.s. For a moment I thought it was his ghost, only bigger and fatter than the man I remembered. I yelled out his name. He saw me and smiled that same impish smile and winked that same wink, and over a glass of *cana* recounted all about the man he loved, with whom he had been sharing an apartment in Rio de Janeiro for all these years. He must have sensed my confusion, for, anticipating my question, he explained: "A duel is a duel, my dear Little Star. The accepting of the prize is the victor's prerogative." He downed what was left of his drink and concluded that, like me, he was never the marrying type. I thought about Zé do Cangaço, how he'd seemed almost happy the night Caruso won. He had known but had never revealed the man's secret to me.

The announcer called me onstage, and I mentioned to Caruso how all these years I'd been wondering whether he'd fallen victim to the same fate as my young astrologer, vanishing into an astral void on the way to claim his bride. He laughed, holding his huge belly. "Little Star, your imagination and skill are unparalleled. It was pure luck that I beat you that night." He curled his arm around my shoulder. "Now come on, old girl, obey your husband," he said. "Go up there and give these hippie-hoppers a good lesson in poetry."

The Ecstasy of São Mercúrio

Padre Miguel Inácio Malpica da Gama leaned his head against the sticky plastic of the seat, closed his eyes—eyes bruised by deep rings of insomnia—and tried to distance his mind from the lies, truths and half-truths that had resulted in this expedition, this turn of events he had never, in his thirteen years of service to the Church, ever envisioned. He knew the futility of wrestling with fate. The succession of events that led him to this end was based on an absurdity; he was well aware of that. But wasn't everything? Yes, he thought, everything. Every dusty town, every hungry mouth, every dry pair of eyes he'd ever delivered sermons to when the need for bread, water, and work was more vital than the need for Christ. He squeezed his rosary, nails pressing against his palms. "Forgive me, O Father, for being blind to your will," he muttered. "Forgive me for my pride."

A jolt of the tiny plane interrupted his prayer.

"Don't worry, Padre," cried the youth from his pilot's seat. "Everything is under control."

The priest hugged his valise to his chest and peered out the window. Beneath him, all around him, only blackness. He tried to visualize the dense Amazonian forest, or the dark river that he had only known through adventure books and childhood fantasies. He had been traveling now—he opened the suitcase and checked his alarm clock—for almost half a day. After a bus and two planes, there still remained a long boat ride up the river to Bororó. The archbishop had informed him that Boca de Ouro's men would be waiting for him at the landing field. The prospect of meeting these men—more specifically, men that belonged to another man, one who went by the name of Golden Mouth—disquieted him more than the whine of the single engine, the imminent landing, and the adolescence of the pilot in whose hands his life presently lay.

It was still night and drizzling when Padre Miguel Inácio descended the short steps of the plane onto the wet, aromatic land. A double row of torches sputtered fitfully in the rain, delineating a crude landing strip. They gave off a smoky light, enough for him to follow the young pilot to a canopy where two men talked in loud voices. The boy shook their hands and introduced them to the priest, who bowed his head. The smell of ripe bananas hung thick in the air.

"This is Américo, and this is Venceslau. They will take you from here, Padre." They emerged into the faint glow, heavy mustaches, dark eyes, rifles hanging from their shoulders. Both men clasped the priest's right hand and raised it to his lips.

"We hope your journey hasn't been too difficult, Padre," said Venceslau, lifting the priest's suitcase. "You can sleep in the boat. Bororó is half a day away. And with this rain—"

"Yeah, who knows when we'll get there," said Américo, the tallest of the two. He handed an envelope to the boy and whispered something in his ear. He then opened an umbrella and held it above the priest's head. "*Vamo?*"

"Yes, let's go," sighed Padre Miguel Inácio. Beyond the banana field, they halted on the bank of a river. A sleek cigar-shaped boat was moored to a rickety dock.

This final leg of his journey he experienced from a certain

distance, as if on the shore watching someone else go by. He managed to remain awake for most of the ride, except for brief losses
of consciousness he attributed to the lulling patter of rain on the
boat's canopy. Gradually the darkness lifted and the rain diminished, leaving behind a dense cloud of fog that swirled around the
vegetation like artificial smoke in a theater. From time to time a
rent in the mist revealed the shapes of giant pachydermic trees,
their leaves dripping slowly onto the brown water. Then the
sounds began. At first one lone bird—an eagle? a *bem-te-vi?*—
hooted mournfully; another answered, then another, and soon the
cries became jumbled, deafening. Thousands of voices joined in
the chaos of a jungle awakening. A pungent odor rose with the
sun, a mixture of rotting foliage and muddy water. They no
longer traveled the main river, wide as an ocean; at some point
they had entered one of its myriad tributaries, a tiny capillary off
the mammoth artery. The forest towered above him, beside him,
barely an arm's length away. At each bend of the channel, Padre
Miguel Inácio felt further removed from the world. He heard the
two men talking to him, asking him questions, himself answer-
ing them, but all their voices held a dreamlike quality that made
each word stretch and twist into the stifling air.

He opened his valise. By his clock it was seven-thirty. Just two
days ago, at this same time in the Igreja da Santa Conceição, he
had been kneeling in morning prayer, already ordered to surrender the congregation he had grown so fond of in the colorful town
of Olinda, in reprimand for his "noncompliance with several
guiding principles of the Holy Church," the final verdict read to
him in person by the bishop of the archdiocese in Rio, who had
flown to Olinda after the callous rumors involving Padre Miguel
Inácio were aired on national television by the popular tabloid
news show *Aqui, Agora.*

"You should thank God every minute of your life for this second chance we're giving you, Padre," the old man pronounced,

his mouth brimming with food from the regional dishes arranged on his side of the long rectangular table. Padre Miguel Inácio sat across from him, pale and silent. With a single, brief sip, the archbishop emptied his wineglass, and while waiting for the maid to bring out another bottle, informed the priest of a spectacular church recently built in the Amazon forest, the Holy Church of the Sacred Wounds of the Blessed Jesus, of the pious Boca de Ouro who funded its construction, and who, in exchange for a residing priest, had promised a donation "worthy of our immediate attention, a contribution that will help the church immeasurably in its many Godly ventures to humanity at large." After two years he would visit in person, to give the church his formal blessing; when that time arrived, he would expect to see many converted souls. "In fact, your top priority, although highly irregular, will be the immediate baptism of all the Indians out there. If we wait for their consent, we might have to wait forever. They're like children, you see; only God knows what's best for them." At this point he stopped chewing and turned the entire force of his baleful glare on Padre Miguel Inácio. "Don't think that I am unfamiliar with your politics, Padre, your ingenious opinions about the Church and the poor, your disaffection with our relationship to them. We are not Lutherans. I should not have to remind you that our primary duty is to their undying souls, and that a man with an empty stomach is always closer to God."

That same night Padre Miguel Inácio packed his scant belongings, among them his Bible, his rosary, a flask of holy water, holy oils consecrated by the archbishop, a copy of Euclides da Cunha's *Os Sertões*, and, before the sun rose, having slept nothing, commenced on the voyage that now, as a soft orange light reflected off the river, filled him with a sense of foreboding.

The sun was high when they reached the final bend. Venceslau shifted the rifle from his knees to his shoulder and asked the priest for his suitcase.

"Don't worry, I'll carry it myself."

"Sorry, Padre, I've orders to follow." He nodded in the direction of the dock they were approaching, toward the distant figure of a man in a broad-brimmed brown hat.

"Oh," muttered Padre Miguel Inácio, faking comprehension, and nervously handed over the small valise. He smoothed his old robe with his hands, tightened the rope around his waist, adjusted his hat, and touched the cross around his neck.

2

"Padre Miguel Inácio!" The man removed his hat, took it to his chest, grasped the priest's right hand, and kissed it. He smiled widely, a row of golden teeth glinting in the noon light. Padre Miguel Inácio bowed slightly and lifted his hand to his hat. *Golden Mouth*, he thought. "I'm Boca de Ouro." He threw an arm around the priest's shoulders, directing him toward the dirt road ahead where two other men stood next to a parked limousine—a strange and unsettling apparition in this primeval place. "You don't know how pleased I am to meet you, Padre. My people need you."

Padre Miguel Inácio tried hard not to form an instant judgment of his host, the generous patron who'd summoned him to this end-of-the-world place and whom he would have to work with for God knew how long; but in such verdant place he could not help but associate Boca de Ouro's shiny red shirt with danger, like the skin of a venomous toad. He told himself that this ostentatious display might not be an indication of Boca de Ouro's character—that maybe his riches were the mere fruits of a lifetime of honest labor, that the expensive boat and the luxurious vehicle and the gold in his mouth, on his neck and wrists had been attained at no one's expense. Like King Solomon, he thought. But the tense deference of Boca de Ouro's men toward their boss hinted otherwise.

Américo opened the door to the limousine and gestured for the priest to enter. Padre Miguel Inácio allowed himself a tiny smile at the sheer irony of the circumstances; he had never been inside one before. The dim interior smelled of raw leather, and even after all six men were situated, there was still enough room for the priest to stretch his weary legs. Between them a small table with a tray of breaded shrimp and colorful sauces reminded him that he had not eaten a proper meal in more than twenty-four hours. Boca de Ouro sat in front of the priest and lit a thin cigarette. The vehicle moved slowly down the road.

"So, Padre, I trust your trip wasn't too tiresome." Padre Miguel Inácio parted his full lips—but before he could speak, Boca de Ouro continued. "Eat, Padre, eat. This is especially for you."

"Thank you, but I'm not—"

"You know, I don't think God's set foot in this place since he made it." He laughed, filling the car with smoke. The priest coughed. "Oh, I'm sorry, how rude of me. Is this bothering you?" He rolled down his window and tossed the cigarette outside.

"No, I—"

"You should see these people, Padre. Just yesterday they were running around half-naked, eating the hearts of their enemies, men like you and me. But, *modéstia a parte*, I've managed to instill a little fear of the Lord in them." One of the men Padre Miguel Inácio had not been introduced to, a saturnine, square fellow with extravagant sideburns, chuckled. Padre Miguel Inácio suddenly felt dizzy and feared that he would faint. "At least now they wear clothes. They don't go around *fudendo*—oh—" he lifted both palms to his chest "—forgive me, Padre, you hang out here too long, you acquire bad habits. I mean, *fornicando* everywhere—I gave them work, a roof to sleep under, I told them all I could about Jesus, God, *e o Diabo*. And now that we have a real temple, and you, a real priest, this whole village, myself included, for I must admit it's been a long time since I've attended a proper mass, we'll all be under the blessing of the Holy Mother Church."

He continued to speak, with occasional grunts of agreement from the other men. He told the priest of God's calling to him, of his mother's deathbed wish that he devote his life to the succor of the miserable, of how his humble gold-mining business provided for himself and so many others, of how he had recently rejected, with the welfare of his own people in mind, offers from American and European companies. "And they offered me *a lot* of money." He rubbed his index finger and thumb together. "But I must tell you, Padre—and forgive me for doing so, I understand you're a man of God, not a man of politics—that this whole *globalização* business is a great pile of . . ." he grinned. "You know what I mean." The priest found himself quietly agreeing, to his own surprise.

The car stopped. They exited the vehicle, and the dampness engulfed him once again. On a slight eminence of land in the middle of a vast clearing stood the church, austere and white, its architecture reminiscent of a Spanish fortress, with wooden double-doors solid enough to block a herd of charging bulls. He began to sweat beneath his robe. Beside each door a full-length stained-glass window displayed the image of an archangel blowing a trumpet. A giant bronze bell hung in the hollowed arch above the entrance, and a tall golden cross crowned the steeple. The priest was relieved. For a moment during the ride he'd had the disquieting vision of the whole church, like Boca de Ouro's teeth, made of gold. Even so he avoided the urge to calculate the thousands of *reais* that this temple must have cost. A lush, well-tended lawn surrounded the building, a bald spot in the hairy jungle. About ten steps from the church stood a smaller building, the stone path leading to its entrance flanked by manicured rose-bushes. My living quarters, he thought.

Boca de Ouro hugged the priest's broad, bony shoulders again and lifted his arms. "Here it is, Padre. The Holy Church of the Sacred Wounds of the Blessed Jesus—your home and God's home. Welcome!"

At that moment, through the haze of exhaustion, a violent vertigo assailed Padre Miguel Inácio; he felt light, his head hollow and terribly slow. His knees trembled, his voice faltered, the sweat on his body turned to ice. And he wasn't sure, as the sun reached the dome of the sky, whether the shimmer he saw before falling unconscious was that of the golden cross or Boca de Ouro's golden mouth.

3

He awoke to a woman's voice singing. He knew he had been dreaming, but could only remember a desperate race and a mounting sense of anguish. He opened his eyes and struggled to make sense of his surroundings, a sweet odor of frying meat in the air. His head throbbed, the ceiling spun, but not so fast that he couldn't discern, through the mosquito netting, the pink clouds and chubby cherubs painted in delicate strokes above him. He examined the rectangular room, the narrow mattress, the ceramic floor, the doors at either end. He mused upon a shaft of sunlight coming in through the high octagonal window, hypnotized by the glittering motes of dust. On the night table beside him lay a folded towel and a small washbasin, fragrant leaves floating on the water's surface. The only thing he recognized was his habit, carefully folded over a simple wooden chair. He sat up and tied the netting into a knot, surprised to be wearing his white nightgown. He noticed his sandals and valise on the floor by his feet, but it was only when he saw the golden cross above his bed that he remembered. The hour on his clock, eleven thirty-five, meant nothing to him. Everything here exuded an unrelenting, mystifying somnolence. He crossed himself and closed his eyes. In a low voice he prayed, fueled by a premonition that some irreversible and important phase of his life had just begun. He recited the Credo, the Hail Mary, the Our Father and other prayers that he improvised, speaking to God in a casual, familiar manner, as one would speak to a childhood friend, asking him to rekindle the fire in him, the same flame that had burned in his chest when he was a young man of nineteen, fresh out of the seminary and starting his pilgrimage throughout the Sertão. "Back when I was filled with purpose," he murmured, "when I would walk miles and miles covered with the dust of the road, barely eating, barely sleeping, baptizing all living things, marrying men and women who cohabited. Remember, Father?"

He thought of all God's clerics, in this world as well as the next, who had inspired him, the ardor of their worship, their passion, their accomplishments, harboring a special fondness for Antonio Conselheiro, hero of *Os Sertões*, performer of miracles, founder of hundreds of chapels and cemeteries in poor northeastern villages. Together with *índios, caboclos*, blacks, *mulatos*, armed solely with rocks and rustic weapons, Conselheiro defeated four expeditions of soldiers in order to protect the Sertão from the new republic, a government bent upon separating church from state, secularizing cemeteries, instituting taxes and, in Antonio Conselheiro's own words, "Reestablishing slavery and returning dark-skinned people to their masters, so as to be able to identify the Catholics when the persecution begins." Then there was Irmão Solano Freitas, his penitent's belt of nails always wrapped tightly around his waist, a man who never slept beneath a roof, kneeling in prayer throughout the night on stones and broken tiles until he'd spontaneously levitate. Saint Francis of Assisi, preacher of abstinence and tamer of wolves, never failed to inspire Padre Miguel Inácio. And neither did *Padim* Ciço, the hunchback patron saint of the Sertão. He called upon all of them to help him in this venture, to work through him, speak through him, suffuse him with their zeal, their devotion, for the truth was that Padre Miguel Inácio—although he dared not admit it, not even to himself—had, along with his belief that the Lord's Hand was present in every endeavor, that Jesus resided even in the darkest of human hearts, watched the flame of his young man's passion slowly diminish over the years.

He made use of the small but well-appointed bathroom. Once showered and shaved, he eschewed his habit, donning a pair of worn but comfortable jeans and a lightweight shirt. He opened the door.

A bronzed, muscular teenage girl stood in front of a stove, still singing. When she spied this wan, rumpled version of Padre Miguel Inácio, a crooked part bisecting the damp curls of brown hair pasted to his scalp, her song halted in mid-note. She stared at him in delighted curiosity. The kitchen was bright, a warm breeze blowing in through the open door. On the doorstep a skinny dog scratched its ear.

"*Bom dia*," he said. "I hope I haven't slept too long."

She laughed and turned to the two iron pots simmering on the stove.

"What's your name?"

She glanced down. "Zumira."

"*Muito prazer*, Zumira. My name is—"

"Padre Miguel Inácio," she said, lingering over each syllable. There was music even in her speaking voice.

He pointed at the stove. "What are you cooking?"

"*Pacú* fish. And this here is *mandioca*. For you." She looked directly at his face, her eyes black, radiant. She had the raven hair and round features he had expected in the people of these lands. How beautiful, he thought. He thought this without the slightest trace of desire; in his thirty-two years he had been blessed with the complete absence of sensual temptation. Even so, God had put him through numerous tests. Many times, particularly during confession, different women had admitted to him, in tears, of the lurid desire they felt for him, of their undying adoration, of imagining him in place of their husbands in bed, of being consumed with passion at the mere sound of his raspy voice at mass. Once, in Santiago, a young woman stood up in front of the entire congregation, unbuttoned her dress, and declared that she could no longer stand the demon of unrequited love digging its claws into her heart. The archbishop from Rio had included this occurrence in his unending list of condemnations against the priest.

A voice yelled from outside: "Zumira!" Boca de Ouro was announcing his arrival. She quickly shooed the dog out and faced the pots. He walked in. Padre Miguel Inácio had never paid much heed to other's choices in clothing, woefully out of touch with the mercurial world of fashion, but Boca de Ouro's skintight jeans, his yellow silk shirt open at the chest to reveal three gold chains amid a mass of curly hair, and the snakeskin boots that almost reached his knees were impossible to ignore. He wore no hat this time, and some of his straight, dark hair—strands that the brilliantine failed to keep in place—fell into his eyes. "Ah! Padre!" He halted his steps, surprised, inspecting the priest from head to toe. "*Porra!* You don't look like a priest anymore!"

Unwittingly charmed by this loud, agitated man, this tacky Roberto Carlos of the Amazon, Padre Miguel Inácio smiled and replied with a familiar refrain: "Yes, but remember, the habit does not make the monk."

Boca de Ouro chuckled at the priest's response; then his expression turned serious. "You had us all worried!" He patted Zumira's shoulder. "You see? That's why we need a doctor here. Thank God everything turned out all right, but you never know, a *cobra coral* could've bitten him; it could've been something bad! *Né*, Zumira?"

She agreed without turning from the stove. "*Sim, senhor.*"

He bent over and whispered in the priest's ear, "I just finished construction on a clinic. State-of-the-art. It's not too far from here." He pulled out a chair for Padre Miguel Inácio and sat next to him. "I see you've met Zumira. Nice girl. She's here to take care of anything you need. She'll cook, clean, wash your clothes. If you ever need anything for the church, candles, saints, whatever, and I'm not available—I'm a businessman, you know, I travel all the time—you just tell her, and she'll know what to do. We've already arranged everything. *Né,* Zumira?"

"*Sim, senhor.*"

Padre Miguel Inácio inched forward. Before he could stop himself, the question spilled out of his mouth. "Shouldn't she be in school?"

"What?"

He leaned back in the chair, feigning nonchalance. "No, nothing, I was just wondering if there's a school here."

"School? Ah! No," Boca de Ouro said in a rueful tone, "no school." He pointed his index finger toward the ceiling. "God willing, if my business continues to prosper like it is now, I'll make sure one gets going right after the clinic. First comes God, then health, then, later, education. Right, Zumira?"

"*Sim senhor.*" She served the food, a bowl of minced fresh fruit, sweet manioc, rice, juice, wine, and a whole fish drowned in coconut milk and cashews. Despite his usual frugal habits and polite table manners, Padre Miguel did not wait for his companion to start eating before taking the first bite. He ate all the fruit, half the rice, two generous servings of sweet manioc, and when Boca de Ouro asked him why he did not touch the fish, he lied: "It looks delicious, but I'm allergic."

In truth, he could not eat the animal—or any flesh, for that matter—ever since his ill-fated encounter with Saturnino, the fish he had erroneously pronounced divine, whose miracles were

akin to the rock doves that rained down upon the wandering tribe
of Israel. The very reason he found himself in this place. Even
now he could hear the doleful voice of the archbishop: "Did you
think yourself so holy that you failed to seek a second opinion?
Are you that close to God, or is it just overwhelming hubris? Even
the great Moses paid for his pride, Padre. Be thankful for this
chance to relearn humility."

After the meal Boca de Ouro showed him the interior of the
church, where every major saint of the Catholic pantheon was
represented by a painted plaster statue—Saint Anthony cradling
a child, Saint Sebastian with the three arrows stuck in his bare
torso, Saint Francis of Assisi, a deer at his feet and a dove on the
tip of his extended finger, Saint Judas Tadeo, *Santa Aparecida*,
Michael the Archangel—and finally, from the cross behind the
altar, a sad life-size Jesus with all his sacred wounds bleeding
unabashedly. The artist had chosen to place the nails through the
palms of his hands, a common but inaccurate depiction that
always managed to annoy Padre Miguel Inácio: The crucified
were nailed through the wrists; palms alone could not sustain the
full weight of the body. He scanned the church with one long
look, the pulpit, the candles, the confessional, the arched ceiling,
and quickly calculated the amount of people—three hundred, at
least—its wooden pews could hold.

"What you think, Padre? Beautiful, no?"

The priest mumbled a faint affirmation and asked when the
first mass was to be held.

"Why, tomorrow, of course!"

Only then did he regain his sense of time. Tomorrow was
Sunday; he had slept straight through an afternoon, a night, and
a morning. Now he would have to spend the rest of the day and
possibly the entire night in preparation his first sermon.

4

He saw him—but first he heard him, the music weaving through the narrow path he walked upon—at that hour when most people slept, when the light of the moon revealed a world much different than that of daytime, inhabited by moving shadows, by birds that did not sing to the sun, the smell of vegetation replaced by the fragrance of night blossoms in full bloom; a world defined by trembling, uncertain edges that seemed to exist under water. In fact all things around him—the trees, the stars, the shadows, the river, himself and the boy he watched, more beautiful than this full, yellow moon, more serene and beatific than any painting of Jesus or the Holy Mary—appeared to float at the bottom of an ocean. He did not approach the figure sitting on the bank, afraid he might be a ghost, an apparition, a forest sprite that would disappear at the sight of a mortal. It was a vision woven from the tenebrous flesh of the night, this naked youth at whose mere sight every hair on his body stood on end, his stomach clenched, his heart pounded in his chest, viscerally awake, maniacally alive. For a moment he forgot everything—the insomnia, the unfinished sermon, the path back to the church, the mosquitoes biting his skin. His name, occupation, God, the devil. He crouched behind a gnarled bole and watched the boy play a *pífano* flute, his silver skin glistening. Near and far, the noise of the forest continued unabated, the liquid notes of the flute like the voice of the river, never once jarring the nocturnal dialogue into stillness. And since no other human ears listened, Padre Miguel Inácio knew that it was in his honor the boy played. He remained there, barely blinking, barely breathing, until the youth put down the *pífano* and dived into the current with such grace that for a second Padre Miguel Inácio wondered if he would transform into a pink *bôto* and swim away. But then the boy climbed back onto the riverbank, covered his wet, lithe body with a thin shirt and a pair of shorts, and just before fading into the shadows, held the *pífano* against his chest and bowed in the priest's direction.

5

Padre Miguel Inácio delivered his first sermon in Bororó on a rainy Sunday morning in January, during the middle of the dry season. Although he had not slept the previous night, he felt revived, animated, and as soon as the one hundred or so Indians settled in the pews, he scanned them one by one with great zeal, their threadbare clothing, the brown, round faces, high cheekbones crowned by slanted, dark eyes that contained a deep weariness and a deeper patience. A kinship with time that city people could never have, he thought. When he did not find the face he hoped to see, his animation faltered. He lowered his gaze, silently moving his lips. "Be with me now, O Father."

At the front bench sat Boca de Ouro, a red rose in the breast pocket of his white linen suit, and beside him, five of his men, their clothes, their features, their hard expressions in absolute contrast to the rest of the congregation. Padre Miguel Inácio, bemused by his thoughts, failed to notice the rifles on the laps of Américo and Venceslau, otherwise he would have asked the men, as he'd had to in past circumstances, to take their weapons elsewhere. It did not matter that he could not remember the sermon he had prepared; after a moment of panic he opened his mouth and the words spoke themselves. Thank you, Father, he thought, Thank you for not abandoning me. He spoke to them in that raspy voice devoid of ceremony, arrogance, or rebuke, that voice that had invariably found the shortest paths to many hearts, well loved throughout all the backlands of the Northeast. He spoke of simple things, of birth, death, nature, love, hate, rarely referring to scripture, peering beyond the congregation of men, women and children, beyond the lit candles and incense, beyond the saints and the colored light filtering through the stained glass, at something or someone only his eyes could see. He spoke of things that were understandable even to these people whose ancestors had been slaughtered in the name of the very God he represented, truths instinctively known to every human, regardless of culture or religion, taken in along with the first breath, the first drop of mother's milk. They listened, curious about this man whose countenance held a radiance they saw only in the faces of the smallest children in the village.

At the end of the sermon, per the superior's orders, he asked how many present had been baptized. Boca de Ouro and his men raised their hands. He then asked who would like to receive holy baptism after mass, and only after Boca de Ouro turned in his pew and gave them a look did the Indians tentatively raise their hands. That bothered the priest. He emphasized the seriousness of baptism, of what they would have to accept—Jesus, communion, confession, the Holy Spirit—in place of what they would have to renounce, including the worship of ancestors, of pagan gods and spirits. He told them to proceed with this step only if they were absolutely willing, not to allow coercion to influence their decision, regretting almost immediately the severe look he leveled at Boca de Ouro as he said this. Had the archbishop heard these words, he would have certainly labeled them as dissuasive, would have added this speech, along with that angry, obvious stare, to Padre Miguel Inácio's list of ecumenical improprieties. Even so, a large majority, perhaps all, approached the altar for baptism, and he could sense, as he poured the water from his cup onto their heads, murmuring, "I bless you in the name of the Father, the Son, and the Holy Spirit," that their decision had not been born of personal conviction.

6

Weary in body, exhausted in spirit, Padre Miguel Inácio locked himself in his room hoping to fall asleep. When Zumira knocked on the door, insisting that he eat something, even if just a soup or a salad, he told her not to worry, to take the night off, he wasn't hungry, thank you.

"But I must cook for you. It's my duty to cook every night."

"Well then, go ahead, cook for yourself and give my portion to someone else."

"Who?"

"Anyone you want, a friend, the dog, anyone."

"How about coffee and toast?"

"No Zumira, thank you."

"How about a little wine?"

"No, thank you."

He heard her steps retreating, and from a distance heard her say, "How about some *chicha*?" Her giddiness suggested that this was some kind of brandy, rum, the *cana* of the Amazon. But so many thoughts were attacking his mind, buzzing along with the mosquitoes outside his netting, that despite his curiosity, he declined that too. For a moment he wanted to ask her about mass, about her feelings on her baptism, now doubting as to whether he had made himself understood, whether anything he said made any sense at all to her and her people. He started to call her name, "Zu—," but gave up, telling himself that everything happened according to God's will. Who was he to question a soul's baptism? I am only a vehicle of Our Father, he thought. Nothing else. I must have no attachment to the outcome. He could barely recall the sermon; the whole day was a blur. In his mind, below the whirlpool of his thoughts, only one image held fast, a persistent, clear image that now, as he covered his face with a feathered pillow and tried to think of Jesus, lay next to him, caressing his skin beneath the brown, worn habit he hadn't bothered to remove, crooning that ancient melody in his ears. He turned on his side, stared at the wall. "The writer is yet to be born who can put such wonder into words," he said to no one.

He waited until the voices of Zumira and what sounded like two, possibly three other girls died down outside, until his room grew dark, until the rain ceased and the moonlight entered his window. He watched as it inched from the wall to the mattress, until it finally fell upon his face the same way it had the previous night when he couldn't sleep and had decided, encouraged by the brightness of the full moon, to take a short walk.

This time he didn't hesitate before plunging into the forest. The whole day had been a long bridge leading to this moment; the sun had risen and set just so the night could return. Padre Miguel Inácio retraced the narrow, distinct path, wondering whether the boy's feet had ever walked upon it, whether what he saw—a tree, a flower, an owl, a bat, the stars, this moon—had also been seen by him, whether the penetrating, intimate scent given off by the wet earth had also been smelled by him, and the thought, Yes, of course it had, this is where he lives, after all, filled him with joy. He walked with his usual long strides.

The river shone in front of him. First he made sure that this was the correct tree. He searched for a distinguishing feature, something that would assure him he had indeed found the right spot, half hoping that maybe he was mistaken, for there was no one in sight. But this was the place, he knew. He closed his eyes and opened them, closed and opened them again, praying each time that the boy would reappear, that he would see him through the spaces between the leaves, *Please God, please*, not even thinking of the blasphemy in the nature of this request. He slumped his whole body against the tree, sweating, disconsolate. Finally he walked over to the rock where the boy had played his flute. He stripped off his clothes—his old pair of jeans, a T-shirt with

Olinda written across the middle, his leather sandals, the only pair of shoes he owned—and slowly, first his feet, then his legs, torso, and finally his head, submerged himself in the cool silver water. He felt the boy's presence envelop him, felt that the gentle river brushing his outstretched arms—its fish, pieces of branches, fallen leaves, and other mysterious detritus—was the same river that had washed the youth's body. And in his unprecedented, feverish longing, Padre Miguel Inácio opened his mouth and drank the silver water, swallowing it with the same deference he used when he drank the blood of Christ.

8

On Monday, much to the priest's contentment, Boca de Ouro did not come to visit. Nor did he come for confession. In fact, nobody came—not Monday, Tuesday, or Wednesday—but still Padre Miguel Inácio sat in the dark confessional every afternoon from three to six. The only person with whom he exchanged any words was Zumira. The girl talked to him incessantly, as if she had known him all her short life, emboldened to ask questions of a personal nature: "Don't you have a girlfriend, Padre? What, you've never had one? What about before you became a priest? Have you ever seen a naked woman before? Well, have you ever *dreamed* of one? Don't you want a son one day?" Questions that, when asked by others in the past, had made him blush. The conversations always revolved around men and women, or, more specifically, the romantic relationship between them. Normal for a girl her age, he reminded himself whenever she tried his patience, not surprised by her similarity to all those other teenagers, from the city or backlands, whose confessions, until the age of nine or so, consisted of small lies told to their parents, their teachers, some treacherous act against an insect or a cat, but then, suddenly and without warning, shifted to confessions, at once remorseful and excited, about small crushes, about touching themselves while imagining various people nude, about kissing their cousins, sisters and brothers on the mouth, *with* tongue, about feeling a friend "You know, *there*," and, finally, the one that invariably followed, sometimes a year, two years, sometimes only months later. Zumira is no longer a child, he thought, But neither is she a woman, her breasts are still two grapes, and her smell sour like a green *carambola*. His musings were interrupted by an abrupt vision, a quick reverie where he saw himself sniffing a star-fruit tree, its scent irresistible, a sensation more powerful than any he had ever experienced, as if he had been blind since birth and suddenly discovered the world of color. He repeated to himself, Sour like a green *carambola*.

She talked as he sat at the table, all the while whisking a broom around the kitchen floor, waving her wooden spoon in the air to emphasize a point, tending to fragrant pots on the stove. He listened to what she said only in the hope that she might mention an otherworldly beautiful boy who played the flute, but all she talked about were Brazilian men, not Indians, not boys, for, according to her, Indians couldn't provide her the future she dreamed of. "They all become crazy, sooner or later."

"Crazy? What do you mean?" he asked, his interest piqued.

"They all become stupid. Plus they're ugly. They have no hair on their faces. I like men with big mustaches, like *Magnum*."

He crossed his legs, uncrossed them, crossed them again, hooked his fingers around his knees, and probed her further on the crazy business she had mentioned. First she made him swear he would never repeat what she said. "If you do, I'll get in trouble. Boca de Ouro doesn't want me telling any of this to anyone. I only do it because I like you, Padre. I don't really know why, you're always quiet, you just stay in your room all the time, or in that box in the church, but I do, I like you." She pulled up a chair, angled the broomstick across her lap, and told him, peering over his shoulder every so often to check the front door, that a few years after Boca de Ouro settled his business in Bororó, many young men in the village had begun to act strangely, walk strangely, talk strangely, do strange things. What do you mean, strange, he wanted to ask, but she didn't give him time, saying that was why Boca de Ouro wanted his own clinic and doctor, since this started happening he'd lost many workers, boys who were sent to a hospital somewhere in the city and never came back, others whose hands, arms, and legs stopped obeying them. "I think they're just making it up so they don't have to work in the *minas*. They're lazy, Padre. They just want to lie around in a hammock all day long. Not me, you see. That's why Boca de Ouro lets *me* work for all his important guests. I told him everything people were saying in the village, all that talk about the mines being cursed, about Tchekum using him to send down his wrath upon our people." She paused. "And you know what else, Padre?"

His mind was spinning. Hospitals, mines, useless limbs, young boys—these words were too familiar. He did not want to know what else, but asked anyway, "What?"

"They're saying Tchekum sent *you*, too." She set the food on the table, prepared a plate for herself, and sat next to the priest. His hands now fidgeted. The delicious smell of the bean soup and its ingredients—cumin, yes, cumin and cilantro, a hint of cayenne, onions, green peppers, red peppers, tomatoes, olives, and the black beans, their scents as discernible and harmonious as instruments in an orchestra—prevented anything else from holding his mind.

8

On Thursday afternoon, his fifth day at the Holy Church of the Sacred Wounds of the Blessed Jesus, Padre Miguel Inácio's increasing restlessness reached a pinnacle. Despite no one stopping by for confession, not even Boca de Ouro and his men, despite not being able to concentrate on a single prayer or read his Bible or *Os Sertões*, the book he loved and that never failed to command his attention, he felt no guilt, no remorse, none of the sense of failure that had saddened him in the past when a congregation did not respond in the way he hoped, that is, the way his superiors expected. No one came to thank him, no widows fingering the beads on their rosaries over votive candles, nothing. In his room he paced back and forth, worried that under such circumstances he was unconcerned. "What is happening to me, O God?" he said, and then, glancing at the octagonal window, "Where could he be now?"

Padre Miguel Inácio sat in bed, rested his head in his hands. Perhaps he should work on this Sunday's sermon, but the desire to write had left him. Zumira knocked on the door, stating she had finished her afternoon work; she would be back later to prepare dinner. Complete silence, except for the carols of a few birds outside his window. This was the hottest time of day, when the entire forest grew hushed in oppressive heat. Unlike the night, he thought, and he lay down, allowing the humidity to calm his senses. He took a deep breath and placed an arm across his eyes, thankful that at that moment he smelled nothing besides his own familiar scent of wet wood. He let out a yawn, another, and yet another. His body yielded to the bed. A mosquito buzzed in his ear; he had forgotten to unroll the netting but was too relaxed to get up, and so decided to ignore the chorus of mosquitoes between his temples. The static crackled in his skull. He tried to stand. Numbness pinned his body down, he struggled to move but couldn't, his limbs prey to an absolute paralysis. He screamed, desperate, but no voice escaped his mouth. I'm dying, he thought, this is it. He gathered all his will and sat up at once, his pulse throbbing in his head as if he had just been chased by all the demons in hell. *Tchekum* came into mind, but the word did not bring any memories or make any sense. He inspected the room, surprised to see it quiet and still. A lone mosquito flew slowly before him. Padre Miguel Inácio observed its flight before smashing it between his palms. He wiped his hands on his shirt, put on his pants, and searched for his sandals. He looked under the bed, where instead of his sandals, he found his hat, covered in dust. He looked in the bathroom, in the kitchen, nothing, checked his suitcase but did not see them there either, and so he left the church barefoot.

9

He followed the main road before veering into the forest, away from the river, concentrating on the movement of his feet upon the spongy undergrowth. The dense canopy overhead formed the dome of a cathedral, its gloom punctuated by shafts of sunlight, its hush barely interrupted by a bird's song. The air was redolent with the odor of plants and animals whose names he did not know, tinged occasionally with a whiff of the river in the mid-afternoon heat, the river he could not see but knew accompanied him in its lazy course behind the wall of vegetation. There was not a soul in sight. The ground he walked on bore no mark of human presence. He recognized some of the plants around him, lianas wrapped in gossamer veils of spiderwebs, their occupants alarmingly huge, immobile as stones. He fought the impulse to stop and smell each one. The diurnal forest was different from that of night, this one more lonesome. He preferred the latter, the forest bathed by moonlight, cool, mysterious, filled with the pulsations of unseen life. He wished it were nighttime now, at least he wouldn't be sweating so much, and the smells wouldn't be so cloying, and perhaps then he would hear that melody again, see the boy again. He tried to recall him but saw only a stylized silhouette, and the song was now contaminated by an insidious Luis Gonzaga tune that had been resurrected from some dark corner of his mind. Again he concentrated on his feet, their dutiful pace. He felt separate from them, for although he had the impression of wandering in circles, they proceeded before his mind did, as if conscious of a destination.

Soon he arrived at a road he had not seen before. He stopped, momentarily blinded by the naked sky. The road led him upward, over the crest of a steep hill. He halted halfway up the slope, and saw off to his right sections of the river, between small breaks in the foliage, and farther away, the clearing where the church stood. Only then did he realize that the sun was considerably lower in the sky; he had been walking for a long time. A light rain began to fall. He had almost reached the top of the hill, and decided that he would turn around once he got there. It was then that an acidic, greasy odor carried by the breeze swept over him, burning his throat and stinging his eyes, a smell that did not come from anything living, or that had ever been alive. The priest, his curiosity aroused, reached the top and froze. A roar of water arose along with the corrosive stench from an immense hole in the earth, a barren wound of excavated land etched with steep steps ascended and descended by an endless stream of men, almost naked, their entire bodies coated with ocher mud, except for the few who held rifles. It was almost impossible to distinguish the men from the huge sacks of stones they carried on their backs. Giant hoses lashed the walls of the pit with whips of water that flowed down like blood, dark and streaked with silver, into a narrow channel. Padre Miguel Inácio tried to distinguish some faces, the ones he had baptized. This resembled nothing more than a human ant pile. He had heard of such places before, he had seen pictures on television, in newspapers, and in magazines, but still the whole scene remained unreal.

A worried Zumira greeted the priest at the door. He walked in, soaked with sweat and rain, slumped on a chair, and laid his head on the table.

"Whatever it is you saw out there," the girl said, "you better forget it, Padre."

10

On the night before his second mass at Bororó, Padre Miguel Inácio slept soundly, free of the nightmares that had consumed him, asleep and awake, since his last walk through the forest, when he witnessed what he now thought of as the black hole— for him, that was exactly what it was, clearly part of the gold mine that bankrolled the archbishop's generous donation, the humble business that had funded the church, the limousine, the boat, the gold in Boca de Ouro's mouth, even this very bed he lay on. No, none of it hounded him this morning, neither the images of ashen men nor the grave voice that accompanied them in his nightmares, *All hope abandon ye who enter here*, something he had read somewhere a long time ago. Adding to his delight, the song now echoing in his room was the one that had eluded him since that haunted night by the river. The flute melody accelerated at certain parts, slowed in others, and the thought that maybe the flutist was somewhere nearby constricted Padre Miguel Inácio's chest and stomach—urging him to rush to the bathroom and empty his bowels. He quickly washed his hands and face, brushed his teeth, and, trembling, stepped outside, searching, but the kitchen and the small study were empty. He opened the door to the patio where the dog slept huddled against the wall. The priest made a hasty circuit of the building, trying to follow that sound that seemed to issue from all directions, but saw no one. He rushed back into the kitchen, seized the church keys from the bottom drawer, ran outside again, opened the church's back door. Except for the Christ and his saints, the church was also empty. He looked around for a radio that might have been left on by Zumira. He raised his eyes to the early sky, and it dawned on him that he could not hear the cacophony of monkeys and birds that greeted every morning without fail. The flute reverberated in what seemed to be a silent vacuum. My God, it's in my head! he thought.

He hadn't thought about God in a long time, it seemed. An overwhelming desire to pray flooded over him. Panting from so much running, he entered his room and noticed the dog, which, taking advantage of the open door, had sneaked into the house and appropriated his bed. It looked straight up at him with round, pleading eyes, ears drawn back, its long, scraggly tail wagging timidly. He sat beside the animal and touched its head. It rolled onto its back, exposing a drawn belly marked by insect bites, much like the ones on Padre Miguel Inácio's arms, legs, and especially his feet. A young female, the same one that had licked his hand on that first morning; hard to believe that was less than two weeks ago. He brought his face close to the dog's snout. The two sniffed each other; it appeared his sense of smell was, at least for the moment, back to normal. The dog licked his nose. "What a sweet soul you are," he murmured, and the fact that he could barely hear his own voice beneath the melody in his head did not bother him, elevated as he was by a spontaneous and unprovoked feeling of love toward the animal, toward God, Jesus, Mary, and the universe at large. He thought of his own mother, whom he hadn't seen since the day he left the brothel in Bahia, his only home until the age of sixteen, when, already too heavily bearded for his age, having seen too much of the depredations of the flesh, he had decided to answer the divine calling in his heart. A profound nostalgia conjured up her face, her hair, curly and brown like his, the warmth of her arms around his child's body, her bosom and the softness of her voice as she sang the cabaret songs that had so often lulled him to sleep. He realized that he'd almost forgotten her features, the thin lips that curled down at the ends, her green eyes, very far apart from each other, the dark mole on her left cheek, and remembered what a professor in Recife had once told him, "Everything experienced in a lifetime, from infancy to old age, gets stored away in the subconscious and may resurface without notice at any time." He thought of the faces of his mother's friends and *companheiras*, Tia Jaciara, Tia Salomé, Tia Zefinha, Tia Luluca, Tia Roberta, women who'd been like family to him, and the madam, Madame Calalú, who had comported herself like a grandmother, now shining and beautiful in his memory.

His priesthood was for them a great betrayal. Since its founding, Casa das Petunias had been a favored target of the local priest, who, along with his parishioners, mostly composed of the patrons' wives, conducted weekly protests on the sidewalk in front of the establishment, complete with saints' statues, crosses, signs with some variation of *mulheres do diabo,* women of the devil, in red Gothic letters, billboards depicting crude illustrations of Sodom, Gomorra, and Jezebel flung from a tower. His mother's words—"Think, Miguel. You set foot outside this house for a seminary and you'll never see any of us again"—still welled his eyes after all these years. He wished she had attended at least one of his services. He would have convinced her that God's love was unconditional, that contrary to what she believed, he did not despise her; after all, Mary Magdalene, the love of Jesus' life, had been a prostitute like herself. The love of Jesus' life. He meditated on that thought for a moment—another one that came from that mysterious pool inside him, as if someone else had thought it. He too had a love now, whether real or imagined it did not matter, and the clear image of the boy, resuscitated by the song, burned his chest as he knelt in prayer. He would have stayed that way—hands clasped, body swaying gently back and forth, lips moving silently—for much longer had the dog not licked the nape of his neck, startling him, and thus prompting him to prepare for mass.

In church, however, the disembodied melody was problematic: He could barely hear his own words or those of the congregation. Not as many Indians showed up this time, and the ones present had clustered in one group toward the back. On the front pew Venceslau, Américo, and the man with the long sideburns whom Padre Miguel Inácio recognized from the limousine ride sat without their boss, rifles across their laps.

"If you'll excuse me, gentlemen," Padre Miguel Inácio said, not sure of either the inflection or volume of his voice. "Take your weapons outside or leave the church. This is the house of God; instruments of violence are unwelcome here." He had the impression of sounding firmer than he intended, for they all left at once, a trace of fear—Godly fear, which he did not need a dog's sense of smell to detect—written across their faces. "Now you," he said. "Yes, all of you, please, come forward. Don't be afraid." The Indians looked at one another hesitantly. Since none stood up, Padre Miguel Inácio descended from the pulpit, sat among them, and, with his internal melody providing counterpoint, recounted from memory his favorite parables.

He had their attention. Slowly the wary faces softened, small children played among the pews, a woman began suckling her baby; during certain parts, the listeners nodded at one another. Everything smooth and peaceful until the story of the raising of Lazarus. The oldest man in the group, his eyes embedded amid the deep elephant lines that surrounded them, interrupted the priest. Padre Miguel Inácio saw the man's lips moving, tried to read what they said, but it was difficult for, like Zumira's the man's Portuguese was heavily accented by another tongue. He prayed for the song to cease: Please Father, not now, please! He

needed concentration. The man stopped talking and stared at him
in a curious way. His face frowned into a question—he looked at
the others and murmured something that made them all giggle.
He walked over to Padre Miguel Inácio, cupped his hands around
the priest's right ear, and said, "Why in the world would your
shaman do that? Here, we do not welcome the dead who try to
return among the living. Even if they persist, we must be very
stern, we must tell them, 'You're of the other world now, go on,
leave us, you have no business here.' We must not let them do as
they wish."

The priest nodded—he understood the question perfectly
well. He closed his eyes, issued a silent prayer of thanks, and
answered, "Because he missed his friend." A woman spoke next.
The old man acted as intermediary, repeating her question in the
priest's ear: Was Jesus, being able to walk on water, related to
Tsunki, god of the river? Here Padre Miguel Inácio did not hesitate either. "Yes," he said. "All gods are related." She sat back
down, smiling a broad and toothless smile.

The doors of the church swung open. They all looked over
their shoulders as Boca de Ouro strode in, overpowering the
incense with his cologne, followed by the men whom the priest
had asked to leave at the start of mass. This time they did not
carry their rifles. Boca de Ouro said something. Padre Miguel
Inácio stared at his lips. The only words he could discern at first
were *delay . . . arrived . . . city . . . late . . . communion*, but fortu-
nately, Boca de Ouro's manner of speaking, his broad, dramatic
gesticulations and exaggerated drawls at the end of each word,
wasn't difficult to decipher. In a hushed voice the priest said, "In
order to take communion, you must first confess."

Boca de Ouro laughed, turned, and said something to his
men. "Excuse me?" Padre Miguel Inácio asked, and this time
understood each word: "I have nothing to confess, Padre."

The woman who had been nursing her baby pulled her nipple from his mouth, covering herself with a shawl. The baby cried, a howl that reached even Padre Miguel Inácio. He walked back to the pulpit, followed by Boca de Ouro. The woman walked outside.

On his way to the parish house, Boca de Ouro surprised him by the fountain. He was lost in thoughts of the handicap this inner music was causing him, how he could not hear others speak clearly. It's only temporary, he said to himself.

At that moment Boca de Ouro frowned and looked directly at him, his lips forming the words. "What is temporary?"

Padre Miguel Inácio squeezed the Bible beneath his armpit and hastened his steps. From now on he must be careful. He pivoted to face Boca de Ouro. "You were saying?"

Boca de Ouro squinted. "You okay, Padre?"

"Yes, yes. I'm just a little tired. I couldn't sleep very well last night. Maybe it was the mosquitoes, or the heat."

Boca de Ouro tapped his forehead with the palm of his hand. "That reminds me! I bought an electric fan for you from the city. It should help." He twirled his mustache as he spoke, which made it hard for Padre Miguel Inácio to see his mouth, but he recognized there the unmistakable formation of Zumira's name, and interrupted, "*What* about Zumira?"

"I just told you, Padre!" He forced a smile. "Zumira is tending to the doctor I brought from the city. That's why she didn't come to church today. But I've arranged for someone else to cook for you." He spoke slowly and loudly, the way one speaks to foreigners or small children. "The lady was at mass. Her name is Josefa Mercedes. People here call her Dona Zefinha." He winked. "She's old and barely says two words, but she's a great cook."

A robust woman of about sixty stood in front of the sink peeling a potato when he walked in, and only when she smiled, revealing broad, toothless gums, did he recognize her. "Hello," he said. She nodded. "Dona Zefinha, right?" She nodded again. He sat on a stool facing her, not thinking of anything, his eyes focused on nothing in particular, simply looking. The rhythm of her hands—one turning the potato clockwise while the other, the one with the knife, sliced off the peel in the opposite direction—drew him into a hypnotic daze. Her legs, brown, thick, rose from the ground like tree trunks; her hands, much younger than the rest of her body, moved like two minnows in a mating dance. Her hair was a cloud above her head, and her yellow, slanted eyes like chips of amber. The song in his head had not relented; it rose and fell, paused and hastened; by now, he knew the points where it slowed and accelerated. He eased into the chair, tapping out a beat on the wooden table.

Dona Zefinha filled a small pan with peeled potatoes. He stayed while she set the food before him, an aromatic stew of vegetables, rice, potato salad, and warm bread. He wanted to ask about Zumira, but didn't. He motioned for her to sit and eat with him, which she did. He did not heap praise on the exquisite meal, and she did not ask how he liked it—they understood each other perfectly without words.

But such harmony was short-lived. He had just retired into his room for the remainder of the afternoon, intent on reading the song of Solomon, a favorite, when the door opened and Boca de Ouro's head popped in, his expression apologetic. "I've been knocking." He entered the room carrying a bulky apparatus and positioned it beneath the window. "Here's the fan I got for you," he said. Padre Miguel Inácio sat up in bed and thanked him, hoping that he would turn around and leave, but Boca de Ouro called out a name then said, very slowly, "I brought someone I'd like you to meet."

A man walked in, his beard and mustache unkempt, his smile wry and irreverent. He had the dreamy eyes of someone who had slept in many beds and spent many nights singing out-of-fashion love songs. Padre Miguel Inácio knew the type; he had seen them day in and day out during his childhood in Casa das Petunias. Boca de Ouro curved an arm around the man's shoulders in a sideways hug. "He'll be staying with us for a few days. But hopefully we can persuade him to move to Bororó for good. Right, *Doutor?*"

The man did not answer. He extended his hand to the priest in a firm handshake. "Claudio M. *às suas ordens*, Padre. It's a pleasure to meet you."

11

Padre Miguel Inácio did not entertain the idea of personally consulting the doctor about his baffling affliction—not so much an affliction, more a divine distraction, he had decided—until five days later, Friday, when the inevitable happened: a young woman whom he had not met barged into his quarters seeking confession, introducing herself as Venceslau's wife. By then he had given up spending three hours of every afternoon in the dark confessional, waiting for sinners who never appeared. He felt embarrassed that she had to fetch him at the parish house, embarrassed that not only did he open the door still dressed in his nightgown and bedroom slippers, sporting a patchy stubble that darkened his chin, but that he could not find his priest's attire. "I'm sorry," he yelled from the room as she waited in the kitchen. "Dona Zefinha must have washed my robe and set it somewhere to dry. Just give me a second."

He knew that his appearance constituted the least of his problems. The prospect of administering confession deaf, to a penitent behind a partition, left him on the brink of panic. He turned, startled to see her in the doorway of the room, arms crossed, exuding annoyance. "I'm sorry," the priest said. "Did you say something?"

"Yes," she stated, squinting at the priest as though he were a sign in a foreign language. She made no gestures as she spoke. Her thin glossed lips moved minimally, impossible to read. He understood enough to conclude that the woman was in a hurry, that she was supposed to be elsewhere but had rushed over here. He had to do something quickly or this could be the greatest disaster of his career. He walked past her to the kitchen and, pointing at the table, suggested that they go about confession then and there. He was pleased with this ingenious solution. Here he could see her mouth and body language, allowing him to divine her sin—which he already suspected to be of an adulterous nature— and prescribe the proper absolution. Years of hearing the same confessions over and over had sharpened his ability to recognize the sin before it was voiced, to an almost prophetic degree, something he believed anyone with a keen eye for observation could determine—just look at this young woman, for example, the tense shoulders, the downcast eyes, the lips trying unsuccessfully to smile, the shirt buttoned up to the collar, the hands gripping the handles of her purse to keep from trembling; everything about her indicated sensuous guilt.

How many times had he tried to imagine the world without guilt, going as far back as Genesis, where he always arrived at the same question: Would it have still been a primordial sin had Adam and Eve not felt shame, had they not hidden from guilt? No sooner did someone confess—"I have sinned, Padre, yesterday I slept with my brother-in-law"; "I have sinned, Padre, I impregnated my lover"; "I have sinned, Padre, I cheated my business partner"—than he or she would be back again, the same confessions, the same tears, the same absolutions, a pointless cycle of sin and repentance, a snake biting its own tail. He leaned over and whispered in her ear as if God had just confided it to him—"Actually, my dear, forget about confession and go home. You have not committed any wrong. You see, there is no thing, I tell you, no such thing as sin!"—This was a great surprise even to himself.

A few hours later, as soon as he saw, through the kitchen window, Dona Zefinha approaching the house, Padre Miguel Inácio ran outside, took into his arms the bundle of fresh laundry she balanced over her shoulder, and asked if she could please show him the way to the clinic, right now. "Something is wrong with me." She nodded, her expression one of genuine concern. He rushed into the house with the laundry, set it down on the kitchen counter, and hurried back outside, thanking the woman over and over.

They left the church grounds. "Is it far?" he asked. She shook her head no and remained silent during the entire walk until she halted, not nearly as winded or sweaty as he, at a narrow dirt alley that ended in a white, square building. She cupped her hands around his ear, and said, "He will not be able to help you, my son." That was the first time, not counting her question in the church, that she had spoken to him.

The waiting room was deserted. There was no receptionist behind the desk to schedule his appointment or announce his arrival, so he simply opened the door that led to the rest of the building. "Excuse me!" he yelled, but still no one. The hospital could very well pass for any modern clinic in Recife, Salvador, or even São Paulo; he walked down the empty corridor to the sole door and peered in to the square glass window, through which he saw the naked back of a woman seated on an examination table. He lowered his chin and tapped the window nervously with his nails, sucking his bottom lip. After a moment the door swung open; he felt arms hugging him and realized it was Zumira, who jabbered in fragmented speech, recounting in one minute the entire three days they had not seen each other. Dr. Claudio M. walked out, tucking his white linen shirt into his baggy pants. The girl glanced back at the doctor, smiling proudly, then faced the priest, said, "I'll talk to you later," and left the men to themselves.

The jubilant doctor ushered him in, one hand behind the sweaty priest's back, and gestured to a black leather chair. He drank from a water fountain and said something that must have been a joke, for when he turned around he laughed heartily. The priest, still trying to regain his breath, offered a dutiful chuckle. He accepted the paper cone the doctor handed him, swallowed the cool water in one gulp, drank three more. The air-conditioned room made him shudder. The doctor sat facing him, behind a cluttered metal desk with no pictures, only papers and a calendar that said *Pantelmin* across the top, and below, in smaller letters, *Mebendazol*. The doctor propped his legs amid the papers and produced a cigar from one of the drawers, lit it, and asked the priest if he minded. Padre Miguel Inácio shook his head from one side to the other. He was not ready to speak just yet, and felt relieved that, although the doctor spoke on and on, looking at the ceiling, taking long puffs from his cigar, his words evidently required no answer. The priest sighed, slumped in the leather chair, and clasped his hands between his legs. He focused his eyes on the doctor, intent on reading his lips, but instead noticed something peculiar about the man's head, something that helped him momentarily forget his condition altogether: The delicate, pink skin right above Dr. Claudio M.'s forehead contained symmetrical rows of red dots, as if a thin needle had perforated it. Sprouting from every hole—*sprouting* was exactly what came into the priest's mind, for the parallel points reminded him of a neat plantation—were tufts of coarse blond hair that did not match his mustache, his beard, or the scarce strands above his ears. Padre Miguel Inácio felt an empathetic crawling of his own scalp, making him aware of his own impending baldness. He wished he had worn his hat. Ever since his thirtieth birthday, brushing his hair had become a disquieting chore, one that caused a slight pang of agony each time he looked at the brush only to see it overflowing with hair.

"*Doutor*, I can't hear a word of what you're saying."

The doctor removed his legs from the desk, shifted the cigar to the side of his mouth, and asked, "What?"

Padre Miguel Inácio told him everything: the sharpened sense of smell, the intermittent visions, his inability to sleep, and most importantly, the repetitive melody that even now, as he spoke about it, was circumnavigating the inside of his skull. He did not mention the boy.

"This . . . song," the doctor said, slowly, eyes wide open. "Does it mean anything to you? Have you heard it before, somewhere?"

"Not particularly, no." The priest lied. "It could have been from my childhood. Who knows."

"Strange, Padre." He made a gesture on the palm of his hand, inquiring if Padre Miguel Inácio would prefer that he write, but the priest said it wouldn't be necessary, as long as he spoke slowly and loudly.

"That's the oddest thing I've heard in years. And I've heard some pretty damn weird things, let me tell you. But are you sure you're not—"

"Going mad?" interrupted Padre Miguel Inácio. "I don't think so. I thought mad people didn't hear music, they only heard voices. You tell me."

"Honestly, Padre, I don't know. Only a psychiatrist could answer that, and I'm not one." He shrugged. "You can understand why I ask, right? I mean, did something happen to you? Did you fall and bang your head, suffer an accident of some kind? Some heavy stress, perhaps?"

Padre Miguel Inácio told him no, nothing like that had happened. Then he remembered the day of his arrival in Bororó—how he'd fainted at the sight of the church only to awaken many hours later—but he remained quiet. Anyway, he didn't think his

fainting had any bearing on this problem, there had been no bruises, no exterior pains the next day. Dr. Claudio M. stubbed out his
cigar and stepped into another room. When he returned, screw-
ing his ophthalmoscope together, he instructed the priest to sit on
the examination table and strip his shirt.

The doctor's disquiet seemed eased by the routine of a medical exam—heart, lungs, throat, ears, coordination, reflexes. The
priest released a childish giggle when Dr. Claudio M. scratched
the sole of his left foot with a key. He asked: Was he epileptic, dia-
betic? What operations had he ever undergone, what diseases?
And his family, what sort of health history? Padre Miguel Inácio
told him all he knew—nothing that indicated problems such as
this. The doctor shielded his mouth with his hand, an odd look on
his face. He murmured something, shaking his head slowly from
side to side.

"*Que foi, Doutor?*"

Dr. Claudio M. didn't answer. He reached into a closet and
obtained a syringe and a plastic cup. Padre Miguel Inácio almost
burst into tears when he felt the needle go in and the slow,
painful suction of the blood from the vein. The doctor then
directed him to the bathroom, and when the priest handed him
the warm cup of urine, Dr. Claudio M. told him to wait—the
analysis would only take an hour or so. He gave the worried priest
a friendly pat on the back. "Didn't expect results so soon, eh? Shit,
even I'm amazed at how well-equipped this clinic is."

Padre Miguel Inácio was busy envisioning himself committed to a mental institution, shipped back to his mother as an
invalid, her only son a baby all over again. "You see," she would
say. "I *told* you God was no good." But part of him recognized even
these thoughts as overwrought, completely unlike his usually
pragmatic view of life, and therefore abnormal, symptomatic of
this altered state.

"This clinic." The doctor rubbed his thumb and index finger

together. "Dirty money. Lots of it." He gazed past Padre Miguel Inácio's shoulder, toward the window, and said, close to his ear, accompanying the words with broad gestures, "Boca de Ouro is a very smart man, but sleazy. All this money—where do you think it comes from, Padre? Ha! And then he wonders why no doctors want to work for him. "My people' need you, 'my people' need you." He improvised a clumsy strut, a mime's impersonation of Boca de Ouro's walk that, had the priest been in a better mood, would have made him laugh out loud. "Well, his people, sure, they need a general surgeon for when they shoot each other—" He paused in response to the priest's astonished expression, nodding emphatically. "—Yeah, Padre, that's right. What, you think those are toy guns they carry? But what I was saying, my friend, is that the majority of his people need a fucking neurologist more than anything."

He excused himself and withdrew into the other room until the results were ready. He emerged in spectacles, a sheet of paper in his hand, and sat on the table. "Yep. Yep," he repeated, studying the white sheet he held at arm's length.

The priest could wait no longer. "What is it," he asked. "Tell me, what do you see?"

The doctor slapped the paper with the back of his hand. "Son of a bitch." The doctor shouted so his deaf patient could hear him. He removed the spectacles, sighed, and said, "You, too, need a neurologist, and soon. Perhaps even a neuropsychologist . . ."

His next words the priest could not discern, for they were clinical terms, something like *eletro . . . falo . . . grama* and *temporal lobes.* "What are you saying?" Sweat beaded the priest's forehead. "What does all that mean?"

The doctor wiped the sweat from his own brow and looked directly into the priest's eyes. "It means that you're fucking poisoned up the ass, my friend. I've never seen this level of concentration, even in the Indians who've worked these mines since they began operation." The doctor said, "Mercury. Organic fucking mercury. That's what he uses to separate gold from sediment. I know it. Everyone knows it. He denied it when I asked, but I'm no idiot. All these sleazy Amazonian miners use it. Everyone I examine, specially the youngest workers, they all have the same problem." He glanced down at the paper. "It shoots straight for the nervous system. Yours is the worst case I've ever seen."

The priest felt disconnected from himself, as the doctor continued, saying he had no idea how so much poison—6.5 times higher than the acceptable amount—could have been accumulated in such short time, unless Padre Miguel Inácio was eating the mercury-impregnated river fish for breakfast, lunch and dinner, and when the priest told him that he hadn't eaten fish in a long time, more than two years, the doctor's jaw dropped, he threw up his hands.

A painful contraction at the pit of the stomach returned Padre Miguel Inácio to his body, shivering on that cold examination table. He managed to hide his pain, behind a mask of shaky stoicism. "Promise me you won't tell anyone."

"But you can't play with this," said Dr. Claudio M., holding out his hands.

"It doesn't matter," the priest told him. "Please, think of it as professional honor, a confession, if you must. Keep this between us, *Doutor*."

"Fine. Whatever you say, Padre." He scribbled a name and a phone number on a piece of paper and tucked it into the priest's clammy palm. "He's a good friend. And a great neurologist. You should get in contact with him as soon as possible. You have a chemical time bomb inside you."

When the priest stood up, he felt as if someone had suddenly planted him on top of a ladder. He braced himself on the table and waited for his head to stop spinning.

12

The room stretched forever into the darkness. Once again he lay under the closed canopy of the mosquito net, arms behind his head, staring at the ceiling. The only difference today was the new fan, which brought him some small relief from the night's stifling heat. What exactly was happening to him? What mystery? What magic? What blessing? What curse? In his mind he searched for a foundation, a starting point, any rational explanation that would satisfy his need for logic. But each justification offended even more against common sense. The doctor's explanation, mercury, was the most absurd of all. How could it be that in less than a month Padre Miguel Inácio, who hadn't eaten fish in two years, didn't have a single mercury filling, and had never, at least to his knowledge, had any contact whatsoever with the chemical, could be more poisoned than those who lived here their entire lives? Yes, highly unlikely, he thought. But not impossible. Nothing was impossible in this world. He knew that every disease, no matter how small the symptoms, merely reflected the state of the spirit. But how to apply this knowledge? What state was his spirit in? He stood, naked, and when he saw that the kitchen was dark, he opened the refrigerator, lifted one of the glass bottles to his lips, and gulped the cold water. He sighed, calmed by the simple pleasure. He pivoted on his heels and glimpsed, from the corner of his eye, a figure seated at the table: Dona Zefinha. His shock was such that he covered his penis with both hands like a bashful boy. No one had seen him naked in a long time. He managed to mumble her name, but before he could ask her what she was doing there, all alone in the dark, she motioned with hands that were barely discernible in the gloom for him to follow her. He retreated to his room without question, fumbling around for the clothes he had been wearing earlier, but found his robe instead, clean and neatly folded on the back of the chair. He dressed, returned to the kitchen, put on the muddy pair of tight tennis shoes Dona Zefinha offered him in lieu of his still-missing sandals, and stepped into the night behind the old woman.

13

No moon or stars hovered above them. Here and there a firefly flickered, a single fluorescent eye that winked in the darkness. The dependable odor of earth. They walked for a while, the priest trailing Dona Zefinha along narrow pathways. The air was still warm from the departed sun, and the ground was dry, but frequent thunderclaps shook the trees.

Through a fine drizzle Dona Zefinha quickened her pace, checking behind her every now and then to make sure Padre Miguel Inácio followed closely. She grabbed his wrist and pulled him along. He was once again five years old, about to cross Avenida Treze de Maio with Madame Calalú. The light rain grew to a fierce shower that lasted no more than five minutes—enough to drench them—and then evaporated into steam rising from the hot humus beneath their feet. Despite the wetness of his robe and the constant bites of mosquitoes, the priest felt sedated. Slowly his thoughts evanesced into the night. The great, deep drum of his heartbeat joined the flute in his head. He thought he heard voices now, children laughing, men and women talking, sighing. If he listened closely, he could almost hear what they said. But just when it seemed he recognized a word, it was lost beneath the surface of all the other sounds in his head.

Without warning, the forest disappeared, replaced by a clearing crowned with clustered straw rooftops floating above the shroud of ground mist. The presence of a human world was incongruous beneath such absolute night. They walked past the village, around the foot of a cliff that curved and ended in a mound. A great dead tree, striped by fungus, lay at the foot of the incline directly across their path. They clambered over it and ascended the hill. Finally, in the middle of what resembled a vegetable garden, Dona Zefinha released his wrist and, facing him, opened a hand on his chest. He waited, watching her disappear into a small hut and return minutes later with a slender, shirtless man, his walk distorted by a limp. He stopped before the priest, and nodded toward the small structure behind him. A flickering glow of firelight emanated from within.

The house they entered had only one wall; its chapped paint revealed cracked, red bricks surrounding a single square window. The entire interior could be taken in at one glance. A pinkish beaten-earth floor held three benches that surrounded a lit hearth, a drum, and several vertical wooden logs that held up the roof and delineated the small square of the dwelling. A hammock swung between two posts adjacent to the wall, and various domestic tools and utensils—machetes, clay pots, hollowed tortoise-shells, stakes, fishing lines—hung neatly from several of the tie beams that crisscrossed the thatched roof.

The man, whom Padre Miguel Inácio was certain he'd never seen before, appeared no older than thirty, with short, curly hair, a hooked nose, and inscrutable eyes. He sat down on a low, ornately carved wooden bench shaped like the head of a lizard. He grunted as he positioned his lame leg against the muscular one. He then stared downward, elbows resting on his knees, apparently absorbed in profound meditation. Dona Zefinha squatted on the ground next to the man, leaving the bench opposite them for the priest. Padre Miguel Inácio removed the tennis shoes, raised his wet robe, and sat down. A large clay pot simmered atop the glowing coals in the hearth.

Somehow Padre Miguel Inácio sensed he was about to undertake a voyage, beyond the forest, beyond the earth and sky, beyond the stars, to a forbidden place. But God did work in mysterious ways. So when the man filled a coconut shell with liquid from the simmering pot and passed it to him, Padre Miguel Inácio didn't hesitate; adhering instinctively to the rules of a ritual he could not have known, he drank the dark, bitter potion only after first washing his mouth with it and spitting it on the ground. He handed the half-filled bowl back to the man, who looked at the priest directly for the first time. Without averting his eyes, he repeated Padre Miguel Inácio's actions. Dona Zefinha, witness to their ceremony, leaned over and said, "Now you will know what's troubling you, my son."

First came the nausea, a violent revolt at the pit of his stomach. Padre Miguel Inácio staggered to the edge of the hut, leaned against a wooden post, closed his eyes, and vomited. Then he fell.

He fell into the middle of the house, into the middle of the forest, into the middle of the hard ground. He continued falling, always into the center of something—a tree, a star, a circle, a triangle, things real and abstract, a subtle continuum of falling into every shape and pattern invented by nature, for a time that could have lasted five minutes or five hundred years—until he realized that all these things were actually falling into *him*. The entire night and the entire forest spun around him, a colony of frantic hornets in a bottle. So many things fell into the priest that his body, no longer able to contain them, exploded and dispersed in every direction—but gently, quietly, a whispering that rose from the air, at once loud, barely audible, modulated, indistinct. It was the boy's voice, who was not young at all, he now saw, but ancient, ancient like the song he was singing.

> *Me, Tsumai, Tsarim, me, me, shaman of this earth, me!*
> *Wi, wi, wi, wi, wi . . .*
> *Me, me, while I make my projectile penetrate,*

Submerging everything, penetrating everything,
Me, me, me, me, the shaman, I am in harmony
Tsunki, Tsun, Tsun, Tsun . . .
You, the extraordinary one,
Tsunki, Tsun, Tsun, Tsun . . .
Tsunki, Tsunki, my spirits, I am summoning you
You, multicolored one of the river, pasuk, I make
    myself a necklace,
. . .Tsumai . . .Tsarim . . .
This is what I do, I make myself a necklace,
The one that is almost unreachable,
The one who sings,
It is you I wear as a necklace,
Your necklace of music is a river on my neck,
You who have gone inside his body,
It is you I summon, Tsumai . . .Tsarim . . .
I open the exit, so you can speak, I invite you,
Me, me, me, me! From the womb of the earth,
I summon you, brushing you with my sheaf of leaves
Tsunki . . .Tsumai . . .Tsarim . . .

The song waned into a more subtle harmony, without words, without recognizable instruments. The priest's body, shattered into a thousand pieces, no longer belonged to him. His spirit breathed peacefully, along with the entire forest, on a continuous bass drone. He opened his eyes and watched, from a distance, the young man stroke his face and neck with a bundle of tiny green leaves, and next to him, Dona Zefinha puffed smoke from a large cigar. Padre Miguel Inácio's naked body looked as heavy and inert as the robe next to it. The boy glided through this world like a seal in water, his movements swift and gracious. Padre Miguel Inácio closed his eyes, losing all notion of himself. Death and life, it occurred to him, were simultaneous and inseparable. Dying was indispensable if he wished to live.

At some point the flute melody returned. He could not say how long it had stayed outside him, where it went. He only knew it had gone somewhere and now it was back. It reentered him like water. It was the only way he would have been able to explain it, a huge waterfall that fell from his forehead to his feet, drowning the whole world in sound. He managed to whisper, "I need the river."

Padre Miguel Inácio threw himself into the silver water. He did not feel as if he had passed from one element to another, for water and air seemed interchangeable. Now he breathed freely. Little by little his skin regained its sensitivity. The cold river touched his entire body, and he saw him; he who caressed his skin, he who had brought him here. Tsunki, god of the river. The boy with the flute.

"You."

He wanted to ask why he had he chosen him. From the river around him he heard a voice.

A fish told me about you.

It was impossible to tell how long they looked at each other. Padre Miguel Inácio—or whoever he was at that instant—saw, in the beautiful youth's eyes, stars; and, deeper inside him, maybe where his heart should be, a great tree, its roots cast throughout his limbs, its branches populated by colorful birds. In the boy's stomach he saw all the people he had met since his arrival in Bororó: Boca de Ouro and his men, Zumira, Dona Zefinha, the shaman, those he had baptized, the workers in the gold mine, Dr. Claudio M., the woman who had come for confession. There were also those he hadn't met, people of the forest who had long gone and people who had yet to be born. Their laughter and joy, and likewise, their pain and struggle were all inscribed upon their faces, upon their bodies. A little girl's smile, radiant like Zumira's, and her eyes, dreamy like Dr. Claudio M.'s, was enough to tell him exactly what had occurred between the two; a man's bruises and broken arm showed the priest what happened when one refused to work the mine; the shaman's lame leg, damaged by a bullet, revealed the punishment for rebellion and practice of one's beliefs.

Padre Miguel Inácio vomited for a second time, a bilious stream that burned his throat. The shaman still sang, stroking his body with a bundle of leaves. Dona Zefinha continued to blow smoke over them. The song stopped. They helped him to his feet. He no longer heard the flute. All he could hear, as the sky lightened, was the call of a bird in the distance. He was back, but not as he had departed.

14

Padre Miguel Inácio delivered his third and last sermon in Bororó on a bright Sunday morning, the first Sunday of February, in a church so crowded that even after parents made their children sit on the floor and all the adults huddled shoulder to shoulder on the pews, some still stood by the doors, which remained open, so air could circulate through the congested space. With air entered mosquitoes, butterflies, and the dog, who laid her head on the lap of a child seated against the feet of Saint Francis. Boca de Ouro was at his accustomed place, accompanied by all his men and their women, including Venceslau's wife, who acknowledged the priest with a slight nod once he took his post at the altar. The only one missing, he noticed, was Dr. Claudio M. and the shaman, who was waiting for him by the river with a small canoe.

He crossed his hands upon his stomach and smiled, looking over the congregation. The muttering of soft voices and bodies shifting ceased immediately. "Friends." He paused, sighed deeply, and it was with great relief that he said: "I am of absolutely no service to you."

They calmly regarded one another. Only Boca de Ouro seemed startled. He coughed loudly, staring at him as if to say, "Be very careful with the next words you say, Padre," an expression that might have intimidated the priest some days ago.

But Padre Miguel Inácio realized that no one here was quite as lost, as afraid as this *patrão* who wore his bravado like one of his gaudy shirts. Once more the priest faces his erstwhile flock: "I can give you nothing that would equal the gift you've given me. You were a mirror that revealed my foolishness and arrogance, for only a fool believes that any man can save another's soul, and only a egotist believes he is the one to do it." Boca de Ouro bolted to his feet.

"Padre, what are you saying!" A murmur of hushed voices swept through the crowd. Boca de Ouro turned to the people. "The priest is not well today. Everyone go home!" He faced the priest. "Padre, we definitely need to—"

"No." Padre Miguel Inácio raised his hand. "Please sit down. I'll be brief."

"You're not well, Padre." The man's clenched jaw betrayed his attempt at feigning composure.

"On the contrary, I'm very well."

Boca de Ouro ignored the priest. He strode down the main aisle, gesturing for people to get up and leave. His men filed behind him, hustling their wives along.

"Boca de Ouro, they don't have to leave. *I'm* leaving."

"What are you saying," he yelled.

"It's very simple. The only way I can help these people," the priest chose his next words carefully, "is by leaving them." They have everything they need." His raspy voice held an unaccustomed intensity.

"What is wrong with you?" Boca de Ouro clutched his head with both hands, causing several of the smaller children to laugh at this comical pantomime.

The priest descended the altar and walked toward the door. Boca de Ouro fell into step behind him, claiming he'd known Padre Miguel Inácio was suspect from the moment he'd arrived, that he was a sham whose soul was bound for the fiery pit. But Padre Miguel Inácio remained unruffled. He paused, removed his robe to uncover the jeans and T-shirt he wore underneath, and handed it to Boca de Ouro. "You're right. I'm not a real priest. Here, take this from me. Do what you want with it."

"My friend the archbishop will hear about this, you understand?"

"Yes. I understand, Boca de Ouro." He nodded, inches away from the other man's face. "Tell His Holiness I went crazy and disappeared into the jungle. It will save me the trouble of writing a resignation."

The throng followed him outside. He stopped by the cherub fountain and faced them. Suddenly Zumira had him in a fierce hug, and he remembered what he had seen the previous night, remembered the child in her womb that she would remain unaware of for at least another month. He placed a hand on her head. He knew the doctor would leave at the first signs of morning sickness, the first missing period—that is, if he hadn't already fled. He looked around, at their faces, at their ageless, serene eyes. They'll survive anything, he thought, for such was his optimistic nature, but immediately afterward he had a moment of doubt. Their spirit would survive because, after all, spirit was eternal. Besides that, he was sure of nothing.

Dona Zefinha ran out of the parish house, his small valise in one hand and in the other, his lost sandals. She smiled the smile he had grown to love, and when she gave him his luggage, he kissed her forehead. Boca de Ouro stood by the church doors with his men, fumbling with his sunglasses, unable to conceal a look of abandonment. Miguel Inácio muttered a silent prayer for him. Of all of them, he would suffer the most.

He turned his back to the church, donned his sandals, and strode into the forest, the dog trailing at his heels. Behind the trees, the river sang.

Ouroboros

Quando Deus quer, água fria é remédio.

The men who spied the skeletal figure in the distance took it for an apparition, another restless ghost shimmering in the afternoon heat. It shuffled toward them slowly, shirt and pants limp on a bare pole of a frame, hands enormous at the end of spindly arms. The men exchanged glances. Some sipped their drinks, pausing the domino game once they could discern the face, the flesh tight like the skin on a drum, the loose hat shading eyes that shone like glass. It was a man all right, and he looked as ancient as the dirt caked on his feet. When he opened his mouth, his breath seemed to give off smoke. "Where can I find a seer by the name of Pascoal?" he asked, his voice the creak of a leather hinge.

He might as well have asked the date of their deaths, for they remained silent, ivory pieces frozen in their cupped hands. They turned to the establishment's owner, who half rose from his stool and, eyes fixed on the man, yelled, *"Ô menino!"*

A boy of about nine emerged from inside the tavern, holding a broom.

"Take this gentleman here to Old Man Pascoal's."

The boy darted a nervous look at the owner, then set the broom against the tavern's outer wall.

And so the stranger followed the boy down the sun-baked

streets, devoid of life at that hour except for dogs lying in the scant shade of a few scraggly trees. The terrain was remorselessly flat, not a hill or hummock to relieve the monotony. Overhead the blue of the sky promised no rain. They wound through five or six identical roads where houses butted against one another, separated only by the bright, simple colors of their facades, and arrived at an empty lot. At the far end stood a shack—its stance so lopsided and precarious it seemed that the next decent gust would complete its downfall. The roof on one side had decayed, only the bleached beams of wood and a handful of tiles remained. The cement that had once covered the outer walls clung in irregular, scabrous patches to the posts.

"Here you are, mister," the boy announced, heading back immediately.

The man clapped his hands, signaling his presence.

No answer.

"*Ô de casa!*" he called out.

Still no answer. He peered through the open window. In the gloom of the hut, amid a clutter of boxes and bottles, he discerned two feet hanging over the back of a dirty, white couch. He tried the door. It fell open, wobbling in its warped frame. He entered and removed his hat.

"Excuse me, Senhor Pascoal?" he said. He heard a loud snore, inched forward to inspect the body. An old man on his back—black, skinny, a gray beard and a drunkard's distended belly, wearing nothing but shorts. A shaft of sunlight shone through the rotted roof directly onto his face. His right arm extended over the edge of the couch; his hand clutched another hand, white fingers laced with his dark ones. The man, startled by that other person, craned his neck in curiosity.

It was a doll. Life-size, the kind common in Olinda during Carnaval: cotton-stuffed body, hard plastic head, pale face, black mane of hair that reached a tiny waist, blue button eyes, red heart-shaped mouth. On her dress, sunflowers; and on her feet, high-heeled leather shoes.

As if sensing this spying on his beloved, the man stirred. He opened his eyes and gawked at the dust-coated revenant, hat clutched against his chest. "Are you Death?" he asked.

"No sir," the stranger replied, calmly, a note of melancholy in his voice.

"Are you a ghost, then?" He lifted the doll from the floor and settled her beside him, hugging her waist. One of her arms flopped onto his ribs.

"I wish I were, sir." He came around to face the couch. "Are you Pascoal the Seer?"

Pascoal laughed, a dry, toothless cackle. "*Meu amigo*, all I see these days are cockroaches, spiders, dust, bottles. And my sweet honey bun here."

"Does the name Saturnino mean anything to you?"

Pascoal's laughter became a fit of coughing. He pounded on his chest. "Who are you?"

"My name is Uriel Augusto. I'm one hundred and twenty-four years old. I was cursed by a fish long ago, and now I cannot die. I'm hoping you can help me, Pascoal. Because I don't know of anyone else who can."

Pascoal sat up, grunting, hacking, moving the fluids in his chest and throat. He propped the doll upright beside him, pressing her knees together so that Uriel could not see under her skirt. His movements released a pungent cloud of stale alcohol. He coughed again and asked, "How did you hear of me?"

"From a woman on her deathbed in Caruaru, who had been in Jatobá during the time of the fish. She remembered that, in the entire town, you were the only one who saw the thing for what it was: a curse. She told me you had arcane knowledge. I've been looking for you for a decade, under every rock in this god-forsaken wasteland."

Pascoal said nothing, just felt along the ground for his bottle, found it, and took a long pull. He held it out to Uriel, who waved it away. Pascoal then held the doll's knee and whispered something to her that the old man couldn't hear. He shook his head, muttered over and over, "I'm not surprised, not one bit." Then he addressed his guest. "This, by the way, is Lindalva. Please have a seat."

Uriel moved some wooden sticks—ceiling fragments—from a chair and sat down, his back erect, feet crossed at the ankles. He exuded the bemused air of someone who no longer expects anything from life. To the right of the single room was a kitchen, filled with an assortment of cardboard boxes and wooden crates, and a corroded cast-iron stove squatting in the corner.

"Okay, old man. Tell me your story."

Uriel's words flowed in a monotonous stream, a cadence that did not vary or falter. His travails originated forty-four years ago, when he was eighty years old and extremely sick. "Good as dead." His heart had failed three times in the space of three months. He would not have lived through another attack; of that his doctor was certain. An operation was risky and financially impossible. "And had I been rich, I would have prohibited it all the same; at that age, what is the point?" He spoke so softly that Pascoal had to cock his good right ear toward his guest. "You see, the idea of dying didn't bother me one bit. I raised three daughters. Saw them bear children of their own. Saw their children's children, even their children's children's children."

"I get the idea," Pascoal said, shifting his feet impatiently.

But his mule-headed wife, Uriel continued, refused to let him go. "Everyone in the Sertão had heard of the fish, how the water from its bowl cured ills. It was at the height of its fame."

But he couldn't recall ever seeing it. All he knew was what his wife and youngest grandson later told him, and each one told a different version.

"In my wife's story I *begged* her to take me to the creature, after awakening from a feverish sleep in which I'd been talking to someone in the room—whom only *I* could see; she waited until the sun rose and summoned the two boys, who bore me on a stretcher to a bus filled with other pilgrims. She swore up and down that I was lucid the entire time, imploring to God to let me live. The fish lady—"

"Otália?"

"Yes, her. According to my wife, Otália had been expecting me, which meant I didn't have to wait with the others. She saw me in immediately, sprinkled some of Saturnino's water on my head, told my wife and grandsons to pray, that I'd be better in a day or two. My wife said I fell into a deep sleep and later woke up bothering her."

Pascoal chuckled and winked at his doll. "You keep talking that way, you'll make Lindalva blush." He took another swig from the bottle. "Sounds like horseshit. And what did your grandson have to say about it?"

"I was just about to tell you."

"Well, go on."

"This second version was told to me, as I mentioned, by the youngest of the two, who died at fifty-five. Poisoned from so much *cana*." He lowered his gaze to the bottle by Pascoal's feet. "My wife had already passed. Two years after the fuss with the fish, she went peacefully, in her sleep. And since she was dead, and no one knew the whereabouts of my other grandson, I kept close to the boy, the only one who knew what had really happened. By then I was one hundred years old; my daughters, old women. I knew something was wrong with my biology; something had gone awry after my meeting the fish. There were many signs, some great, some small.

"Once a cholera epidemic swept through my town, and I contracted the disease. Although I had every symptom, I didn't die, just suffered until the fever burned itself out in my dehydrated, malnourished, breathing carcass. Another time I tested myself and went two months without eating a bite of anything. I became so weak I couldn't bear the weight of my own head. I just stayed in bed talking and cursing ghosts, wife, and others. But my heart wouldn't stop. I could look into their world, but couldn't cross over.

"Years later, when I had gained a fearsome reputation as some sort of walking blasphemy against God, someone slipped rat poison into my food. I puked bile, shit blood and stomach lining for three days, and on the third day, like Jesus himself, I got up and walked outside, and none would meet my eyes. That's when I confronted my drunk of a grandson. Finally he told me." Uriel stopped talking, morbidly still in his silence.

"What? You think this is a soap opera?" Pascoal asked impatiently.

"I need some water, please. I didn't think I still had all these words in me."

Grumbling, Pascoal stood, slipped his feet into his sandals, and shuffled out the back door, to a spigot that sprouted in the shade of the outhouse, returning a minute later with an aluminum cup filled to the brim. He handed it to Uriel and flopped back down, stretching his arm along the couch behind Lindalva's head. "Now. Your grandson's story?"

Uriel drank with the same lethargy that suffused every movement of his body. He smacked his flaccid lips, wiped his mouth with the back of his hand. "Yes. My grandson's story. This is what he said, before he passed: My wife—who always ruled the house through nagging and coercion—summoned the brothers, telling them their grandpa was in dire need of their help, and naturally they obeyed her. Once at our house, they saw my stiff figure on the bed, covered by a white sheet. My wife assured the two that I was not *dead*, but very sick; that we didn't have money for my operation, that my only hope was this miracle fish out in

Jatobá. That I must not be seen by anyone lest I fall prey to the evil eye. So he and his brother hustled my inert body across the desert on a stretcher. Even though it was the season of the blood moon, when no sane man crosses the Sertão, they endured two nights under its hellish stare to get me there."

"You were dead!" Pascoal blurted, as if solving a riddle.

"I believe so. By the time they got to Jatobá, the fish lady was so fatigued she could barely stand, let alone discern the condition of every penitent. He said they forced some of the damned thing's water down my throat."

Pascoal widened his eyes. "You *drank* it?"

"I had no choice. I wasn't present. Only my body was."

In response to this tale a different Pascoal, suddenly solemn, sober, rose and paced the room, scratching his grizzled beard, speaking aloud. This would require arduous work, he said. He would need to realign himself with the cosmos, once again become a conduit for the ancient knowledge he'd been granted at birth. "The rampant ignorance of these lands has made it impossible for me to exercise my talent. An *alchemist*—for that is what I am, Uriel—is, ultimately, an artist, you see, and what is the use of an artist without an audience?"

Uriel looked to his feet. "I have nothing to offer you," he said. "But my life."

"Your life is sufficient payment, Uriel. We have a deal."

And so Pascoal embarked on his most ambitious project: the quintessential alchemy, the grand transformation, life and death. He felt the fire of his youth rejuvenating his worn body. Felt, simply put, fated to solve Uriel's dilemma. He felt needed. Had Pascoal not prophesized, as a young man of thirty-four, the arrival of Saturnino? Had he not warned the citizens of Jatobá? If only he could have shown them a window into the future, shown them what eventually became of their beloved town: an accursed spot given wide berth by all travelers, a cluster of abandoned buildings inhabited only by vultures and the haunted desert wind. His intuition told him that, indeed, Uriel embodied the last living plague of that apocalyptic damnation, the last link in that reprobate chain. He saw, with his astral eye, the divine orchestration in this turn of events.

At sunset Pascoal excused himself and took a walk with Lindalva, to meditate on a proper course of action. When he returned to the dark house, he set Lindalva on the back porch and entered silently, in case Uriel had fallen asleep. He pulled the cord of the single naked lightbulb in the center of the living room and found Uriel still on the chair, in the same position as before. He waved a hand in front of the man's face.

"Yes?" Uriel said.

"You haven't moved?"

"No."

Pascoal sighed. "We'll have to get used to you, old man. You act like a corpse already." Then he announced his plan.

First and foremost they would need to clean up the place: "For a tidy workspace leads to an uncluttered mind." Next, he would need to clean *himself* up. Meditate. Dust off his notebooks. Reconstruct his laboratory. Study. Practice. Stop drinking.

"That is why, tonight, I will have the *cachaça* of my life, Uriel. Whether you join me or not, I will finish all the bottles I have left in the house. As of tomorrow, mark my words, I will drink again only at your funeral."

The night was clear but moonless, cool after the torrid heat of daytime. In August the winds would start, but now the air lulled, the stars poised in their rotation. While Uriel, from the porch, manned the old radiola, switching records and skipping ahead to or repeating his host's favorite songs, Pascoal danced with Lindalva in the center of a circle delineated by candles. He wore his best clothes: black trousers too tight for his waist, a dingy white shirt, black shoes (his only pair), and black socks. As for Lindalva, it was obvious that she had been made for dancing. Her feet expertly hooked onto her partner's, their outstretched arms glued onto each other's. Her hair fell over his right hand, which pressed her tightly to him. Pascoal was a head shorter than she, his face buried in the crook of her neck, his hips moving in ways quite inappropriate for his age. After a few tunes he would exit the circle either to visit the outhouse (in which case he would prop Lindalva against the zinc wall) or to drink another shot. He tottered his way to the porch, beaming, negotiated the two concrete steps, and refilled his glass from the clay urn into which he had emptied three bottles of homemade *cana de cabeça*— bequeathed to him by the illiterate Dona Cândida for writing last month's correspondence to her sister in Minas. The more he drank, the slower he wanted his songs. "Play only the *xotes* in this one, Uriel," he ordered, handing him a Luis Gonzaga record. At another point in the night, he crouched next to Uriel, setting Lindalva on his right leg. Gazing at her in rapt adoration, he remarked, "Isn't she something? Tell me, Uriel, isn't she? Blessed the hands that transformed cloth and cotton into this masterpiece. A true alchemist!"

Seated on a beer crate, Uriel nodded. All traces of the serious, scientific man he had glimpsed that afternoon had vanished. Tonight Pascoal was the universal drunk, aware of nothing but the moment he inhabited. Such blatant display of lunacy, however, did not cause Uriel to second-guess the trust he had conferred upon Pascoal. On the contrary; he accepted it as an affirmation of fate, for he had lived long enough to bear witness to the fine line separating genius from madness.

"I'm telling you, Lindalva is *formidable*! She knows my movements before I know them myself. Why don't you try a song?"

"No," Uriel said, his chin resting on his palm.

"Oh, come on. Let her teach you," Pascoal insisted. He persisted with variations of this same request throughout the night until he could no longer stand, his sweaty body slouched on the porch, dawn fast approaching: "Come on, Uriel," he slurred, an arm flung across his forehead, "dance with Lindalva . . . This woman's too much for one man."

Uriel stared at the doll, lying beside her incapacitated partner on the floor. It occurred to him that she seemed happy, more alive than he'd ever be. He stood and helped the two into the house, removing Pascoal's shoes and wet socks before laying the old man and his darling side by side on the couch.

They spent the next two days dusting, sweeping, throwing away trash, chipped pieces of tile, wooden beams, chunks of dried red clay from the walls. Afterward they set up Pascoal's work space, which he insisted Uriel call *the laboratory*, not *the kitchen*. He explained to Uriel that henceforth he should consider the cast-iron stove a contraption responsible for "divine transmutations." They stacked all the sealed cardboard boxes in front of the stove, releasing a wave of roaches and spiders that Uriel squashed with his flat feet. They stretched a clothesline across a wall in the living room and neatly hung all the clothes scattered about the floor. Pascoal wasted little time eating or sleeping, and his guest less so—in fact, Uriel barely ate anything besides the nuts and seeds Pascoal saved in plastic containers for the crows in his backyard. He slept upright on the hard chair, his head lolling forward, his eyes half-lidded, like a lizard's or a snake's.

As they worked, Pascoal recited the basic principles of alchemical lore, "so as to charge up the atmosphere." Sometimes he would halt in the middle of a chore and lose himself in long passages, his tone pedantic, his gesticulations didactic, as if directing his words to a classroom. The more he remembered the more he spoke, so that most of the tasks ultimately fell to Uriel.

He spoke of the two wisdoms: the king's vs. the queen's, or solar versus lunar ways of knowing; of a man named Aristeus and the famous letter he once wrote to his son, wherein he counseled the boy on the importance of air, the key of nature. He spoke of mercury, "the philosopher's gold"—as well as the philosopher's stone, the philosopher's fire, and the philosopher's egg. He quoted the principle of Occam's razor, in which the simplest theory has the best chance of being correct, at times addressing his words to Uriel, at times lecturing Lindalva. His eyes glazed over with fervor when he spoke to her: "the philosophers' stone, Lindalva, is unique, and one, but veiled in a multiplicity of different names. It is watery, airy, fiery, and earthy, phlegmatic, choleric, sanguine, and melancholy."

He kept circling back to the Prayer for Ancient Knowledge— according to him, the one thing that must be perpetually ongoing, mantric, unfailing, in some part of the alchemist's mind:

The resurrection of the Word.
A tear has occurred
in the infinite fabric of knowledge and meditation.
The Light of God is here again.

Once he deemed the house sufficiently organized, Pascoal began the emotional task of opening the boxes, carefully, one by one. Emotional because each item—be it an old, yellowed notebook; a thin, brittle parchment; a magnet, mirror, or beaker; Bunsen burner or microscope; a block of lead, a crystal, a test tube—elicited a long-forgotten memory in him. He pondered each thing as though it were a photo of a dead sweetheart.

Uriel, in his infinite patience, waited on one end of the sofa, seated beside Lindalva. Once Pascoal emptied all the boxes and organized their contents, he joined them in the living room, a

pencil behind his ear, a large book in his hands. He situated himself between them and, taking advantage of the midday sunlight
directly overhead, placed the heavy, gilt-edged *Manual of
Practical Alchemy* over his skinny legs. He pointed a finger to the
elaborate, colorful drawing on the cover and said, "*This,* my
friends, is a sacred mandala. *The Azoth*—" here he affected a pro-
longed sibilant "—*of the Philosophers.* The *a* and *z* of the Word
itself," he continued, arching his eyebrows, "relate to the Greek
alpha and *omega,* the beginning and end of all things." He
opened the manual ceremoniously and blew on the first page,
releasing flecks of gold dust that shimmered in the light shafting
through the roof.

"And now I must study," he announced. "Please, you two.
Quiet down."

Pascoal leafed through dozens of alchemical facts, recipes,
and illustrations, until he realized, after a while, he'd lost the
focus of his search. He closed the book and intoned the Prayer for
Ancient Knowledge, as well as a prayer to Our Lady of the
Lamps, asking for divine illumination. He opened the book somewhere toward the end, closed his eyes, and lowered the yellow
nail of his index finger onto the page. He looked to where it
pointed and read the following excerpt:

On Material Decomposition:
    The body in which the soul and spirit resideth we
are not concerned for; it is mere earth, and must return
from whence it came, whereas the soul and spirit are
paradisiacal, if the artist can free them from their
earthy prison without loss; but this can only be done by
Death. In order to achieve this Ultimate
Transformation, the artist must follow the seven steps of
the Emerald Formula, respectively, applying them without deviation in the following order: Calcination,

Dissolution, Separation, Conjunction, Fermentation, Distillation, and Coagulation.

He set the manual on Uriel's lap, sprang from the couch, and knelt on the newly swept concrete floor, thanking a host of angels, philosophers, and saints, among them father Cícero Romão Batista of Juazeiro and *Nossa Senhora das Candeias*, for he now had a clear, concise plan of action. He raised his arms, palms upturned, and sang, "Blessed and praised be the Light that illumines me." He felt armed for the combat against the curse of Saturnino, his loins girt. He plucked the pencil from behind his ear, a crumpled sheet of paper from the pocket of his shorts, and jotted down a list, handing it to Uriel. "We're in business, my old friend," he said. "Go to the *mercadinho*, up on the asphalt road," he stretched his arm westward, "two streets over, next to the school, and ask Jean-Pierre to put everything on my account. Tell him I'll settle it next month. Meanwhile, I'll meditate on the Seven Steps."

CALCINATION

Uriel donned his hat and stepped out into the sunlight, walking the path of sand and stone that led into the middle of town. Three days had passed since his arrival. At this hour most sprawled in their hammocks, immobilized by heat. The handful of citizens he encountered along the way acknowledged his presence with a wary "Good afternoon," which he returned by touching the brim of his hat. Once on the asphalt road, Uriel heard the shrieks of children at play that issued from behind the high stone wall to his left. This was the school Pascoal had mentioned. He paused at the wrought-iron gate, watching the youngsters, their tireless movements and high-pitched cries reminding him of a flock of crows. Just past the schoolyard he came to the Armazém do Francês, the town's only grocery store. An adolescent girl slouched beside the entrance, smoking a cigarette next to a giant sack brimming with rice. As he stepped under the awning, she straightened and said, "Hey, are you the man who's staying with Pascoal?"

"Yes."

"Are you his father?" she asked, dipping her free hand into the pool of brown grains.

"No," he said, and passed her the list. She fixed her eyes on him—a look of unabashed fascination—before taking the paper from his fingers.

"Oh, I don't work here. But I can help you find these, if you want."

"Thank you."

She tossed her cigarette on the road, picked a basket from a pile by the cash register, and handed it to Uriel. He followed her down the narrow aisles. A fat cat and her kittens scampered underfoot. A birdcage hung from a roof beam beside the front counter, its canary whistling a three-note phrase that sounded like a question.

They found the first item on the list, a box of Olho matches, against the back wall. She read the second item aloud, haltingly, attempting to decipher Pascoal's handwriting: "*Seven-day* . . . candle, white, *pref-ferra-bly* Our Lady of the Lamp. Ah!" She knew exactly where the candles were. She squatted in front of the colorful glass cylinders, shuffling through the images of saints until she held up, triumphant, the one featuring a perfect flame floating above Our Lady's extended palm.

She read the third item and frowned. "Oil of vitriol? I don't know what this is." She skipped to the next thing on the list: "Sodium . . . what?" and the next: "*Hydro-gen-sul . . . huh?*" and the next: "Okay! Salt. Finally something I recognize. What kind of groceries are these, anyway?"

Uriel shrugged. At that moment a voice said, "May I help you?" The girl jumped, and even Uriel startled at the sudden appearance of a disheveled man with a bristling white mustache and drowsy blue eyes.

"Jean-Pierre!" she shouted, a hand over her heart, "you almost killed me!"

"I'll take over from here, Ninha." He retrieved the list from her hand. "Skipping class again?"

She strolled away, throwing an insolent glance over her shoulder. "I'm fifteen years old, Jean-Pierre. It's no one's business what I do with my time."

He introduced himself to Uriel. "You must be Pascoal's guest. Frankly, we're all surprised that he's got company. This is a first."

"Yes, I'm Uriel. Pascoal will pay you next month," he added, and did not speak again until the man had packed all the items in a brown paper bag, at which point he murmured a barely audible thank you.

He took the same path back home and entered through the open front door. He found Pascoal by the stove, bent over a boiling pot.

"Ah, perfect timing," Pascoal said, seizing the bag from Uriel's arms. He asked Uriel to follow him to the backyard where, a few meters behind the outhouse, rose a motley pyramid of wooden trusses, planks, fragments of furniture, a legacy from his short-lived flirtation with carpentry. He burrowed into the mess and produced a hammer, a tin can full of nails, a rusty saw, and a measuring stick. "How tall are you, anyway?"

"I don't know," Uriel replied.

"Well, let's see." Pascoal moored the stick in the ground by Uriel. It reached the middle of his thigh. He placed a palm there and raised the stick once again, pinching off the point where it came level to the top of Uriel's head. He squinted at it. "One meter seventy-five. Remember that. Here's what I want you to do next. Listen closely."

And Pascoal revealed to Uriel the formula for assembling his coffin.

DISSOLUTION

Shortly before sunset Pascoal emerged from his shack, carrying a tin cup covered by a saucer. "I have something I need you to drink," he said.

Uriel put down the hammer—he was prying nails from the top of an old dresser—accepted the cup from Pascoal's hand, and summarily drained it. Stupefied, Pascoal asked, "Don't you want to know what it is? What it will do to you?"

"Not really," Uriel said, wiping his chin.

"Well, *that* was the dissolution from the ashes of calcination in water, my dear Uriel. This stage represents a further breaking down of the artificial structures of the psyche by total immersion in the unconscious, nonrational, feminine, or rejected part of your mind; it is, for the most part, an unconscious process in which your conscious mind will let go of control, allowing the surfacing of buried material. It will open the floodgates of—"

Uriel handed him the empty cup, picked up his hammer, and returned to the nails on the dresser without excusing himself. Pascoal stopped talking and marched toward the house, indignant.

SEPARATION

Uriel spent most of that balmy, starred night in the outhouse. Pascoal escorted the diarrhetic man each time, a worrisome doc-

tor, meeting him by the door with a glass of water, assuring him
that this reaction was normal. "You're being cleansed. On *all* lev-
els."

Though he said nothing, Uriel worried that this was the most
life his body had shown in years.

To make matters worse, when he drifted to sleep in his chair,
he dreamed.

CONJUNCTION

He awakened to see Pascoal seated on the sofa, smiling inquisi-
tively at him, holding a steaming aluminum cup over his knee.
Lindalva sat beside him, legs crossed, hands clasped in her lap.

"Good morning," Pascoal said, and it occurred to Uriel that
he had been the subject of examination for some time. "Feeling
any better?"

Uriel rubbed his eyes, looked at the window, then up at the
broken ceiling, at the sun high in the sky. Pascoal passed him the
cup, containing "the recombination of the new elements saved
from separation into a new substance." As an afterthought, he
added, "Don't worry, it won't affect you the way the previous con-
coction did."

"Tastes salty," Uriel said. He finished it and promptly
returned to his project.

He couldn't stop thinking of his dream. In it he and his
brother watched their father tame a wild horse, and it didn't seem
that long ago that he'd witnessed the man being catapulted from
the back of a frenzied mare, flying over her neck and head to land
perfectly on his feet. It happened during the drought of 1870,
when they'd been caring for the ranch of a Portuguese baron.
Uriel replayed that scene in his mind all morning as he broke and
sawed and hammered together pieces of sun-bleached wood. The

same two crows he'd noticed the previous day contemplated his actions with beady, corvine curiosity. He christened them Becente and Becenta.

At lunchtime he heard Pascoal calling his name from inside the house. "Maybe I should tell him my dream," he thought, then decided against it. He didn't feel like speaking. He walked in, temporarily blinded by the change of light, and made out the figure of Pascoal sitting in his chair. He'd been eating sardines from a can. He wanted to talk, he said, licking the oil from his fingers. Uriel sat down on the couch across from him and removed his hat. Pascoal asked did anything feel different, had anything changed.

"I need to know that I'm on the right track." He peered into Uriel's eyes. "Conjunction is often when synchronicities begin to occur."

Uriel said nothing but motioned for Pascoal to follow him outside. Behind the outhouse he showed him the nearly completed coffin. Only the lid was missing. Overhead the two crows rose and fell on a current of wind.

FERMENTATION

That night Pascoal went out alone. He didn't bother inviting Uriel. He kissed Lindalva goodnight, gathered some of his dwindling savings from the kitchen drawer, and left, walking slowly along the shoulder of the narrow dirt roads to Severino's bar. He was brooding and morose. A seed of doubt germinated in the stony soil of his heart. He should have had a vision by now. He should have heard voices. Or at least a voice. Something.

"Nonsense, Pascoal," he said to himself. "Quit being so impatient."

But he needed a sign, and he needed it badly. A drink would help him; it would dull the mundane rationality of his scientific mind. What day was it, anyway? He couldn't remember, but by the flickering blue lights and the drone of televisions in the windows and the young couples dallying in doorways, under streetlights, he deduced that it was Saturday.

At least half of the town's men were at Severino's bar. They filled the three tables outside, playing cards, dominoes, smoking, telling loud jokes. Drinking, of course. Someone hailed him as he walked in, but he pretended not to hear. Tonight he didn't feel like talking with any of these folks, these men of simple minds, whose thoughts and conversations never strayed from women, soccer, the lack of rain. Tonight he wished he'd been nameless and anonymous, in a city the likes of Prague or Budapest. He sat at the end of the counter and ordered two shots of *cana*, the first of seven pairs. On this protracted, insufferable night, his mind roamed the crooked tower of his life, opening old boxes, dusting off old thoughts, until at some point, unaccountably, he recalled the first time he'd succeeded in purifying, isolating, and fusing the right ingredients that make up the substance of philosophical mercury. "The liquid which does not wet the skin," he said out loud, staring into space. What divine rhapsody, what inexplicable ecstasy he'd felt then, as a young man of forty-five, having transformed kinetic energy into inert substance. Being able to *touch* magic, to palpate his convictions. What a blessing!

He waited, but the sign he longed for did not come, not even when his rational mind was so affected by the alcohol that his eyes merged objects and people and earth and sky into a single whirling vortex. On his way out he bumped into a table and heard the sound of shattering glass, followed by laughter and cries of *Vovô!* from the men who grabbed his arms to steady him. He shook himself loose from their grasp, mumbling, "*Grandpa* is the mustache of your hairy mother, you hear?" and stumbled back home. He tripped on the stairs, sprawled onto the back porch, and stayed there, glancing up at the universe that revolved around him like the feathers on a peacock's tail. "Death is a slow poison," he said. "When and why did I begin to die?"

DISTILLATION

"Pascoal," Uriel called out. "Pascoal!"

His head throbbed; his eyes did not want to open. When they did, what he saw brought back the full force and seriousness, the gravity, of his predicament. The portrait of Uriel, the pathetic concern on his decrepit features as he knelt and offered Pascoal a cup of coffee—coffee made by his own hand—wrenched the alchemist's heart. He would not abandon this creature, who had been discarded by God himself. Not he. Not Pascoal Agamemnon Gomes da Silva.

"Thank you, my friend." He struggled to sit up, feeling the malodorous wetness inside his pants. "Not to worry—what happened last night was part of the fifth major step." He leaned in to Uriel's face, rubbing his hands together. "The vision I needed descended upon me; I am now vivified, ready for the next two major operations." He clapped briskly. "Back to work. Not much time remains."

Pascoal filled a bucket from the main water tank. He bathed and shaved himself, a luxury in these parts, since the city of Xoroxoxó gave them running water only once a week. But he needed to be cleansed, and absorbing himself in the ritual kept guilt at bay.

He toiled away in his laboratory all morning, producing foul smoke and sour fumes, boiling and reboiling black antimony with purified sulfur to create *bezoar*, the representative compound for the sixth major operation. But he knew that in order for an effective alchemical product to be realized, the mental and astral influence of the alchemist had to be infused into the substance; his doubt, coupled with his behavior the previous night, could very well prevent him from achieving the desired result. He felt that, like Orpheus, he had looked back too soon. His mind sabotaged him. And he might as well admit to himself that Uriel wasn't acting, or looking, any deader. If anything the man seemed more vital than ever, working indefatigably with an otherworldly strength off a limitless reservoir of energy. No, he had to admit. His alchemy wasn't working properly.

Every so often he would leave his brew on the stove and visit the outhouse, where he could hear the clangor of Uriel's hammering through its thin walls. "If only I had the courage," he thought, "I would push a knife right into his heart."

And it was then that an idea took shape in his head.

"Uriel!" he shouted. "Come here."

He rushed outside, pulling up his waistband so that it covered his belly button. Uriel approached him, dusting off his hands on his frayed jeans. The sun was right above them; their shadows pooled under their feet.

"Yes?"

Pascoal patted Uriel's back. "Let's bring the coffin into the house. It's ready enough. You won't go beyond today, my friend."

Uriel felt disappointed, for he had grown attached to his handiwork and believed the coffin still needed work; he had not yet smoothed its edges. He also wanted to install a mirror on the inside of the lid. And perhaps paint it an appropriate black, or a dark purple. But he didn't dare question the alchemist, so the two old-timers hauled the coffin into the house. They set it down inside the back door. Pascoal retrieved a handkerchief from the pocket of his shorts and wiped his forehead. He breathed heavily, more so than Uriel. From the other pocket he removed a piece of paper folded in half. When he'd gathered his breath he said: "Now go to Jean-Pierre's and give him this."

———————

Yes, the plan was extreme, the solution inelegant, and, strictly speaking, not entirely alchemical, but he had given his word. An oath was an oath. Besides, every alchemist must devise a fallback scheme. He retraced the steps in his mind: He would grind the pills down to a fine powder and mix them with orange juice. Uriel would drink it and lie down in his coffin. Once he fell asleep Pascoal needed to be brave. He would use a knife. Extract the heart. Burn it. Blend the ashes into lead, make a ball from the mixture, and perform the *Plumbum Excommunicatum:* burying of the object in holy ground.

He turned off the stove, set the simmering emulsion on the back burner, and lay on the sofa with Lindalva, waiting for Uriel to return from Jean-Pierre's with the bottle of Deep Sleep. His head spun from the previous night's excess, his limbs like concrete. He pressed Lindalva to him, closed his eyes, and immediately began dreaming.

In his dream he could hear the liquid boiling and rushed to shut it off; but upon entering the kitchen he saw no formula or even a fire on the stove. He witnessed instead a clay bowl giving off a flickering, prismatic light. He was afraid to look inside, but it didn't matter, for the bowl became translucent, then transparent, revealing a fish swimming within it. And what struck him most about the fish was not its fins of riotous colors, or its fan-shaped tail, but the mournful expression he'd seen only on widows, gamblers, and statues of Jesus on the cross. He thought that this must be the saddest creature in the world.

COAGULATION

For the second time that day, Uriel tried to awaken Pascoal.

"Pascoal." He shook him by the foot, lightly. He raised his voice. "Old man Pascoal!" The alchemist just lay there grasping his beloved, his position almost the same as when Uriel had discovered him seven days ago. He didn't bother checking Pascoal's pulse.

He would have laughed bitterly, had he known how. They should have foreseen this. This was no garden-variety Indian hex, some old woman's evil eye, but a malignant force that could snuff out whoever dared meddle with it. Pascoal must have been close to releasing him from the fish's malediction.

He strode into the laboratory and saw, sitting inside a pan on the stove, a smooth black stone, the size and shape of a glass marble, still exuding heat. It was small enough that he could swallow it.

But first he must adorn Pascoal for the afterlife. From the clothesline he removed the pants and shirt the old man had used for dancing. They still smelled like cheap alcohol, and Uriel thought, "All the better," for it had to be Pascoal's favorite scent. He disentangled Lindalva from Pascoal's arms and carried her into the kitchen. He wrestled off the man's shorts, the single piece of clothing on his body, and maneuvered the pants onto his skinny legs, cinching them at the waist. The shirt proved a bit more complicated. Once Uriel succeeded in lifting the torso, the head lolled back, the arms dangled at the sides. He stretched the two halves of the garment together in order to button it across Pascoal's chest. He carried him in his arms like a bride and tucked him inside the coffin, which proved too narrow to accommodate the distended belly. He had to squeeze the sides of the stomach inward and shoehorn the corpse into the box so that it would lie flush with the bottom. Lengthwise, however, enough space remained so that Pascoal could stretch his arms above his head, had he been capable of such a thing.

Uriel sat panting for a moment, soaked in sweat, then rose and retrieved Lindalva from the kitchen. He placed her on top of her beloved, her face tilted upward. He smoothed the sunflowers on her dress and wrapped Pascoal's arms around her waist. Before shutting them away forever, Uriel fetched the mirror from the outhouse and glued it to the inside of the lid.

After that, he dug. He picked a spot about fifty yards from the house, next to a mandacarú bush, and sank the shovel into the soil. It took him the afternoon, and well into early evening as the shadow of the bush lengthened over the hole. Becente and Becenta watched him avidly, at times darting into the deepening pit, unfazed by the flying dirt and the flailing shovel, fishing for fat grubs. There, among the blind crawling things, inside the hole that by all rights should have been his, Uriel forgot his predicament, lost in the choreography of shovel and dirt. The darkness inside the raw earth was preternaturally still.

Only when he finished digging, a hole as deep as his height plus two heads, did Uriel realize his singular mistake: He couldn't possibly lift the coffin. He thought about fetching help—but there was no question in his mind that the alchemist would have wanted him as his sole mourner. He had to remove Pascoal and Lindalva from the box, transport them separately to the burial site. But then, how to lower them—gently, respectfully—into the hole? He crawled out of the grave and returned to the house. He yanked on the light cord, causing the shadows in the room to dance beneath the swaying bulb. He reopened the casket's lid.

"Didn't think I'd see you two again," he said.

After Herculean effort, Uriel managed to deposit the alchemist and his doll on their couch.

He carried the empty box to the hole and levered it into the ground. He did the same with the couple. He curled his forearms under Pascoal's armpits and pulled. The dead man's heels dragged twin furrows in the dirt. He placed Pascoal and Lindalva next to the mouth of the pit, then sat on the edge. He jumped onto the coffin's lid, which he'd fashioned from an old door. There was just enough room for him to stand beside the coffin and ease them into it from inside. "If the dead only knew the work they leave for the living," he thought.

He buried them without ceremony. Perhaps if he hadn't been so exhausted, he would have tried to remember a prayer or included some of Pascoal's revered books, his pans, his writings.

Uriel staggered back to the house. With a last bit of energy he swallowed the black stone Pascoal had left atop the stove. Then he remembered the bottle of Deep Sleep by the couch, and he swallowed those too, all thirty of them, recalling the popular adage, What doesn't kill you fattens you.

He turned off the light and sank into his chair, rubbing the muscles on his lower back with the palms of his hands, sighing deeply at the prospect of returning to a life of wandering, of sand and wind and sun.

Uriel looked up at the ceiling, at the approaching dawn, and wondered where the night had gone. The world seemed outlandish, make-believe, far away. As the last star faded into the dome of the sky, he wished he could follow it. Then he closed his eyes.

AND STORIES

Antonio de Juvita

1

A ntonio Didier, better known as Antonio de Juvita after his mother, the fine maker of liqueurs Juvita Didier, would return to his home only in May 1945, two years and three months after leaving for war. It was the first time Antonio had set foot outside Pesqueira, a town hidden in the innards of Pernambuco, whose citizens took pride in its appellation Atenas do Sertão, Athens of the Desert, given in honor of the abundant cultural activity thriving within its humble limits.

Antonio's decision to join the National Armed Forces came to all Pesqueirenses as a surprise, for he'd announced it in the heat of his campaign for mayor, when his only opponent was the incumbent, Marcelo da Farmácia, who had already served in office for eight years and was everything Antonio was not: hardworking, direct, a man of few words. A man of tradition. A family man. But over this serious rival, Antonio de Juvita possessed three serious advantages. He was thirty-one years old, two decades younger than Marcelo, and therefore catered to the generation which presently constituted the largest slice of Pesqueira's electoral pie; after eight years even old-timers were tired of Marcelo's voice, his mustache, the tuft of hair that sprouted like quills from the top of his head. Antonio had sympathizers —behind doors, beneath bricks, in dark corners and questionable establishments everywhere, women, men, children, hoboes, lunatics, prostitutes. Even mangy street dogs couldn't resist his contagious jubilance, his tales, his pranks. And he possessed what Dona Juvita referred to as a devil's gift for the word.

"This son of mine could sell a hairbrush to a bald man."

For all anyone knew, Antonio could have been fabricating half the fancy talk he used in his speeches; but no citizen could deny that the words from his mouth fell on common ears like pearls from the beak of a swan, starting with the title of the political party founded by Antonio himself, scrawled anonymously on numerous walls throughout Pesqueira: PPPPT—PARTY OF THE PROFOUND PRAGMATIC PLURALIST TRANSFORMATION.

And beneath it, in yellow letters, an alias: PARTY FOR THE PLEASURE OF THE PEOPLE OF PESQUEIRA TOWNSHIP.

Even listless children listened when Antonio de Juvita, impeccable in his imported clothes—Lee jeans and a linen Lunfor shirt with a gold pen clipped over his heart, Passo-Doble chrome-colored shoes, and a wide-brimmed Ramenzone, never worn, always held in his left hand—ascended the platform on that last Sunday of January, a month before the elections, took up the microphone, the one with a yellow rag around the base to represent his party, and did what he did best.

"Ladies! And gentlemen! The political post-Aristotelian logic of Pesqueirense politics that we have been encumbered with thus far has caused profound moral, Celtic, Stoic, and especially existential decodification to those of us who long to find, above all, a strong, although dogmatic, sectary political hemogeny! If elected mayor of this fine township, the Athens of my heart, I will enact a program utilizing plutocratic pseudo-progressive means in an evident demonstration of discretionary resistance, appropriative and antiplutocratic!"

Deafening applause. His Adam's apple, the exact proportions of his nose, bobbed with emotion. He produced a silk scarf from his back pocket and wiped his neck.

The square had the air of a celebration. Among those present were Father Tenório and his loyal sinners, long-faced on the steps of the luminous Our Lady of Grace, waiting to return to their Credos and Ave Marias; Colonel Altamiro, making leisurely rounds on his white horse; ladies from Casa Prelúdio, radiant in the yellow dresses Antonio had ordered for this special day, their lips lustrous like the *jambos* on the canopy of branches above them; his diehard childhood companions, Beto, Arnaldo, and best friend, Vladson, chairs hauled up onto the sidewalk outside Lindalva's Bar, glasses raised to him in a toast.

The sun now reflected off the riotous facades of houses at the east end of the square. The Didiers' was the one at the very corner, with the freshly painted yellow door and window, next to Teco's Guitar & Mandolin Repair Shop and Tiradentes Street. Antonio scanned the crowd for something, perhaps a glimpse of red hair or the feather of a peacock in an elegant hat. Here and there dogs, chickens, and drunkards milled about, indifferent to the chaos around them, while teenagers took advantage of the tumult to flirt or kiss or conjoin body parts that could never meet in daylight, in open air. Popcorn, peanuts, *churros*, beer, Orange Fanta and Coca-Cola bottles flowed through the crowd in labyrinthine currents. Xucuru Indians, who'd been in the hills surrounding the town for as long as anyone could remember, also capitalized on the event by setting up kiosks that sold jewelry blessed by the shaman—powerful amulets against the evil eye.

After the cheering subsided, Antonio continued, smiling magnanimously:

"Unlike my pharmaceutical opponent who, if you will notice, follows the formula of three promises per minute!—I hereby promise only two promises!—for the entire duration of my mandate. Number one! To put not only meat on your plates and milk in your cups, but fine clothes upon your bodies, clothes like mine, books upon your shelves, and money in your pockets for whatever fancy your hearts desire, because you deserve it! Yes, thank you, thank you, my friends! "

He waved toward his right:

"Secondly, I promise to put Pesqueira on the map!—not only of Brazil but of the entire world! Greek Athenians will be modeling themselves after us! It so happens that I've been meeting with a friend, a fine architect from Recife, and I have a little surprise for you! Gabriel!"

He stepped aside and up came Vladson's seven-year-old son, carrying a thick roll of posters, one inside another. The boy struggled until he held them open, barely, eliciting delighted *oohs* and *aahs*. He stood on tiptoe and stretched his spindly arms as wide apart as he could.

"Do you know what your eyes are beholding, ladies and gentlemen? These seemingly insignificant drawings! these blue scribbles you're witnessing on this historic page! are nothing more, nothing less than plans for a future spa"—he snatched the top poster from the boy's hands and tossed it behind him, exposing the one beneath it—"a five-star hotel"—repeated the gesture— "and movie theater, ladies and gentlemen! Tourists from the seven continents, even cold explorers from Antarctica, will bypass Rio and come directly to Pesqueira!"

He ruffled the boy's head. "Now let's hear it for little Gabriel!"

The cheers rose in pitch and volume. Antonio formed a V with his fingers, shouting, "The V of Victory!" and folks in every corner of the square mimicked him, chanting, "Out with the old! Out with the old!"

Marcelo da Farmácia waited behind Antonio, inscrutable, hands interlaced beneath his belly, his oldest son at his side. The juvenile, whose vertical shock of hair mirrored his father's, made a final adjustment to the snare drum around his waist. A banner taped to the drum read WPP, for Workers Party of Pesqueira, in red block letters. Marcelo nodded, and the boy, eyes locked ahead, began playing a crisp military march. Antonio bowed deeply and passed the microphone. Marcelo gave him a look of stern disapproval, his mouth hidden beneath his mustache, a sober gray suit complemented by a sober gray tie. The only splash of color in his attire was a tiny red button with WPP over the left lapel of his jacket. He reached down to untie Antonio's yellow rag from the microphone's base, used it to mop the sweat from his forehead. Someone in the crowd booed. The boy played a final flourish, and Marcelo spoke:

"My fellow Pesqueirenses:" His voice cracked. He coughed while gesturing for silence, but the jeers grew louder, forcing him to press his lips to the microphone.

"It was out of respect for my opponent's father, *Doutor* Flávio Didier, the finest dentist to ever set foot in this town, my dear childhood friend, godfather to my firstborn, Arlindo, here, that I've refrained from telling you what my throat can no longer contain. Dona Juvita, forgive me, I have nothing but respect for her person and her talent, I *am* and will always be her faithful friend and customer—but I refuse to stand here and let this clown, this charlatan, bamboozle the citizens of the town I've served and loved my entire life. What does he think leadership is—winning at dominos? I, my friends, am familiar with the workingman's hardships. I personally know the despair of sitting at an empty table after a long workday. Of nothing but bread and coffee for weeks. Of multiple mouths to feed. I *know* the value of work, it's all I've known from the time I was nine years old and my mother dressed me in long pants and said, "'Go and help your father, Marcelo.'"

"Unlike my opponent, who still milks his poor mother even for the cigarettes he smokes, I can say, with a clear conscience, that I have nothing to regret, that I've honored my mother's name, that I've repaid her in double for her sacrifice. And I hereby promise to provide for my dear city with the same loyalty and care I have shown for the past eight years. If at *any time* any of you need anything, you know you can come knock on my door, even at midnight, with the certainty you'll find me ready to serve you. Now I ask, if my opponent is elected, where would you find *him* at such hour? Casa Prelúdio? And how would you deduce which room, which bed to look in? And if you *did* find him, with what potion would you awaken him from his drunken slumber? You would have to go to the Xucuru witch doctor, because I assure you, my pharmacy carries nothing strong enough for *that* job."

One of the women under the *jambo* tree threw a bag of popcorn at him. A dry wind dispersed the kernels over the audience. Marcelo smiled ruefully, shaking his head from side to side.

"Thank you." He extended a hand in her direction. "You've made my point for me. Look at the fine manners of your candidate's companions. 'Show me who you walk with and I'll show you who you are' is a truth we've heard from the mouths of our grandparents since the time we've considered ourselves people. What examples can these plebeians provide our children?"

By now the heckling was giving way to bored indifference. People sat on the ground, drinking, chewing, chatting. Marcelo contorted his face into an expression of deep pain.

"I only feel sorry for Dona Juvita, a fine woman who's had no luck with the men in her life. One left her too soon. The other has yet to leave her breast. I rest my case."

His son started a roll on the snare drum, which Marcelo immediately cut off. A smattering of applause came from his wife and children and a few deaf old-timers who resorted to visual cues, clapping whenever anyone else did. The boy tried to help him down, but Marcelo brushed his hand brusquely from his elbow. Antonio met him at the steps. For a moment both men stared straight into each other's eyes, then Antonio blinked, walked past Marcelo, and said into the microphone: "Let's hear it for my opponent, ladies and gentlemen! Let's show our old Marcelo that we, too, have English manners!"

People hollered. Marcelo da Farmácia was making his way along the edges of the crowd, trailed by his family, when Antonio said:

"*Ei*, Marcelo!"

Marcelo stopped and faced the platform.

"Lighten up, my friend. I have just the cure for your ill humor. Pay attention, for this is something else that cannot be found in your pharmacy!"

More laughter.

"Dear friends! I know we've barely entered February, that we're in the mood for Carnaval, but tonight I want every one of you to pretend it's June! and that tomorrow there's no work because it's Saint John's and you're obliged to celebrate! Senhor Valença!"

A renowned accordionist from a neighboring town appeared onstage in full São João regalia, playing the chorus to a popular *forró*. Another man joined him with a triangle, a third with a *zabumba* drum. Antonio leaped from the platform and joined the people, shaking hands and kissing cheeks and hoisting babies into the air.

At some point in the night, when everyone was too drunk and tired to notice, he disappeared, but the music only ceased once the last couple exited the square, when the sun already shone on the statue of Our Lady of Grace, carved in the previous century and placed on the highest hill of the region so that from any point in town one could look up and see Pesqueira's patron saint, in her blue and silver gown, watching over her people in benevolent glory.

Dona Juvita was already awake when Antonio arrived the next morning. He smelled her coffee as soon as he unlocked the front door. The curtains had yet to be opened, the white hammock rolled on its hook. He set the Ramenzone on the coatrack, next to the peacock-feather hat she reserved for special occasions; more of a decorative item these days, like the porcelain plates handed down through generations of Didiers, hanging on the walls among oil paintings of the Virgin made by the lady of the house herself. He dropped the posters on the wicker sofa, balancing a chocolate cake on his right palm. The house was nearly fifty years old, narrow and deep, its tiled floor painted to match the celestial blue of the ceiling. He crossed the corridor, lined with family por-traits on either side, and peeked into the windowless display room, stacked from top to bottom with shelves of his mother's famous vintages, the most popular flavors sporting such labels as Virgin's Sweat, Indian Prick, Angel Piss, Lazarus Juice, Perdition Nectar; others simply named by their essential fruit: passion, manga, *cajú*, orange, *mangaba*, fig. The names, along with their respective recipes, had been passed down to Juvita from her grandmother, whose mother had brought the basic formula from the Old World.

He found her on the back patio, still in her camisole and slip-pers, sturdy and erect as a coconut tree, changing the water bowl in one of her birdcages. He placed the cake on the wrought-iron table, kissed her tight red curls, and asked for her blessing.

"*Benção, Mainha.*"

"*Deus te abençoe, meu filho.*"

He sat on a stool and removed his shoes, watching her go about her morning routine. Of the twelve canaries, eight still remained. As she approached each cage, the proprietor sang and fluttered its wings.

"I heated up some *cuzcuz* from last night," she said without looking at him. "It's on the stove. There's cheese and bread in the basket. And coffee in the pot."

He thanked her as he withdrew to the kitchen, saying she was the best mother in Pesqueira—no, in Pernambuco, no, in Brazil, in all of South America, and Europe and Greece, in fact. He filled up a plate and a cup and returned to the patio. He put a spoonful in his mouth. "*Mainha?*"

"*Diga, filho.*"

"Were you there yesterday? I looked for you."

"I was busy with Carnaval orders. But I heard everything from right here."

"Did you hear them chanting my name?"

"I *thought* that's what I heard."

Antonio sipped his coffee. "Mother, you should have been there. The people love me. You're going to have a mayor for a son."

"Yes, Antonio, I'm happy for you. Though you know I worry. Marilita will be giving birth any day now, and Marcelo's been a fine mayor, really. He will be hard to surpass." She thrust her hand inside Azulão's cage and rubbed the little blue neck. The canary closed his eyes, leaning into her fingers.

"*Ora*, come on, Mother. Politics is politics. People are ready for something new. And I'm not the one knocking up the poor woman. Making babies is an easy thing to do, you know."

"You have a point. But still." She moved on to the next cage. After a moment of silence she said, "Antonio, I think there may be something wrong with Ulysses. He hasn't been cursing at anything, won't sing his *marinheiro* song. I've never seen him this way, so sad like this."

Ulysses was the household parrot. Dona Juvita found him on a June morning about eight years before, swaying from one leg to the other on the edge of the cement laundry tank and screeching passionately at the birds in their cages, "Shut up, bitches, shut up, bitches!" When he wasn't cursing, Ulysses liked to sing a well-known coastal ditty that went: "O tell me mariner, tell me mariner [*marinheeeiro só*], O who taught you how to swim . . . ?" The parrot entered the household not long after *Doutor* Flávio's infarction, and naturally, Dona Juvita accepted his sudden appearance as a gift from the Virgin—a little laughter to ruffle up the sadness her husband's absence left behind. Antonio, of course, took to him instantly, named him, clipped his wings, told everyone that he flew in all the way from a ship in the Atlantic, for he could only have learned such obscenities from a sailor's mouth.

Antonio greeted Ulysses on his *sapoti* tree—"*Bom dia, Ulysses, bom dia*"—and lifted him from his perch, kissing his smooth beak. Ulysses wobbled from Antonio's finger to his shoulder.

"So, we can finally have our chubby chicken here for lunch!" he tugged lightly on a green breast feather. "Should I start plucking?"

"*Te fode, te fode,*" Ulysses muttered, nibbling Antonio's hand.

"Ha! *Toma!*" Dona Juvita said. Antonio cut a piece of the chocolate cake and offered it to the bird. It stuck out a black, dry tongue and licked the icing.

"*Mainha?*"

She was spreading newspaper at the bottom of the last cage. "*Diga.*"

"You didn't give any ear to the things Marcelo said in his speech yesterday, did you? Because I tell you something, a desperate politician is like a rabid dog, no one knows when, how he's going to attack. How dare he bring up your name, that *fela da puta.*"

"*Fe-la-da-puuu-ta!*"

He petted Ulysses' head. "That's right, old duck. You're fine, aren't you? You just missed me, that's all. Come on, now. Repeat after me: *Mar-ce-lo-fe-la-da-pu-ta.*"

"Stop that, Antonio. You *know* he'll say it when Marcelo's people come over. Look," she emptied a dirty water dish into the laundry tank, then opened the spigot to refill it. "You think I'm throwing away all these years of friendship because of politics? Your father was godfather to his firstborn. And Marcelo helped cure your diarrheas and your bow-leggedness when you were still a little *porrete* running and shitting around. Don't you forget."

"How could I? You remind me every day. You said I used to pull at his eyebrows."

"That's right. In your diapers, from his lap."

"You see?" Antonio yawned. "Rivals from the start. This is just another way of doing what I did as a baby."

"Antonio!" she placed both fists on her hips. "This is no joke. You know how serious Marcelo is about all this."

"Yes, Mother. So am I. Serious *and* worried. Just look at what this election is doing to *me*." He bent over and parted his hair.

"What?"

"A bald spot. See? I saw it this morning." He pointed to the back of his head. "Look, look, it's right there."

"All I see are flakes from that dried-up cow drool you use. Wash that head, Antonio!" As an afterthought, she added, "I'm not even going to ask what mirror you spotted this *bald spot* in."

"The mirror in Vladson's bathroom, Mother. Where else would I be?" He placed Ulysses back on his perch, stamping his feet to knock off the ants that speckled his toes, and declared that he was going to sleep for a few hours before the boys showed up. "Campaign business. Today I'm delegating my cabinet ministers."

"Pass me that shirt right now. It's putrid. Ana is coming today."

He didn't unbutton but slipped it over his head and handed

it to his mother, who tossed it in the tank. She asked if Ana should make lunch for a battalion, and he, rubbing his hairy, thin belly, said not to worry, as long as there was plenty of cold beer, "or some of your miraculous Lazarus Juice," the boys would be more than happy.

He fell asleep in the hammock in his father's study, the room farthest from the street, best for daytime naps, although in truth, sleep came to Antonio anywhere, for he was blessed with the easy and deep slumber common only to children and drunkards.

Acauana, the Xucuru helper who came over twice a week, had to shake his foot repeatedly, and with a certain violence, before Antonio opened his eyes.

"Your friends have arrived, Senhor de Juvita." Her accent was singsong and archaic, the accent of the rustic Indian.

"What time is it?"

"Almost one o'clock."

He held on to the girl's arm. "Lazy bastards," he said, struggling to sit up. "I told them to be here at noon."

The conference convened at the kitchen table. While Acauana shuffled about with a broom, the birds screeched in their cages, and Dona Juvita filled orders in her workshop, Antonio appointed Vladson treasurer, Arnaldo secretary of educational affairs, and Beto minister of culture, respectively. Vladson, an accountant at his sister's father-in-law's shoe factory—the only of the four men married and presently employed—declared that his first mission upon assuming his post was to create a one *vintém* coin with the emblem of the Virgin on both sides. He claimed that he owed it to his wife, who in turn owed it to Our Lady of Grace. "She made a *promessa* in all our names, gentlemen. The woman spent two nights on her knees, promising Our Lady that if we came out victorious, no household in Pesqueira would be devoid of her holy image—" he looked behind him to make sure Acauana wasn't within earshot "—and that includes Evangelists and Indians, who you all know would shit on the face of the Virgin if they could."

Ulysses, from the back patio, cried out:

"Shit on the Viiiiiiiiiirgin! Shit on the Viiiiiiiiiirgin!"

The men laughed. "Well, gentlemen," Antonio said, "one thing I've learned in this life is not to mess with a *promessa*. Especially promises made to her." He wagged a finger at the drawing on the calendar hanging by the refrigerator. "Cursed the Christian who doesn't follow through with that lady. And believe me, I've seen her vengeful side. Jehovah has nothing on her."

"Yes, well," said Beto, the youngest of the four, who had the habit of cocking back his head before he spoke. "We'll have to make sure that, *somehow*, the coins don't circulate outside of Pesqueira. Any ideas?"

Antonio draped his head over his folded arms and sighed wearily. They had finished three bottles of Lazarus Juice, a case of beer, two bowls of boiled peanuts, a cauldron of barbecued chicken hearts—courtesy of Vladson's wife—and the chocolate cake Antonio had brought with him that morning.

"And you, Mr. Secretary of Educational Affairs," Beto addressed Arnaldo in an affected nasal voice, cupping his hand around an invisible microphone. "What are *your* plans for the higher learning of Pesqueira Township?"

Arnaldo, eyes slitted, seized Beto's fist and, fixing an invisible tie, answered, "The interviewing of fresh-minded, well-prepared, avid young women—*ahem*—pedagogical professionals to serve in our illustrious town's respectful bedro—*ahem*—our illustrious Desert Athens's classrooms."

At that moment they looked up and noticed Dona Juvita, leaning against the door. It wasn't clear how long she'd been standing there. She dried her hands on her apron, picked up a couple of empty bottles from the table, and uttered a few phrases they'd heard countless times while growing up: "Boys, your mothers must be worried. Time to go. Sweet dreams."

That night Marcelo da Farmácia's pharmacy, Farmácia Bom Modelo, burned to the ground—an act of arson with the dubious distinction of being, up to then, the single most heinous crime in Pesqueirense history. The perpetrator did it very late, when the town, still hungover from the previous night, slept soundly, not a dog or horse or chicken in sight. A gasoline-filled soda bottle thrown from the street shattered the display window, starting the fire, whose smoke quickly reached the apartment directly above the business, Marcelo's living quarters. Luckily all seven—Marcelo, his wife, his three boys and two girls— fled the building in time. There was much crying and hair-pulling, oh-my-Gods, *puta merdas*, much astonishment in the gesticulations of the townfolk; for once, a crime worthy of all the melodrama present there. Some bystanders just stood motionless, hypnotized by the tableau of flames that curled into the sky.

By the time the volunteer fire unit arrived, anonymous knocks and shouts of "Fire!" had awakened the town, including Antonio and his mother, who rushed immediately to the scene. Dona Juvita removed Angela, Marcelo's two-year-old, from the arms of a hysterical Marilita. Marcelo sat on the curb in his blue pajamas, holding his head in his hands. Even through the black smoke Antonio caught the searing look of intense loathing when Marcelo eyed him. He elbowed his way through the throng of people and blurted, "Don't even *think* that I have anything—"

Marcelo flew at him, landing a blow on Antonio's head. It took four men to hold him down. Onlookers were deliciously scandalized. This was turning out to be a most memorable night, with not only a fire but a political fistfight to keep tongues wagging for the rest of the year.

Antonio staggered up, wobbled over to Colonel Altamiro, and

demanded a private audience with him, immediately, in the *del-egacia*. At first the colonel didn't hear him. He was yelling at a group of boys to stop throwing firecrackers into the flames, at the same time petting the neck of his skittish horse. "You idiotic little anarchists, the place is full of flammables!" The animal snorted, making nervous pirouettes. "Have pity on your mothers!"

Antonio called out again. The colonel jerked on the reins violently until the horse stood absolutely still. "What is it, de Juvita?"

He repeated his demand. Colonel Altamiro reached inside his pocket, retrieved the jailhouse keys, and told him to go ahead and wait there, he'd be over once things calmed down.

All the municipal buildings bordered the square. Antonio walked the few blocks to the plain, unassuming structure, unlocked the door, lit the kerosene lamp, and rolled a cigarette. Before lighting it he switched off the metal fan on the desk, which hummed like a giant horsefly. Outside, the frogs' whistle sounded almost human. The place was empty, no prisoners, no deputies, no watchman or receptionist. There were only two rooms, one to the right of the entrance—the colonel's office—and, at the end of a short corridor, a rusty iron cell built like a cage, whose bars had, at one time or another, imprisoned a transient and motley roster of inmates that included jealous husbands and lovers, professional gamblers, Paulista cat burglars, feuding Xucurus who'd knifed each other over land, an endless stream of drunks, and more than a few kids, incarcerated at the behest of their parents for dipping into their father's wallets. It had never contained the kind of men Colonel Altamiro heard about on his radio, like those men in Recife, who raped and killed for fun.

The colonel (who years before gave up explaining to the populace that he wasn't a colonel but a captain), was single, middle-aged, with pronounced bones, more respected for being the owner of the sole radio in town. Some speculation ensued behind closed

doors about his private life, partly because of his manicured fingernails and his predilection for tight trousers, partly because of
his long bachelorhood. The radio, an OuveBem the size and shape
of a shoebox with a long antenna facing northeast, nestled inside
an alcove on the wall. The saint, a replica of Our Lady's monument, rested atop a pile of papers on his desk. While searching for
an ashtray, Antonio inspected the device, twiddling the dial on its
face until there was a click and a burst of static. He then fiddled
with the antenna and a second dial, stopping only when a voice
came through.

The show host spoke of Roosevelt, the United States of
America, and a first bombing raid upon German troops in a town
called Wilshemshaven. Williamshaven? Wilhelmshaven. Also, of a
conference in Morocco between Roosevelt and Churchill, at which
the American president had announced that the war could end
only with *an unconditional German surrender.* The announcer
then joked with a sidekick about the Brazilian general Leitão de
Carvalho, first mocking his name, "Big Pig," then his current
negotiations with the United States to send Brazilian forces into
the war, saying that Carvalho should wait at least a week *after* the
end of Carnaval, when he could guarantee sober troops. Or in fact,
any troops at all. Antonio listened intently, rolling one cigarette
after another, until he heard the colonel reining in his horse outside. He shut off the radio and assumed a rigid stance by the doorway, as if posing for a portrait.

Colonel Altamiro walked in, his whip attached to a braided
belt which he tugged over his girdled belly. His spurs scraped the
floor. He let out a sigh and, shaking his head from side to side, laid
a heavy hand on Antonio's shoulder. Both men stank of smoke.

"What a mess, no? Who would ever've imagined?" He sat
down behind his desk, removed his hat, and gestured for Antonio
to sit.

Antonio fidgeted on the plastic chair facing the desk. "I'm

here for obvious reasons, Altamiro." The colonel nodded. "I feel for Marcelo; I really do. But you know very well whom he is going to blame for this."

The colonel reached into a cooler under his chair, wrapped a few cubes of ice in a bandanna, and handed it to Antonio, who pressed it to the red lump above his eyebrow.

"Listen, Altamiro, you've known me since I was a kid. Okay, fine. Fine!" he held up his hands like someone being robbed. "I'm guilty of many things. I'll admit here, on this image of *Nossa Senhora*, which you're using as paperweight," he pointed to the wooden statue on the colonel's desk, "that most of the things people say about me *are* true." In a harsh and rapid cadence he mimicked Marcelo: "Antonio's lazy, hates hard work: true. Antonio loves a bottle: true. Antonio knows, *biblicamente*, all the girls from Casa Prelúdio: true. His mother bankrolls even the cigarettes he smokes: true, too, all of it, true." At this he produced a bag of tobacco and a pack of papers from his back pocket and expertly rolled another cigarette. Just as he was about to light it, he offered it to the colonel, who accepted. "But I swear, Altamiro," he jabbed a stiff index finger toward heaven, "I swear on the soul of my father, may it leave the Lord and travel straight to Satan's side right this moment if I'm lying, that I didn't have a thing to do with what just happened to Marcelo's pharmacy." He leaned on the desk, narrowed his eyes, and whispered, "You know, he probably had some secret business going on with the wrong people, some *capangas brutos*, like those farmers from Muro Alto or Assunção, the kind of *machos* who resolve anything with fire or lead." He raised an eyebrow. "I wouldn't be surprised, Colonel Altamiro."

After a short silence, the colonel spoke. "I hear you, Antonio." He clenched his hand into a fist, so that the cigarette stuck out from the middle like a finger. The kerosene lamp lit the left side of his face, stained black from ashes. "But in a town like this, no secret is kept secret for long. All I have to do is sit and wait." He smoothed the ends of his mustache. "Trust me, I will uncover the culprit. Soon I'll smell the gasoline on the son-of-a-bitch who did this to Marcelo. And then we'll see who's the *macho* around here!"

The whole of Pesqueira mourned the tragic fate of Farmácia Bom Modelo, an establishment that had provided faithful service every day of the week, except Sundays, since 1898, the year Marcelo's late father, Marcelo senior, finished school and started the sort of pharmacy-cum-general-store, the kind of typical interior city *venda* where nearly everything could be found. Not one envelope of *Aspirina*, not one bottle of Orange Fanta, *Lavanda* Iracema, Atkinsons English Lavender, Cepacol Cures All or Cibalena, rubbing alcohol or Perfume Helena Rubenstein, not one package of cotton balls or Modess, a jar of the ever-popular Capiloton for male baldness, Robustelth for Feminine Health, Peanutonor for a Gentleman's Honor, not a tube of Colgate toothpaste or a pocket comb Yolanda, a bag of tea leaves or a carton of Gillette or a single Tek toothbrush, nothing, absolutely nothing was salvaged from the fire. A rusty Coca-Cola sign survived above the display window along with the shady *mangueira* Marcelo senior had planted in a small earthen square on the pharmacy's first day of operation, and whose enormous roots had long since cracked the surface of the adjoining sidewalk. The tree bloomed with thousands of small white flowers. In the still air they drifted, like silent snow, onto the scorched ground beneath.

Once again Antonio de Juvita didn't come home to sleep. He found his mother on the sofa when he walked in around lunchtime. She looked up, puffy-faced, blew her nose, and said,

"Antonio, we have to talk. Sit." She patted the space next to her.

She had decided: She was going to help Marcelo's family reconstruct their business, no matter the cost. She had saved enough money to buy bricks, sand, and cement for the building, and with a few months of her widow's pension, she could afford the *mão-de-obra* as well.

Antonio bolted from the couch. "Mother, are you insane? Those are your hard-earned savings!"

"Yes, but I don't have small children to raise, the house is paid for, and we have everything we need—including good health, thank God. Besides, I still have my liqueurs."

"It makes no sense whatsoever. Marcelo is a man. You're an old woman. You *need* your savings, Mother. His pharmacy is probably insured anyway! He's always spouting his proletarian dogma, but let's not forget that he is, above all, a greedy *businessman!*" He hissed the last word.

"It's our duty, Antonio. His firstborn is your father's godson."

Antonio raised his finger, his voice shrill with indignation. "Mother, get it out of your head. I, as the man of the house, *forbid* you to offer Marcelo any money, do you understand? Where would that leave *me?* Disinherited, out on the street! Have you stopped to think how humiliating that would be for your son?"

Dona Juvita glanced toward the front door, where sunlight filtered in through the iron grillwork. The birds chattered in the back.

Antonio concluded his harangue. "Now I'm going to go into that kitchen and have me some lunch, and we'll no longer talk about it, agreed? Subject finalized."

He walked into the corridor, and she called out after him from her seat on the couch, "I'm sorry, Antonio, but this is not for you to decide. My mind is made up."

He emerged a few moments later, holding a piece of toast, speaking with mock indifference. "Fine, Dona Juvita. I know once something gets in your head there's no negotiating." He started walking away again, stopped, turned back. "Why did you even tell me anything?" His voice quavered as if he were about to cry. He crammed the bread into his mouth. "Godammit, Mother. I'm the one who was sabotaged here."

She regarded him incredulously. "You?"

"Yes, me. Have you stopped to think who'll get blamed for this?"

Dona Juvita stared at the floor, hands locked between her knees. Then she told Antonio that of course she had no doubt that he had no part in the fire. That the people responsible for it had bad hearts.

"Well, good, Mother. At least that, thank you."

"But Antonio, my son, tell me something: you really don't think this could've been politically motivated? That maybe one of your friends . . . wanting to help you . . . set this up?"

Antonio paced around the room, hands on his head, "Nononononononono. God," he cried, "not my mother, too. *Please!*" He slapped his thighs.

"Don't be dramatic, Antonio. I just asked a question."

"Mother, how can you let it cross your mind? What kind of *friends,* as you say, would do something like that? You should have seen the looks I got on the way home today. My political career is over! *O-ver!* This damned fire has ruined my life! Fuck!"

"Antonio."

His shoulders slumped and he said, in a tone of mock resignation, "Go ahead, Dona Juvita. Offer that self-righteous, pompous prick the money, and let's see if he'll take it. For him, you're nothing but an old, sad, widow—he'll never accept anything from you."

Dona Juvita stood, brushing the lint off her black skirt. She plucked her purse from the coatrack and strapped it to her shoulder. "We'll see about that, Antonio," she said. "Now excuse me. I'm going out."

2

It was the hottest part of day, when the town shut down for the sacred two-hour nap. Most afternoons around this time, Dona Juvita played solitaire in the back patio under her birdcages or, on the days Acauana came, sat and chatted with the girl, asking for news of the families who lived in her village. She moved through the shadows cast by the rows of mango trees, but the deserted stone sidewalks shimmered with heat, enveloping her in a blast of hot air that singed the hair of her nostrils. A hushed stillness enclosed the town and the hills behind it, yellow at this time of year; nevertheless Dona Juvita had the odd sensation of being pricked by tiny needles on the back of her neck, and knew that somewhere, behind warped fences, through cracked blinds, hidden eyes marked her passage. She tightened her grip on the parasol's handle. During siesta, doors and windows stayed open in the unlikely event of a breeze, so that she caught glimpses of private lives inside those houses: bodies stretched on a mat on a kitchen floor, a teenage girl shucking beans into a metal bowl, a pair of feet dangling from a hammock, the flash of a hand and a fan.

Once at the entrance to Marcelo's mother's, Dona Juvita clapped her hands and was answered by one of his children, a pale, plump girl with saucer eyes who showed her in and disappeared into the house, calling her grandmother.

The room smelled of lavender. Dona Juvita sat on the edge of a rocking chair, by a bookshelf, her purse in her lap. She studied the painting of a beach on the wall, deciphering the tiny, neat signature on the bottom right: *Nair*—who at that very moment shuffled into the living room.

"Only a tragedy to make you visit me, huh, Juvita," the old woman said with a smile. Dona Juvita stood and kissed the soft, powdered cheeks, accusing her of hoarding some secret elixir of youth. She asked about Marilita and the kids.

"They're all sleeping, except for Áurea, here." The girl ran and hugged her grandmother's side, looking up at Dona Juvita curiously.

"What about Marcelo?"

"He's in the shower. *Pobrezinho*," she shook her head from side to side, "still hasn't slept. Spent all morning on the phone with Recife."

"Could I have a word with him?"

Senhora Nair ran her hand over the child's short brown hair. "Go get your father, honey." The girl ran inside, and Senhora Nair informed Dona Juvita that she was about to brew a *cafezinho*. "*Aceita?*"

"Sure, thank you." As the old woman retreated, Dona Juvita added, "Look, Senhora Nair, my house is also available, in case yours gets too crowded. Talk it over with Marilita." Senhora Nair nodded. At that moment Marcelo walked in, combing his tuft of hair. He slid the comb into his back pocket, held Dona Juvita's extended hand in both of his, and pressed it for a while. She hugged him, patting his broad back. They sat side by side on the sofa.

"Marcelo, I'm here in the name of my husband, your son's godfather." She opened her purse, found the thick brown envelope encircled by a rubber band, and held it out to him. "This is for you."

Marcelo took it, but when he realized what it contained, he returned it to her, indignant, "What is this, Dona Juvita? Do you really think—"

She placed it in his lap, pressing it down for emphasis. "Marcelo, if you don't take it, you'll be offending not only me but the memory of Flávio. So do me the favor: take this and let's not talk about it."

He protested; she insisted. The envelope passed back and forth.

"Dona Juvita, if this has anything to do with Antonio —"

"This has *nothing* to do with Antonio. I am doing it because I need *my* pharmacy back, as soon as possible." She brushed the sides of her hair. "In a couple weeks I'll need a new coat of Wella's Auburn Rose; where do you expect I will get it?"

Marcelo's face softened for a moment. "Yes, well, I've just put in another order with Recife for the most crucial items, *penicilina*, some prescriptions, alcohol, shaving cream, and so on. You'll be happy to know that I included your Wella in it."

She poked his hand with a forefinger to drive home her point. "Okay, then. I'm sure that was an added expense. You must have just received your order for February before it all went up in flames."

A truck drove by on the street, rattling the floor. He replied that yes, it was true, he wouldn't get a refund on this month's order, which he had, in fact, received just Monday, yesterday. Once again he attempted to hand back the envelope, but his mother shuffled into the room bearing a tray with three small coffee cups. With the flash of her eyes, Dona Juvita compelled him to conceal it, and he discreetly, resignedly, inserted the envelope in his back pocket. After she finished her coffee, Dona Juvita expressed her sympathy once again, reminded Senhora Nair of her offer, and left as swiftly as she had come.

In the days that followed, while the town prepared itself for Carnaval, Antonio hardly set foot at home. Not even for afternoon naps. Now Dona Juvita only saw him in passing, like an apparition, from the bathroom to his bedroom, chewing something in the kitchen, foraging in the laundry baskets, showering. Always on the verge of walking out the door. Whenever she directed her words at him, his responses were short and nonchalant. And when a very pregnant Marilita along with her girls, two-year-old Angela and eight-year-old Áurea, accepted Dona Juvita's offer and moved into the guest room, Antonio, like a saint, became rumored about but never spotted. Dona Juvita only heard him from her bed at odd hours of the night, knocking around like a rat inside the walls. In the morning when she checked his room, she'd notice more items missing from his dresser. A few of her liqueurs, too, vanished from their shelves in the stockroom, mostly bottles of Lazarus Juice.

Antonio faded from the eyes of Pesqueira as well. People talked, of course. Some said his disappearance proved his involvement with the fire. Others, the ones closer to him, testified that he had gone on a retreat to Casa Prelúdio, that only the girls of that esteemed house could distract him from his pain.

On the night before the official start of Carnaval, Dona Juvita and all her houseguests were awakened by the sound of someone forcing open the rear door, followed by a loud crash that left the canaries in an uproar, with Ulysses screeching profanities over the commotion. Áurea was the first to brave the living room and discover Antonio, supine on the floor, snoring, his left hand still clutching his hat. The entire room stank of *cana*. The girl yelled, "*Mommm!*" and the baby started crying. Marilita ran out, as did Dona Juvita, and with much difficulty—first by the torso, then one leg, then the other—the three managed to prop Antonio on the sofa.

But he was gone, remarkably, before dawn, and this time he appropriated whatever remained of his things: the brilliantine, the Capiloton, his two-tone shoes, pants, shirts, socks, underwear, even his hammock and the last of the Lazarus Juice.

In the morning, as the children slept, the women found two folded notes on the kitchen table, under the porcelain vase. One read "Juvita" on the outer half, and the other, "Marilita e Família." They prepared a pot of coffee and sat down, facing each other. Dona Juvita unfolded hers and read the elaborate penmanship to herself.

> *Pesqueira, 06 February 1943*
>
> *My Dear Beautiful Mother,*
>
> *Please make sure you're at the square this afternoon for the Commencement of Carnaval Ceremony. As soon as time permits me, I'll send you a more detailed letter.*
>
> *Loves you more than you'll ever know:*
>
> *Antonio*

She folded and tucked it in the pocket of her gown. Marilita then opened hers and read it aloud: "Pesqueira, 06 February 1943. Dear Senhora Marilita, Accept my deepest condolences for the tragedy that has befallen your family. I wish the eight of you nothing but the best. Thank you for keeping my dear mother company. With gratitude, Antonio Didier."

Dona Juvita leaned forward and rested her elbows on the table, almost in a trance. The birds' morning chatter filled the patio. Marilita shrugged, tugging her from her thoughts, "Maybe he's finally found a woman he wants to settle down with."

"I doubt it." She stood and placed her full cup in the sink. "This son of mine is up to something, Marilita. I can feel it. A mother always knows."

Despite the ashy space where the pharmacy had once stood, contrasted by the colorful storefronts and residences around it, Pesqueira was ready for Carnaval. Each year, no matter how bad the general economic conditions of the country, a generous, sacred fund was set aside for the festival, which in 1942 won the Most Traditional Carnaval in the State of Pernambuco award, largely due to its unparalleled *frevo* orchestra.

The town expected visitors from every neighboring state this year. Confetti dappled the streets and sidewalks, and rolls of serpentine adorned every available tree. Food and beer stands sprouted along the four sides of the square. Boys darted across the streets holding their ears, a sure sign of an imminent explosion of fireworks. Girls, dressed like odalisques, ballerinas, as "women of life," sprayed each other with lavender or rose solution from their *lança-perfume* bottles. This year the stage had been assembled in the center of everything, facing away from the church. A huge truck from Recife had arrived the day before, and the workers spent at least twelve hours installing electrical fixtures and mounting the aluminum beams. The end result was a beauty.

The collective anticipation hung in the air along with the heat.

By five o'clock in the afternoon, the square was filled to capacity, many strange faces among all the familiar ones. The orchestra musicians ascended the stage one by one, dressed in white, strands of colorful ribbons adorning their instruments, and took their posts to thunderous applause. Marcelo's oldest boy stood among the rhythm section, smiling shyly, his drumsticks poised above the head of his snare drum. The last to go up was Silvio Peixe, the conductor. He walked to the front of the stage, removed his hat, and placed it over his heart as the multitude cheered.

Dona Juvita watched all of it from the back. Silvio took the microphone, agitating the crowd, asking if they were happy and ready to party and so on. He then informed them that, before the festivities could start, an important municipal announcement needed to be made. He stepped aside and a nervous Vladson emerged from the back of the stage to take the microphone.

Vladson explained to the onlookers that he was making this announcement in his official capacity as treasurer of PPPPT. In his right hand he held an open letter, which he waved in the air. He removed a pair of wire-rimmed glasses from his shirt pocket, adjusted them on the tip of his nose, and began reading slowly and without preamble:

"Fellow Pesqueirenses of my heart: It may have come to your attention that a brutal world war is being fought outside our country borders. As you celebrate this evening, ladies and gentlemen, know that a very evil man is carrying out his plans for the domination of our beloved Europe, and maybe the world. I have heretofore decided, after a period of intense soul-searching, that the *best* way for me to serve my people is to join whatever forces are fighting this man, this lunatic, to leave the comfort and safety of my hometown and travel whatever distance I have to in order to impede the success of his infernal Machiavellian schemes and ensure that he never sets foot anywhere near my beloved hometown."

Vladson cleared his throat, an expression of intense preoccupation, or perhaps faint pain, on his face.

"It is with a heavy heart that I announce my abdicacy of the candidature so as to join the National Armed Forces. By the time you hear this from the lips of my beloved treasurer Vladson Lino—" Vladson stuttered over his name"—I should already be aboard a ship in Recife with my fellow soldiers and General Leitão de Carvalho, on my way to England. May the Virgin's Grace stay with you. Forever Yours, Antonio Didier—your humble servant Antonio de Juvita."

A murmur rippled outward from the stage and spread in all four directions of the square. Vladson's voice cut through the babble.

"It's not over yet! There's more! Quiet down please. "P.S.: I hereby publicly cast my vote, in absentia, for the reelection of Marcelo Nóbrega, our old Marcelo da Farmácia; a good and honest man who, in his long tenure as mayor, has done well by our town and who, after myself, is best qualified to hold the reins of our local government."

Dona Juvita had to leave, quickly, the cloying scent of *lança-perfume* lodged in her throat.

When she arrived home she locked herself in the bathroom, knelt before the toilet bowl, and threw up her lunch. Marilita, feeding Angela in the kitchen, saw Dona Juvita rushing in, holding her mouth. She stood outside the bathroom door, asked if she was well, but Dona Juvita turned on the shower and ignored her inquiries until the persistent knocking finally ceased. Dona Juvita removed all her clothes, dropped the lid of the toilet, and sat down on it, drained, weary.

"He's too old and lazy to be a soldier," she told herself. "They won't take him."

She reached into her purse and fumbled for a plastic rosary she used on occasion, at funerals, at church on Sundays. She picked off the strands of hair knotted between the beads. There, on the toilet, she wrapped the rosary around her hands and mouthed an Our Father and an Ave Maria. She then spoke aloud, offering a promise to Our Lady of Grace: "Dear Senhora das Graças, please let this be a prank, another of Antonio's fabrications. For whatever reason, it doesn't matter. You do this for me, and I promise you . . ." she closed her eyes, pressing the beads to her forehead. Azulão, the only canary who sang after sundown, warbled three bright descending notes, and she continued, "I promise that I will release *all* of my babies from their cages, the very moment I discover that Antonio is nowhere near any war."

Dona Juvita sold most of her liqueurs at Carnaval, more than the sum of all other holidays of the year. She worked incessantly from that Saturday evening until first light on Ash Wednesday, assisted by Áurea, Marilita, and her second oldest boy, whose name Dona Juvita could never remember. Although she refrained from displaying a price list on her windowsill, people still came at all hours of the night and day requesting the most popular brands, which sold at one *vintém* per bottle: Lonely Wife, Indian Prick, Ambrosia, Bull Tamer, and Angel Piss, among others. Whenever someone asked for Lazarus Juice, Dona Juvita bit her lip to keep from crying.

"I'm out of them," she would say.

After the second day, the reek of makeshift latrines set up throughout the city became unbearable. Side streets and alleyways stank of urine and vomit. The music shook the floors and walls of the house. She removed the more delicate plates from the wall, a precaution. Ulysses screamed nonstop from the backyard. Friends and acquaintances, including Father Tenório, stopped by to confirm that she was all right. Others, folks who claimed to be friends of relatives or relatives of friends, to use the bathroom.

"Each Carnaval is the same thing," she complained to Marilita. "That's Flavio's fault, for insisting we build a house right on the square."

Marilita nodded and smiled from her stool by the window, always poised to help her hostess despite her swelling belly. She now divided her time between the two houses. Whenever she stayed at Dona Juvita's, the kids adopted a kind of rotation scheme in which a different one slept with her each night—all but the oldest boy, who took cat naps at the *conservatório* whenever he could.

Marcelo showed up once to have coffee with Dona Juvita and express his gratitude at her selfless display of friendship, yelling so that he could be heard over the pandemonium outside. He never mentioned the fire, Antonio's letter, war, or politics—but at one point he said nothing and sat still awhile, tapping rhythms on the side of his empty cup. He then put a hand over hers, and his eyes filled up with tears.

But everyone else who turned up at the house, however briefly, *did* ask about Antonio: Had she heard news from him, had she any idea when he was returning, and to all she offered the same answer: "I only know as much as everyone."

This year's Carnaval moved at an awkward pace. Pesqueira appeared dulled under the sweltering heat. She noticed more revelers alone, seated against walls, vomiting on sidewalks, especially pathetic in the midst of the bacchanalia around them. In the morning the young men and women passed out on the street looked like dead cattle she'd seen strewn about desert trails.

On Ash Wednesday afternoon, when it was all over, Dona Juvita showered meticulously, donned her black wool dress, and left for mass at Our Lady of Grace. She went in honor of *Doutor* Flávio, who considered it imperative that they attend each important mass of the year. This was the only mass Antonio ever graced with his presence. No matter how tired and hungover, every year he accompanied his mother to Ash Wednesday mass—his feeble attempt at penance, to atone for the debauchery of the previous four days.

This year Acauana went with her. She arrived at the house early that morning to clean the residual mess, and since the time coincided, and the church was on her path back to the hills, she informed Dona Juvita she'd attend the service with her. She said it while standing on tiptoe behind her back, fastening the clasp on a thin chain weighed down by a gold crucifix.

"You don't have to, you know," Dona Juvita said, in case Acauana, much keener than her veiled demeanor let on, had offered out of pity.

"I understand. But I've always wanted to stand in line and feel the priest putting his mark on my forehead." She released a short laugh. "I've never had the courage to go before." Then she added, after the chain was secure on Dona Juvita's sweating neck, "Poor Mister Antonio. So far away from his home. I'm going to miss him."

"Me too, Ana. Me too."

Outside the church, the ritual of mass unfolded. Father Tenório's most fanatical followers wore sackcloth and ascended the long steps, littered with the wreckage of festivity, on their knees. Acauana plucked the sleeve of Dona Juvita's dress and pointed to an empty glass bottle labeled "Indian Prick." Dona Juvita bent down and quickly hid it inside her purse.

Father Tenório stood in a cloud of incense by the altar, before a long line of people, dipping his thumb into palm ashes and marking the foreheads of his flock with the sign of the cross. Over and over he intoned the words: "Remember man that thou art dust and unto dust thou shalt return." By the time Dona Juvita's turn came—right after a dubious Acauana, who looked back with dread on her face—she realized her mistake in choosing a dress made of wool. She had never felt so hot in her life. She was barely conscious of waving to Senhora Nair, Marilita, Marcelo, and their children, who together occupied a whole pew. She teetered to the last bench and sat down. She rolled up her sleeves, slipped her heels out of her shoes, and undid the first three buttons on her lapel, exposing enough of her bosom to attract the attention of the young couple beside Acauana. While Father Tenório's voice droned on and on, she reaffirmed her promise to the Virgin, wondering if she had been a little disrespectful for doing it nude the first time, in the bathroom. Her thoughts were a confused hodgepodge of evangelical hymns, birdsongs, and gunshots. She praised God's mysterious workings, thanking him for granting her enough strength to come here on this day, and was startled when the collection plate nudged her. She took it with one hand and reached inside her purse with the other, but couldn't get her fingers deep enough to feel the small wallet, which managed to settle at the bottom. She removed the green Indian Prick bottle and handed it to Acauana, this time winning reproachful looks from the same couple as a breath of alcohol rose into the air.

On their way out Acauana asked Dona Juvita to please make sure the ash was gone from her face. "The chief will punish me if he sees it," the girl said. Dona Juvita licked the cuff of her dress sleeve, held up Acauana's black bangs, and rubbed away all traces of the mark from her brown forehead.

In many ways Carnaval was the purgative process by which the town shed its skin for a new year, like a desert *jibóia*. After a period of rest the duties and habits of everyday life gradually resumed, the plans for reconstructing Marcelo's pharmacy moved forward and all of Pesqueira pitched in to help, whether it be manually, financially, morally or, in Father Tenório's case, spiritually. True to form, the burned area became one-half social club, with provisional domino and card tables everywhere, and one-half construction site.

With only two weeks left until election day, Colonel Altamiro decided to run against Marcelo da Farmácia, forcing the town to line up at the elementary school early on the last Saturday in February, sit behind the cardboard ballot box, and cast their votes. A Voter's Ten Commandments were printed on a banner at the entrance gate:

01　DO NOT VOTE *AD NULLUM*
02　DO NOT VOTE IN CONTRADICTION TO YOUR OPINION
03　DO NOT VOTE TO SATISFY YOUR FRIENDS
04　DO NOT VOTE TO SATISTY YOUR PARENTS
05　DO NOT SELL YOUR VOTE
06　DO NOT TRADE YOUR VOTE FOR FAVORS
07　DO NOT VOTE WITHOUT KNOWING A CANDIDATE'S PLATFORM
08　DO NOT VOTE WITHOUT KNOWING A CANDIDATE'S PAST

09 DO NOT VOTE WITHOUT KNOWING A
    CANDIDATE'S CHARACTER
10 DO NOT ALLOW ANY STATISTICAL REPORT
    TO INFLUENCE YOUR VOTE

Marcelo won again, but by a surprisingly small margin. In a stroke of bipartisanship, he appointed Vladson as treasurer. Dona Juvita smiled to herself when the results were announced; a substantial number of citizens had checked off a hand-drawn square on their ballots and scribbled "Antonio" beside it. Then there were the usual votes for horses, roosters, dogs, and vagrants; twenty-three votes for Father Tenório, more than on any other election; two for the pope; and approximately thirty cast for assorted philosophers, saints, literary figures, and deities, including Jesus, Socrates, Don Quixote, and God.

On the third day of March, after waking from a dream of an infant Antonio wailing in his crib, Dona Juvita hastened to the jailhouse to ask the colonel if he'd heard any news from the war on his radio. She brought with her two bottles of fig liqueur, the colonel's favorite, and congratulated him on his successful campaign.

"Why don't you stay a moment, Dona Juvita," he said, waving toward the plastic seat across from him. He turned up the volume on the device. "The morning news is about to start. They may mention something."

And so she heard about the heavy air attack on Berlin, just the previous day. "With many casualties," the announcer added.

"Were those *Brazilian* casualties?" she asked, pointing to the radio.

"I'm sorry, Dona Juvita." Colonel Altamiro shrugged. "They don't let us know. War reports are vague in these parts. It's as if we were excommunicated from the rest of the world."

She laid her head on her folded arms. The colonel stood calmly, adjusted his tight belt, and poured some water into a plastic cup for her. "If I hear any more news, I promise I'll personally ride to your house and let you know, Dona Juvita," he said, patting her back.

At the hour of siesta on March 8, six days later, while Marilita napped with the baby and Dona Juvita played solitaire on the patio, Áurea arrived home from school waving a yellow envelope that the mailman had just dropped off. "It's from Senhor Antonio!" the girl squealed, and sat facing Dona Juvita. Ulysses muttered something unintelligible from his perch. Acauana left her dishes and stepped into the patio, rearranging the bouquet of artificial roses on the table.

Dona Juvita ripped open the envelope. Inside she found a smaller envelope, labeled VLADSON—TO BE READ PUB-LICLY, and a folded letter. She opened it, saw the heading and signature, and for a second held the sheets of notebook paper to her chest. She read the careful handwriting silently.

Berlin, 20 February 1943
Dawn

Dear Mother:

This is the first chance I've had to write you since my departure. I'm writing this by candlelight, while my comrades sleep, many of them moaning from their night-mares or their wounds. We've been without leadership now for a week, since at the last minute General Leitão de Carvalho realized that our boys needed more time for training and only sent the ten soldiers he deemed most qualified and ready for the mission, myself among them, naturally.

So far we've fought two battles beside the Allied forces, the first one in a cold and bitter rain you could never imagine; it was like ice cubes falling from the sky,

with my comrades' blood running as freely as the rain-
water in the gutters of the German streets. In that first
battle, my ammunition spent, I had to resort to cold-cock-
ing a huge German in order to save the life of my fellow
Pernambucan Zé Brindeiro, who was being throttled
mercilessly as the Nazi sang "Deutschland Über Alles"
at the top of his lungs. In the second battle the Virgin
spared me. I reacted without thinking and threw myself
on top of a German grenade that was lobbed into our
tank. The grenade never went off. After the fight every-
one talked about it without cease.

War is hell, Mother. You, more than anyone, know I
am a man of peace and good cheer, but every time I think
of these brutal Huns marching into Pesqueira to enslave
you and Vladson and Ulysses and all of the town, I find
it easy to pull the trigger and apply the expert marks-
manship I inherited from Father.

I've also seen lots of beautiful things, like the majes-
tic family of killer whales swimming alongside our ship
in the middle of the Atlantic, and Berlin's fascinating
achitecture, with streets and houses that are older than
our whole country. The German people are very beauti-
ful, very tall and very blond, like movie stars, their eyes
an ocean blue. It's sad to witness what this lunatic has
done to their morals, and to the morale of the people he
persecutes. I have seen some of them, these Jewish people.
They remind me of our people, with their earthiness and
love of family, dance, music. In Brazil, their skin would
be considered white, so you can imagine, if this Hitler
does such things to them, what he would do to our poor
mulatos and Indios. Not to mention our neguinhos.

My closest companion is an American soldier
named Butch. He wears his guns on his hips and a white
hat on his head, constantly chews tobacco, and never

*misses a shot. Between the two of us, we took out a whole
unit of Germans in that first battle. Afterwards he came
over, asking if all Brazilians were such great shots, and I
replied that if they came from the Sertão they were. That
was the beginning of our friendship. We don't understand each other fully, but between his broken Mexican
Spanish and my fractured seventh-grade English, I've
figured out that he is a cowboy from a town called Texas,
as well as a professional rodeo star, and father of two.
Some nights he pulls out his harmonica and plays popular American songs, and for a moment we forget there is
a war outside our encampment. I've told him about
Pesqueira and about you, but your Lazarus Juice spoke
for itself. After Butch sampled it he made such a fuss that
the other soldiers wanted to try it too, and since I could-
n't say no, all the bottles I'd brought with me are now
history. Even the men who'd been wounded in battle
were thankful to you, Mother. For a moment your sooth-
ing elixir allowed them to forget their pain.*

*I'll refrain from recounting more horrors, Mother,
as you have always had such delicate sensibilities. Just
know that your son is healthy, strong, and filled with
courage, thanks to the Didier blood running in his veins.
Please do not worry. Your happiness is of utmost importance to me, and I'm sorry if on my last days in
Pesqueira I wasn't the exemplary son you're accustomed
to. My mind was crowded with important decisions and
doubts; I knew that if I consulted you, you would have
convinced me to stay, and this is a sacrifice I'm willing to
make for you, my continent, and my people. I hope you
can find it in your heart to forgive me.*

*Yesterday, while walking down a desolate street, I
left my unit and followed the sound of a distant, sad
waltz until it led me to an abandoned mansion. I opened*

the gigantic jacarandá door, all fancifully carved and inlaid, and walked through endless dusty rooms full of debris, riddled with bullet holes, following the music. Finally, in the middle of an enormous marble salon dominated by a giant flag with a swastika emblazoned upon it, I discovered an old German hausfrau, sitting alone with an accordion on her lap, and the body of her dead husband, in full SS uniform, at her feet. She just kept on playing, staring out into the distance, unfazed by my presence. Something about her, maybe her resolute concentration, or her infinite sadness, or her strong, agile fingers, reminded me of you, Mother, and for a quick instant, I was a boy at your side once again.

With all my love,

Your son Antonio

P.S.:Write me at the address on the outside of the envelope. I have a contact there who will forward anything you send to wherever I'm staying. I have two requests: first, if you could send some liqueurs, especially more Lazarus Juice, all of the men would be unimaginably grateful. Second, Mother, I'd like to ask you for money. Anything would help. The money I brought was only enough to last me through training in Recife. I spent the very last of it just yesterday on a little Jewish boy who lost his entire family. It's freezing here, and I'm in dire need of jackets, socks, gloves, and so on. In fact, if it's not too much to ask, some kind of monthly allowance would be a godsend. Whatever you can afford. When I return to Brazil as a decorated veteran I will resume my political career and pay you back for everything. This I promise.

Dona Juvita turned the envelope over and read the return address, running her fingernail across the bold script on the front:

Forças Armadas Nacionais c/o Carmelita Santos
Rua da Soledade, 128
Torre, Recife, Pernambuco—50.000

"So?" said Áurea.

"What does it say?" said Acauana.

Dona Juvita smiled and took a breath that filled her whole chest. She was truly impressed this time, and in her heart of hearts, even a little proud. In the entire race of humans, she thought, I am the only person Antonio could never fool. She tried to rock, forgetting that she wasn't in a rocking chair. "He's in Berlin, Germany. He's fighting in the war, alongside the Americans. He's already the hero of two battles." The girls beamed. She handed the small sealed envelope to Áurea. "Do me a favor, Áurea. Go and give this to our new treasurer. He must be at the site with your father; they never take any breaks, those two."

Áurea bounded out of the house. Once the front door slammed shut, Acauana approached Dona Juvita's stool, crouched in front of her, and whispered: "I asked the chief to say a special prayer to Tupiama. Mister Antonio will be fine." She nodded. "He'll come back. And then he will be president."

"Mayor, you mean?"

"Yes, that's it."

"Thank you, Acauana. He sent you his greetings, you know."

"I know." Acauana grinned and returned to her work.

Áurea ran the four blocks to her father's pharmacy. A lazy cloud rolling in from the hills promised rain, something the town hadn't seen since the previous winter. The streets were quiet except for a group of kids still in their school uniforms, two of her brothers among them, playing soccer in a shaded lot. They screamed for

Áurea to come join them, that they were short a goalie, and she screamed back that she'd be just a minute.

At the site, deserted in the noontime heat, she found the mayor and the treasurer dozing under the mango tree. She approached them very lightly, like a cat, and stuck the tip of her pinky into her father's ear. He smacked the side of his face and jumped up. "Dammit, Áurea! You want to give your father a heart attack?" Doubled over with laughter, she held out the letter to Vladson—who had awoken with the commotion and was brushing the sand from the backside of his pants. Both men read the directions on the outside of the envelope. Marcelo frowned and Vladson shrugged, hiding it in the front pocket of his shirt.

Above them, above everything, a flock of canaries traced an elliptical path in the sky. Five times they flew from the monument of Our Lady to the church steeple to the rows of mango trees to the clouded backdrop of hills, their mingled song a rapturous cacophony, returning, before anyone could notice them, to the cards on the table and the parrot on his perch and the open cages hanging in Dona Juvita's patio.

Curado

First there was the affair of the shitty turkey.

The patient, a newlywed, old farmer, grateful for the painless recovery from the vasectomy he'd undergone to satisfy his bride—"Who already has five children from a previous marriage and made it very clear, *Doutor*, what she would, or more specifically, would *not* do"—brooked no refusal. A week after the operation, when Claudio arrived in the mountainous, wind-swept town of Toritama for the start of his Thursday shift, man and fowl were in the waiting room. The farmer stood ceremoniously, touched the brim of his hat, and said, "*Doutor*, because of you, I'm a happy man. Here is the star of my farm, Petunia; me and my wife want you to have her. Look at this beauty." He flicked the turkey's bright red wattle, its plump body wrapped in an entire newspaper secured with twine and a yellow bow. The man winked, pressing the malodorous bird to the doctor's chest. "Take it to your woman. I'm sure she'll like it."

It was almost seven-thirty on a rainy July morning, too early for the overhead TV that, especially during afternoon soap operas, commanded the undivided attention of the entire clinic. Claudio's punctual patients sat side by side on a long wooden bench, while the tardy ones squatted or slouched against the wall, some chatting, others eating breakfast, all holding white plastic cups with cloyingly sweet coffee that Seu Antonio, the custodian, never failed to make.

Claudio, always late, had no time to argue; people here were serious about their gifts. He thanked the farmer, joking about how calmly the turkey passed from arm to arm. He held up an index finger to indicate he'd be right back, swung open the screen doors, and trotted across the parking lot, groping inside his pockets for the remote-control key chain to his girlfriend's Mustang, on grudging loan while his ex-wife used his Landau for the week. Instead of pushing the Unlock button he triggered the alarm, a mistake he committed each time he borrowed the damn thing. It took him two seconds to stop the deafening sound, just enough time for Petunia to panic. She squawked and jerked herself right out of his grasp, dashing toward the gate of the parking lot, a speeding ball of newspaper and twine that, even through his irritation, made Claudio laugh. He considered going after the bird but decided to let her go. What would he do with a turkey in an apartment in downtown Recife? Elisabeth, moody as only a pregnant first-timer in her first trimester could be, wouldn't allow it onto the white carpets, would scold him for accepting it. Watermelon, corn, liqueurs, that was one thing—but livestock? She'd tell him that was what he got for working in a hick town.

He headed back towards the clinic, relieved.

From the street someone screamed: "*Get that tuuuurrrrkey!*"

A gang of kids chased the fowl down the cobbled road that fronted the parking lot. Petunia jumped up onto the high sidewalk and darted into a food shop, where, with the vendor's help, she was quickly cornered against a beer cooler that read BRAHMA in big red letters. Claudio quickened his pace and had almost reached the shelter of the clinic when a voice behind him yelled, "*Doutor!*"

No use pretending; he was the only doctor in town. Here his general surgeon's degree of twenty-five years had expanded to encompass family practice, anesthesiology, obstetrics, pediatrics, psychiatry, marriage counseling, whatever the occasion called for, a necessary adaptation that all doctors in this part of the country sooner or later adopted. A skinny boy in shorts and sandals ran toward him, holding the turkey aloft, smiling a triumphant, toothless smile. "Remember me?"

"Of course," he lied. "Thank you." He accepted the squirming bird. Although he'd examined just about everyone in town at least once, Claudio could not remember names or faces; and after patients left his office, he quickly forgot them, their respective illnesses, their stories. Besides, he rotated between three hospitals in the big city, where bullet and knife wounds were as commonplace as hay fever in this little town; and perhaps not remembering was a defense mechanism he'd developed long ago, also out of necessity. He circled back to the car and opened the trunk—so neat, so vacuumed, so different from his—undid the bow, unwrapped the turkey, and handed it to the boy while spreading the newspaper over the bottom. He then placed the turkey inside, shut the trunk, and promptly forgot all about it until the following morning, when Elisabeth, five minutes after leaving for work, stormed back into the apartment, breathless, demanding to know what the *hell* that smell in her car was.

He was in the middle of shaving. He thought she'd forgotten something, her keys, her dentist's case, her bottled water or prenatal vitamins, but as soon as she barged into the bathroom, Claudio, his face half covered in foam, said, "My God! The turkey!"

"What?"

He wiped his face on a towel. "Shit, Liz, the poor thing, I killed it!" He squeezed past her, wearing only his pants, and jogged down the hall toward the elevator, pressing the Up and

Down buttons frantically. They lived on the fifth floor. The indicator above the door was frozen on eight. "Damn!"

"Now, relax, Claudio, and tell me what's the matter, please." She spoke in the guarded tone she usually reserved for discussing his ex-wife or daughter.

"Quick, give me the keys, I'm taking the stairs. I'll explain later."

"You know, if you would just tell me—"

"Give me the keys, goddammit!"

He had screamed louder than he intended to; as she handed them over, her bottom lip quivered, her hands trembled, and the elevator arrived, filled with neighbors he didn't know—men in ties, women in panty hose, well-scrubbed kids in school uniforms. He stepped into a cloud of aftershave and perfume, shirtless, shoeless, semishaven, nodding and managing a sheepish *"Bom dia,"* which went unanswered. He could almost hear their thoughts, the *tsk-tsks* of reproval, the accusations: *"Bruto . . .   Abusador."* "Shameless, shameless . . . Bad husband . . . Bad father . . . Bad doctor . . . Bad, bad man." His cell phone vibrated loudly. For once he was grateful he owned the damn thing, grateful for the habit of slipping it into his pants first thing in the morning. He hit Talk without looking at the number.

"Hi Dad!"

"Carol! Hi, honey."

"I'm staying home today."

"Huh? Why?"

"You forgot to give Mom the money for the field trip. Remember? But that's okay. I didn't want to go to a stupid art museum anyway."

He muffled the mouthpiece with the palm of his hand. Finally, after stopping at every floor along the way, the elevator opened onto the parking garage. He was mortified to have forgetten about Carolina's field trip and apologized to her profusely while walking to the Mustang, promising he'd make it up to her, he would. He used the key to unlock the trunk, phone between ear and shoulder, almost jumping with joy when the two bright and beady eyes blinked up at him in the sudden shower of light, followed by a throaty *glub-glub* that echoed throughout the dark garage.

"So what are you doing today, Dad?"

"Working, honey!"

Then the stench reached him. The thing had shat everywhere; the newspaper had been ripped to shreds, white and green smudges smeared into the carpet, not one spot devoid of turkey shit. It had managed even to soil the roof of the trunk, which left Claudio truly baffled, imagining Petunia in elastic contortions. My God, he said to himself. I never imagined a turkey could have so much crap in it.

"Dad! Are you at the hospital?"

"Honey, I have to go. I'll call you right back."

"Okay. But be prepared. Mom is mad."

He locked the trunk once again, holding his breath, but the smell had seeped into his nostrils. He looked outside, beyond the gate. A light drizzle fell, Recife's version of winter. As cars lined up to exit onto congested Torre Boulevard, Claudio approached the security guard, a young uniformed man holding open the iron gate, and asked if he had an empty bowl lying around anywhere.

"What was that, *Doutor?*" The guard cupped a hand behind his ear.

Claudio crossed in front of an idling vehicle and repeated his question. The man asked if an empty soup bowl would do—"I just finished some for breakfast"—and Claudio said, "Yes, that would be great, here, I'll take the gate for you, it's an emergency."

Claudio held open the gate, fully conscious of his harried, shirtless, half-shaved, barefoot middle-aged state, trying not to look at the faces of his neighbors. He thought of the bright side:

At least he wouldn't have any reputation to uphold. The guard brought him the bowl. He filled it at an outside spigot and carried it to the car, where he was met by a fuming Elisabeth demanding an explanation, *now*. "And an apology, too."

"Okay, Liz, but promise me you won't be mad," he said, his voice all charm and sweetness.

"Claudio." She wasn't falling for it, so he opened the trunk, making an elaborate production out of it—"*Tchan tchan tchan tchan*"—and revealed Petunia, like an announcer introducing the star of his show. He proceeded to tell Elisabeth how the turkey was a gift from a patient who wouldn't let him refuse it, how her name was Petunia and he couldn't understand why, how, my God, he'd forgotten her in the trunk. "My memory these days, I tell you . . ." How he would personally see to it that her beautiful Mustang regained its new, imported car smell. He even tried a medical joke, leaning in to her ear conspiratorially: "You should've seen how happy that farmer was when I explained to him he could have a vasectomy *and* keep his balls."

For the first time in their year together, Elisabeth erupted. He was selfish and irresponsible, and she would never let him borrow anything of hers again. She was sure he would've remembered the turkey had it been inside his ex-wife Linara's trunk.

Claudio felt like a roadside accident, painfully aware of the morbid curiosity from people in their vehicles. "She doesn't *have* a trunk," he whispered loudly. "She doesn't have a car!"

"Shut up! This is so typical of you, Claudio." She pulled up the sleeve of her blouse and glanced at her watch. "Now look, I'm late. If you weren't such a pushover to Linara, this would never've happened in the first place! Did you have to give her the Landau for a whole *week?*"

He consulted his own watch, a reflex. He reached inside the trunk and placed the bowl by the turkey's feet.

"What the hell are you doing?"

"She hasn't drunk anything for twenty-four hours."

"You're ridiculous. I'm calling a cab." Elisabeth unzipped her medical bag and retrieved her cell phone, sighing, shaking her head from side to side. She strode toward the gate. "I have patients too, you know. You care?"

He could think of only one person who might adopt Petunia. Zuleide, his daughter's nanny, a woman who had worked for him and Linara since the day Carolina was born. She owned a small *granja*, a chicken farm, outside town. He took the stairs to the apartment, quickly finished shaving and dressing, and drove to his previous home without calling. Instead he called the Hospital da Restauração, his Friday-morning gig of twenty years, and spoke to a colleague who reassured him that things were under control; he'd be contacted in the event of an emergency.

Linara's car—*his* car, that is—wasn't in the drive when he arrived at the house, and though he should have been grateful ("*. . . be prepared, Mom is mad!*"), he felt a tiny constriction deep in his chest. He rang the bell. Carolina met him at the entrance. She seemed taller each time he saw her; taller and more graceful, her impish smile more and more like her mother's, a gap between the two front teeth, the ones Elisabeth referred to as her misaligned central incisors. Her hair, thick and brown, reached below her shoulders now, but she still wasn't keen on grooming, wearing it in a ponytail that always unraveled, leaving a tuft on one side of her head.

His little tomboy. The only part of himself he could ever see in her was her feet. From the time she was a baby, he and Linara marveled at how they were the exact replica of his: a fat, crooked big toe, shorter than all the rest, the nail on the little one atrophied, barely there. But now her chin, too, resembled his, cleft in the middle with a dimple that had become more pronounced within the last year.

Carolina's eyes widened when she saw the bird in his arms. "What's that?"

"Meet Petunia, honey."

"Can I pet it?"

"Here, you can hold her. She's completely tame, *mansinha.* See?" He flicked Petunia's wattle, as the farmer had, and passed her to Carolina. He walked to the front porch and called the nanny, running his hand along the railing he'd scraped, sanded, and painted at least three different times in the eleven years he'd lived there. Soon the entire house would need fresh paint.

Zuleide greeted him, drying her hands on her apron. She gave him a fierce hug. He could smell cilantro on her neck and on the bright bandanna covering her short blond afro. He pointed to Petunia, now chasing a gleeful Carolina around the avocado tree in the yard.

"Boy, she certainly *is* a beauty." Zuleide crossed her arms and considered for a moment. "Sure. I'll take her."

Claudio kissed the woman's forehead. "Zuli, you're an angel."

Carolina ran toward them. "Can I keep her?"

He said she'd have to talk it over with her mother and Zuleide. Then he asked if she would like to spend the day with him, and she ran to her room to change. She never *walks,* he thought. No wonder she's so skinny.

Zuleide offered him coffee. "Linara won't be back until tonight," she added. He nodded, wiped his shoes on the bristle mat, followed the woman inside. It was strange to be treated as a visitor in the home that had been his for so long. The only difference in the decor was the pictures on the wall. In the year he'd been gone, Linara had discovered a latent talent for painting. She signed up at a local college and, at forty-five, produced art that was, at least to him, as good—no, better—than that of most artists who'd been painting their whole lives. She transformed his old office into an atelier, filled it with landscapes, portraits, still lifes of fruit and flowers, filled the whole house with them, in fact—the bathrooms, the kitchen, even Carolina's room had them, all over the walls, stacked atop one another in mismatched, colorful frames.

He sat on the white leather sofa, hands wedged between his knees. If he closed his eyes he'd fall asleep instantly. This was where he'd sat that morning, the worst morning of his life, when Linara awakened him and said, "There's a young woman at the door asking for you." He'd known then it was over. This was where Elisabeth told Linara how they'd met in a medical convention, how they'd been "going" for seven months. How—and she smiled when she said it—they were in love. "Is it true, Claudio," was all Linara asked, disappearing into their bedroom when he stammered his answer. Shortly thereafter he and Elisabeth moved in together, and in two months she was pregnant. So far he had told no one.

While he drank Zuleide's bitter black coffee, Carolina, now in jeans and sneakers, swung on the hammock in the den, telling him to hurry. On their way out, Claudio pointed an accusatory finger at the turkey pecking the dirt in the front yard, and said, "You behave, understand? You've caused enough problems."

Carolina wrinkled her nose when she entered the Mustang. "*Eca!* What's that smell?"

Claudio sniffed the air deeply, closing his eyes. "Ah! The sublime scent of Petunia!"

They dropped the car off at a detailing shop in the center of town, where he was compelled to lavish the attendant with an exorbitant tip before the man would even consider the job. Then they went for a walk. Like him, Carolina loved the chaos of downtown Recife, its trash, fallen mangos, and *sapotis* scattered among the gnarled roots sprouting from the cracked, ancient sidewalks. At the heart of the city, called simply *Recife Velho*, Old Recife, the shaded streets narrowed, grew louder, congested with vendors and shoppers, bars, *cafeterias*, newsstands, juice houses, sailors, transvestites, cops, street urchins, stray dogs, doves, horses, VW vans with crackling loudspeakers on their roofs hawking politicians, movies, department stores. The colonial flavor of the city was most noticeable to him during winter, with the unrelenting drizzle, the leaves ceaselessly drifting from their high canopy of branches onto the cobbled roads and sidewalks, the occasional burst of sunlight through a break in the heavy overcast. A church stood on most corners, its doors wide open, beggars sprawled on the steps. The brown Capibaribe River bisected the entire city, and because of it, bridges, like churches, were omnipresent.

They stared out over the Atlantic, gawked at a monstrous German tanker in the port; a few blocks inland they entered the old jail, a strange structure left over from colonial times, shaped like a giant two-story worm with barred square windows along its sides—nowadays a crafts market called Casa da Cultura, each tiny jail cell transformed into a colorful shop that sold traditional art, sweets, and liqueurs from every city in the Northeast. He told Carolina she could choose a gift, and was surprised when, after five minutes, she approached him holding a foot-long priest in a black cassock, hands clergically clasped beneath his belly, a beatific smile painted on his wooden face.

"That?"

She grinned and pulled a string at the base, raising a huge penis that protruded from a slit in the priest's skirt. Claudio would've laughed, had he not been so embarrassed.

"Mom's gonna love it!" she said.

He tried to hide his chagrin, dismissing the trinket as a sign of rebellion toward the nuns and priests she had to tolerate at school. Carolina had always loved jokes, especially blasphemous ones. The doll reminded him of his brief time in the Amazon, when the turbulence of his life had led him nearly to accept an assignment as the in-house doctor for a gold-mining gangster. While there he'd met the gangster's in-house priest, Padre Miguel Inácio; he wondered what had become of that tormented young man.

"Don't you *dare* bring that to school, you hear, young lady?" he said, wagging his finger at the devilish smirk on her face. "*Nem pensar.* Don't even think about it." He paid the attendant the ten *reais*, asked for a bag, and the two stepped out once again, hand in hand, into the hazy morning.

They bought two tapiocas from a *Bahiana* in an immaculate turban and white dress. As they crossed the Ponte do Comercio, a market bridge designated for commerce alone, his cell phone rang. It was *Doutora* Angela, director of the Hospital da Restauração, informing him that Mariana Almeida, "the teenager you sterilized on Wednesday," was finally lucid, asking the nurses what had happened: Was she still pregnant? Why did she hurt?

The patient had staggered in during the end of his shift, alone and bleeding heavily after a botched back-alley abortion. Unable to stop the hemorrhaging, Claudio rushed away from the operating room, still in his mask and bloody gloves, and barged into Angela's office—"Not to ask your permission for what I'm about to do, Angela," he'd said. "Simply to inform you, because the circumstances are dire." He explained the situation. The girl was an unaccompanied minor. "Her uterus is punctured beyond repair, and there are already signs of necrosis and infection. She must have waited a couple of days, until she couldn't stand the pain any longer, before coming in. Either I remove it this instant or she dies."

Angela reacted exactly as he expected any anal-retentive, career-minded woman riding the high horse of her director's post: "She's seventeen, Claudio. Seventeen. We can't!" she threw her hands in the air.

The job of director had been offered to him on several occasions, but he refused each time. He didn't need the extra responsibility, couldn't even imagine having to organize, hire, fire, reprimand, refuse and grant raises and vacation time. Only five years ago Angela had been in residency, scrutinizing Claudio's every move in the hospital. Now here he was, standing in front of her oversize desk.

Claudio stripped off his gloves and said, "Well, then *you* finish the operation, Angela. I'm not having anyone die on my table today. Not when I can avoid it."

"Fine, Claudio," she said. "Who am I to argue with the voice of experience, right?" She pointed a finger at him, "However, *you* be the one who gives her the news later. Okay? Do not pawn this off on one of the nurses. Make sure *you* explain to that girl there was nothing else you could do."

Claudio informed Carolina that they had to go in to work, just for a moment, and was grateful that she didn't whine. She liked the hospital, the staff, the patients, often begged to accompany him on his shifts, and had even watched him perform minor procedures—the draining of an abscess from a man's chest, the casting of broken limbs. "I just love that smell," she'd confessed on more than one occasion. "You always have that smell, too, even when you get out of the shower."

He hailed the first cab he saw, a blue Parati, and sat in the back with Carolina. Once at the hospital—a squat, functional building with narrow hallways and fluorescent lights—he escorted her to his office, a cramped alcove at the end of a long corridor on the third floor, and instructed her to stay there and wait for him. She wasn't happy. She wanted to make the rounds, "say hi to Sueli and everybody," but he said no, she was to sit quietly at his desk, he'd be only a few minutes. She pouted and crossed her arms, swinging her skinny legs back and forth.

On the fourth floor he halted just before the patient's room. He stared at the digits on the door, the five and the eight, gathering his thoughts. Angela knew how much he hated this. It was her way of getting back at him. He had no problem with the body and its fluids, diseases, excrements. But talking to patients, seeing that mix of fear and longing in their eyes as they hung on his every word, even the ones he fabricated to impart false hope or to soften hard facts, that was something to which he'd never grow accustomed. He tried to remember a passage from *The Power of the Moment*, a book he'd stumbled across in the supermarket through divine guidance, his only consolation during the tumultuous months of his divorce, but all he could remember was "Be in the moment."

After the same nurse walked by and greeted him twice, he knocked. A faint voice said, "Come in." He turned the knob slowly. The girl was lying on her side, facing him, a blue sheet up to her waist. Her long black hair had been done in a braid. The window was raised behind her; a breeze blew past him when he opened the door. He had half expected to find her angry or crying, demanding something. But she just stared at him absently, somewhat resigned, and he had the sense that she already knew who he was, what he was about to tell her.

He dragged a chair from the window to her bedside. He knew better than to ask about her family—that would only put her in a more awkward position. The pregnancy had never been an option, that much was obvious. Most likely her parents, if she had any, would swear by their daughter's virginity—a dubious virtue at best, he thought. He sat down beside her, startled by her ethereal beauty, a radiant aura he commonly saw in patients right after surgery. He looked at her and said, "Mariana, honey, in order to save your life, I had to remove your uterus. A hysterectomy." He drew a breath and held it for a moment. "You can never have a baby." He braced himself for tears, but instead she rolled onto her back, staring at the darkened television set mounted on the wall facing her.

"All right."

He said they could talk more later if she wanted; he'd be available for anything, whatever she needed, she should call him. He'd performed this procedure many times before; all the women recovered wonderfully; in the end they were just fine, just fine. She tightened her lips and nodded, thanking him. He put the chair back under the window before he left.

That evening father and daughter picked up the Mustang from the detailer's and met Elisabeth for dinner at her favorite Chinese restaurant, where she treated an aloof Carolina with almost saccharine sweetness, once again insisting on doing the orthodontic work on her front teeth. "It won't hurt a bit! You'll look adorable in braces." Afterward they took Carolina home, and as they waited in the car for her to walk inside, Elisabeth toyed with her cell phone.

Then Linara was there, opening the gate for Carolina. Claudio sat stiffly, gripping the steering wheel, disappointed when she didn't glance his way. He didn't blink until they disappeared into the house. Later, after making love to Elisabeth, he recalled Linara as he had seen her, fresh from the shower. He imagined her slipping under the sheets next to him, naked, her hair wet, her skin damp, and her excruciating, maddening coolness.

Four months later there was the incident with the bottled snake.

At the age of fourteen Claudio had been cured of the deadly poison of a *cascavél*. He'd gone to fetch his horse, Pó de Ouro, Gold Dust—so called because of his mane, the color of a ripe cornfield—who had the habit of jumping the fence to visit Cibela, a mare from the neighboring farm. It happened on the way back, as he ran barefoot, switch in hand. Pó de Ouro trotting ahead like a shameful penitent, burnished in the sunlight. There was the sting on his ankle, quick and sharp like the prick of a thorn. A segmented rattle vanished into the grass. Claudio struggled onto Pó de Ouro's bare back, and slumped forward in delirium. He remembered his uncle carrying him to the couch, opening the blade of a Swiss Army knife, making two deep incisions, in the shape of a cross, over the bite, and sucking on it fiercely. He also remembered waking momentarily to see a man in mirrored sunglasses, looming over him in a cloud of cigar smoke. He was brushing a palm frond against Claudio's chest, belly, and legs, while muttering in another language.

That night his uncle told him: "Son, few exist who've survived so much venom; you've been born again. That snake chose to spare you. You are a *curado,*" here he looked past Claudio's eyes, straight into his soul, "a *cured* one—which means you may never, *ever* harm a snake, you hear? Don't even *think* of harming one. Don't tolerate any person hurting one, either." He patted the boy's sore ankle for emphasis. "Consider yourself in eternal debt to snakes."

So of course, when Claudio arrived at the clinic in Toritama that hot Thursday in November and found *Seu* Antonio amid a noisy throng, gesticulating wildly—"The *danada* was in the middle of the broom closet staring up at me with those cold evil eyes, and I got my forked stick and I put it around her head and rigged this container and stuck the hissing devil inside"—he remembered his uncle's voice, the way the man's eyes had burned into his. He joined the curious circle of patients, studying the elaborate object in the man's hands. "Good morning! What've we got here?" he said.

"A viper, *Doutor.* Look at it!" *Seu* Antonio had cut out the bottoms of two Coca-Cola bottles, the two-liter plastic kind, poked small holes in them, and sealed them together with duct tape. The labels, as well as the bottle caps, were still in place. The coils inside, intricately etched in stripes and diamonds, filled the space completely. There was no telling where the snake ended, where it began. Claudio asked him what he planned to do with the *criatura*. *Seu* Antonio, always dapper, his Indian hair perfectly parted, his elegant frame belying his sixty-odd years, shrugged laconically. "I haven't thought about it. Kill it, I guess. Or sell it to a Xucuru witch doctor for medicine." He laughed at his own joke.

"How come you didn't kill it in the closet, when you had the chance?" Claudio asked.

The man shrugged again. "Ah . . . I didn't want to make a mess. Besides, I wanted to show it around a little. It's not every-day that we see a cobra this huge!"

"I'll tell you what, *Seu* Antonio: I'll take it from you. I want to show it to Carolina."

"Yes, okay," *Seu* Antonio said, beaming. "Tell little Carol it was a gift from me. Remind her she's due for a visit." He handed the bottle to the doctor.

It was heavier than it looked. Claudio held it by the ends, spinning it backward and forward. "Are you sure it's alive?"

"Oh yes. She's got a lot of life in her, that's for sure. She's a mean son-of-a-bitch. Be careful, *Doutor*. I'm not sure what kind it is, but she could be *venenosa*." At this some ladies in the wait-ing room uttered tiny shrieks.

Claudio carried the bottle to his maroon Landau, which he'd parked in the street beneath a row of mango trees. He lowered all four windows, something he could never do in Recife, and hid the bottle beneath the passenger seat, muttering, "Hang in there, I'll be back before you know it." Here, under the ample shade, the car would stay cool. He marched into the clinic, ready to greet the day's patients.

First was Adriana, a twenty-year-old mother of two with heavy varicose veins, bulbous and blue, all over her calves and thighs. This was her third consultation with Claudio. Each session consisted of wrapping a tight band around her fleshy thighs and injecting the sclerosant, a strong saline solution, into the root of each cluster, using a thin, short needle. He had hoped to finish the treatment today, but after the thirteenth injection, the girl's veins were disappearing under her dark skin.

"The shots are starting to hurt, *Doutor*," she complained, smiling. She was sitting on the examination table, her denim skirt hiked up, her left leg propped on a stool.

"That's why we can't see the veins anymore," he said, holding up the syringe and squinting at her inner thigh. "They're afraid now!"

"I'll just come again next week."

He looked up at her over his reading glasses and asked if she was certain. Each visit cost her thirty *reais*, and although it was nothing, really, especially when compared to prices in Recife, he knew her money was hard-earned, as was everyone's in Toritama.

"Yes, I'm sure." She scooted over to the edge of the table and slipped her feet into her sandals. "That way I get to see you again."

He smiled. "Okay, then. Make sure to wear your compression stockings to bed tonight." He disposed of the syringe, the latex gloves, and sat behind his desk, still uncluttered this early in the morning: an orderly stack of papers, a pen, a calendar with the mayor's picture, and a clay statue of Our Lady of Conception, placed there by Maria José, the clinic manager, who on off days worked as a manicurist in her sister's beauty salon.

He treated the next patient. Then the next. And it was Maria José herself who popped into the examination room as he was finishing with his third patient, a man with an everlasting cough, and said, "*Doutor*, we have a problem."

He squeezed the man's shoulder, urged rest, and handed him a prescription. She cracked open the door and motioned for him to peek into the waiting area. He saw a fat woman standing by the front desk, arms folded across her enormous bosom, sweat stains blooming beneath her armpits, her face mottled as though she were passing a difficult stool. He recognized the grinning man standing beside her. Petunia's farmer. He tried to remember what he'd treated him for, but couldn't.

"It's *Seu* Algenor, remember? The vasectomy? That's his wife." Maria José leaned into his ear. "Pregnant. Blaming *you* for it." She tightened her lips to hold back a smile. "Sorry. You better see her now. She's been making a scene out there."

At that moment the woman spied him from across the room. "*Doutor de merda!*" she yelled. "Yes, you!" she continued, in a vicious voice that made him ball his right hand into a fist. The waiting patients looked on gleefully. In a town like Toritama, a scandal of this nature was prime grist for the gossip mill.

Claudio walked straight to the woman, an ingratiating smile tacked on to his face. He assured her that her satisfaction was his primary concern, that he would get to the root of her problem, and while he mouthed platitudes, his smile never slipping, he hooked his hand around her upper arm, his fingers digging into the soft flesh of her bicep. He hissed into her ear, "Come with me." The farmer shrugged sheepishly, his face at once apologetic and triumphant, the face of a man who was not to blame if modern medicine could not diminish his virility.

Maria José ushered the coughing patient out of the examination room. Claudio closed the door and assumed his post behind his desk. She faced him, her blond hair an electric shock.

"This is your fault, *Doutor*," she went on. "*You* didn't do your job right, and now look," she put a hand on her stomach. "Two months already. I just found out today. My neighbor, who's a midwife, confirmed it."

Claudio leaned back in his chair, studying the woman without out a word. He rolled an imaginary toothpick in his mouth, for effect. The woman shifted her weight from one hip to the other. It was evident her act was falling apart, now that her audience was out of earshot. Her eyelids, heavy with mascara, were beginning to tremble. In the face of his reptilian silence, he could almost smell her righteous anger evaporating. He tapped out a rhythm on top of the desk, staring at her without blinking. He took a deep, audible breath. "I'll tell you what, Mrs.——"

"Cleide."

"Cleide?"

"Yes, Cleide."

"Okay, Mrs. Cleide. I'll tell you what." He leaned forward. He picked up a paper clip and unbent it. He spoke very slowly. "You leave my office right now, *ca-la-di-nha*——nice and quiet. You tell your husband whatever lie you want, but you make sure I don't see either of your faces again. In return, my dear, I won't tell your husband that the belly you're carrying, if indeed you *are* pregnant," he pointed the extended paper clip at her, "is not his." He got up, walked to the door, and held it open. "Because that would be the *easiest* thing in the world for me to prove."

The woman stood there for a moment, her face clenched, indignant. She gave him a look of withering scorn and puffed out her chest as she exited the room and grabbed her husband's wrist as though he were an errant schoolboy.

"*Seu* Algenor!" Claudio yelled. The man stopped and turned to him. His wife turned also, her countenance dreadful. "Petunia is doing great. Fatter than ever. I gave her to my daughter."

Before *Seu* Algenor could reply, his wife pulled him out the door.

The rest of the day went smoothly. By six-thirty the waiting room was empty, save for Maria José and *Seu* Antonio, who watched the six o'clock soap opera, *Bad Angel*, with avid concentration, barely saying good-bye to Claudio.

The drive from Toritama to Recife was Claudio's most cherished moment of the week, when he could be alone, for two hours with his thoughts and music——the music Elisabeth, Carolina, and

Linara loved to ridicule. He had looked forward to it all after-noon: the summer's deep blue sky, stars rising on the horizon, the rawboned mountains alongside the lonely canyon road. Later, a full moon to guide the way. He would crack his window, just a bit, and allow the cool breeze to blow on his face. Before starting the engine he reached into the glove compartment and sifted through his cologne bottles and papers and tapes until finding the cassette he wanted: Andrea Bocelli, the man whose songs soothed his soul, made him forget the world. He inserted it into the player and drove away from the clinic, returning the waves of a few pedes-trians on the sidewalk. When *"Una Furtiva Lagrima"* came on, Claudio choked back his own tears. *"Una Furtiva Lagrim/a negli occhi suoi spuntò . . ."*

How could the women in his life not be moved by this? How could Elisabeth call it pop opera? Couldn't she hear the passion? Then he remembered. They had agreed to meet for dinner. She wanted to have a "serious talk." He decided to call once he rolled into town, pushing away the sinking feeling in his stomach at the prospect of such a talk.

The moment, Claudio. Be in the moment. You're not at dinner yet. You're in the car, with Andrea.

He sang the whole way home, rewinding his favorite songs, pumping his fist in the air, rounding out his rudimentary Italian with fanciful phonetics. He delayed dialing Elizabeth's cell num-ber until he was in downtown Recife.

She was finishing up her last patient, a root canal. She sug-gested they meet at Romulo's Pasta, a new restaurant on Beach Drive. She assured him he'd love the place, she had eaten there with her mother and great-aunt just the other day. He asked should he pick her up but she said no, she'd take a cab. He'd been driving her to and from work for two months now; she claimed that she could still detect the faint smell of turkey shit in her Mustang.

He drove slowly, hoping to stretch the hour into infinity.

The place was dark and intimate. Small tables, couples, candles, wine. Canned piano music. He arrived first, chose the booth nearest the bar. Even with his glasses, Claudio struggled to read the drink menu.

"My little old man!" Elisabeth kissed the top of his head, right on his bald spot, flung her purse on the cushion next to him, and sat down, nudging the table away from her belly. Her pregnancy had just started to show during the past month, a neat curve that could be mistaken for a bit of excess weight. She often joked that it still wasn't as big as his ample paunch. "Here, give me that. Tonight everything's on me."

She called the waiter, a thick-necked, overmuscled surfer type whose long bangs and affected accent annoyed Claudio. She ordered virgin apple martinis and two entrees that sounded Greek to him. He prayed that the dish would be fish-free. He couldn't stomach seafood, hated the smell of it. But he wasn't about to tell her, not now, with her in a good mood, thank God. He slipped his glasses into the breast pocket of his shirt and looked at her, at her glossy, smiling lips, the lipstick a shade lighter than her skin. When she smiles, he thought, she is beautiful, her small and irregular teeth belying the perfectionism she exercised on her patients.

Now, if there was one thing he had to give her, it was this: Elisabeth was direct. She'd barely finished with the waiter when she said, "I have news for you, Claudio. I found out the sex of our baby. We're having a boy."

"What? But I thought —"

"Yes, I know we had agreed to wait, but today I paid a visit to Uncle Modesto's clinic, because it was his birthday and because I wanted to clear up some questions—the man *is* an obstetrician, and he *is* family, after all—and he let it slip during the ultrasound. He said, 'He's got the family's signature Roman nose.' *He.* But I had a feeling, anyway."

Claudio was silent, staring absentmindedly at the tiny flame of the candle on their table. A boy.

"Aren't you happy?"

"I am! I am."

"Then why the long face?"

"*What* long face? I was just thinking about it. Letting it sink in! Jesus." He couldn't help it. His patience with her waned each day, and he felt terrible about it, he did. The waiter brought their sterile martinis, green and chic, a fat cherry at the bottom of each cone-shaped glass. The man crouched down so that his bangs were at the same level as Elisabeth's face, and asked in what he must have thought was a gallant tone if they needed anything else. Claudio said no, but when the waiter turned around he snapped his fingers. "Actually, what beers do you have?"

"Well, let's see . . . We have Brahma, Antarctica, Keis—"

"A Brahma will do, thanks. Here, take this back." He lifted his martini, spilling some on his hand, taking sadistic satisfaction in Elisabeth's irritated sigh. He could see where things were heading. This conversation would end as all their conversations these days: with scathing words, her sulking, his losing his temper and ignoring her until a new truce was negotiated in bed.

"Listen, Claudio. You have to tell them. This is ridiculous."

Just as he'd thought. Her latest favorite power game. His sorest button. He'd promised her a million times that he would tell Carolina and Linara about the baby *when the time was right.* A soft bossa drifted from the speakers; Claudio hummed along with the "*Desafinado.*" He really wanted to flip the table over.

"In a month it'll begin to show, then what?"

"Then I guess it'll be out of my hands. A moot point." Her face clouded. He attempted to backpedal. "Look, Liz. I'm sorry.

Okay? I know I've been an asshole, and I'm sorry. I promise you that I'll take care of it. I *will* tell Carolina." He covered her hand with his. "As soon as she's back from vacation, I'll tell her. She'll be thrilled to know she's having a little brother."

"And Linara?"

"It doesn't matter what Linara thinks. But I'll tell her too, if it makes you happy."

His beer came. He ignored the glass, pulled a long draught from the amber bottle.

"It's not that it makes me *happy*, Claudio. It's just that I don't understand why this is so difficult for you. You act like you're ashamed of me."

Claudio set his beer on the table. "Can we just have one meal, *one*—" he clutched the bottle, his knuckles white "—meal, without a fight?"

Elisabeth withdrew to the bathroom. She returned to her seat as their dinner arrived. Scallops. He pushed the shells to the side and ate the pasta, chewing mechanically. Drank another beer, then another. She only ate half of her dish, certainly so that he would insist she finish it, but he wasn't budging. Not tonight. He was tired of apologizing, tired of playing daddy.

Their silent war ended in the car, at a stoplight on Boa Vista Avenue, where Claudio slammed on his brakes to avoid hitting a group of street urchins who materialized in front of the vehicle with water bottles and dirty rags, smudging the windshield for change. For a moment the dark water obstructed his field of vision. He turned the Landau's wipers on, reached into his pockets, "Here, here, don't bother." He held out his fist and distributed the change into the sea of brown hands gathered at his window. "Try asking next time, will you?"

He looked at their ripped shorts, the luminous eyes gleaming from their pinched, soiled faces, their ribs clearly visible through their skin, thinking, In a few years they'll figure out taking is easier than begging, and I'll be pulling bullets from their bodies. And for the briefest of seconds Claudio forgot his own problems, the woman sitting next to him whom he couldn't love who was carrying his second child, a brother whose existence he could not explain to Carolina or Linara.

From the corner of his eye he saw Elisabeth reaching under her seat, tugging at something.

The snake. Oh God, Jesus Christ, the snake. "Have you seen the full moon tonight, honey?" he planted a hand on top of her skirt and squeezed her thigh.

"You got something—" she yanked out the first half of the bottle "—stuck here. It's warm. It bumped into my leg when you almost ran over those boys."

"Ah . . . Liz, baby, don't worry about it. It's a Coke bottle Carolina forgot there."

Horns honked behind them. He stepped hard on the accelerator.

"But it's hot, and heavy."

"Trust me, Liz, leave it there," he pleaded in the softest, warmest tone he could muster, but she had jerked the container out and was now studying it in the same way he had done before, asking him, "What the hell is this" while patting the ceiling for the inside light. She flicked it on; Claudio pulled to the side of the road, tires screeching. He turned to her, his palms against his chest in a posture of supplication. "Honey, promise me you won't panic," he said.

But it was too late. Her face drained of color, and he braced himself for the scream. It came—shrill, hysterical. She dropped the bottle between her legs, flung the door open, and jumped from the vehicle. She slammed it shut, shaking the whole Landau. "What is that thing doing in there?"

Claudio threw his upper body across the passenger seat, rolling down the window while his seat belt tightened around him, constricting the pasta in his gut. "Honey, it's okay. It was *Seu* Antonio at the clinic, he caught it this morning and I was just holding it here until—"He could feel his dinner climb his throat.

"What, and you couldn't tell me before I got in? You want to kill me! That's it! You want me to lose the baby so you won't have to explain your bastard to anyone!" She started to walk away. Claudio idled along beside her. Passing motorists slowed down to gawk. A few of them honked.

"Please, Liz, get back in the car, I'm begging you."

"Throw that thing away."

"I can't!"

She stopped and looked at him incredulously. It was a test now. "Get rid of it or I'm not coming in."

"I can't, Liz. I'm a *curado*." He offered a crooked, despairing smile.

"A what?"

"A *curado*, baby. I'm cured, cured!" She laughed—a nasty, sneering sound. He felt like crying. "From the venom of a poisonous snake, when I was a kid. Please, Liz, it's late. Liz!"

Elisabeth stuck her arm into the open window and snatched her purse, rattling off a long and unflattering litany of names that ended with a rhetorical question: "When will you grow up, Claudio?" He tried to formulate an answer, but before he could say a word, she stalked across the busy square, toward a row of parked taxis. Claudio sat there awhile, his head against the steering wheel. Her taxi drove off in the opposite direction, eastward, toward her mother's house. Her mother, a lover, it made no difference to him. If only *he* were carrying his own baby.

Claudio picked up the bottle from the floor and set it on his lap. It *was* warm. The snake must have absorbed the day's heat. "That was quite an entrance, my friend." He parked the car in an empty lot just ahead. About half a mile behind the avenue were the Dois Irmãos woods, and the lake. Some night air would do him good. He retrieved a scalpel from his medical bag, raised both windows, locked the doors, and stepped out, bottle in hand, under the full moon. He crossed the avenue and headed down the path leading onto Recife's virgin soil. He expected beggars, prepared himself in the event of robbers, but the woods were serenely calm. As he neared the lake, a light wind sprang up; he heard the sound of leaves rasping against one another, whispering sighs. Overhead a few bats reeled back and forth. The dark earth was sprinkled with patches of moonlight.

He picked a space between a gnarled banyan tree and the water. He gingerly cut through the layers of tape until the two halves of the makeshift container came loose, like an odd, synthetic egg. He squatted down and set it before him with utmost care; a mass of shiny coils spilled through the crack and onto the ground, unfurling into a long, elegant *jibóia*. It lay still a while, as if savoring the coolness of the earth. All at once it moved, gliding toward him in a straight line; his heart beat harder than ever, but he remained still, unafraid, even when, mere inches away, it stopped and raised its body to the level of his face, and its opaque eyes stared directly into his. Later, when he told the tale, he would swear on the life of his children that the snake had thanked him—"It looked straight at me and said 'Thank you' with its eyes. Can you believe it?" But for now Claudio was frozen, delighted, mesmerized, not a thought in his mind save that he and the snake were together, in the moment.

The Whirling Dove

By the rhythm of his breathing and the weight of his arm on her belly, Cloé knew her lover had fallen asleep. She squirmed away from the damp body that only moments ago she had savored and explored, that body she had housed with excruciating pleasure, not because it was particularly beautiful—no, the pitiless light of dawn revealed every wart and blemish with surgical clarity—but because it too had given freely of its senses, of its caresses, opened its passages and doorways. She managed to free herself, replacing her belly beneath his arm with the bundle of covers, her chest beneath his head with a rumpled pillow. She found her right shoe under the bed. She scanned the bedroom for the other, then stumbled to the living room, where she discovered it beside the piano along with her white dress, her book of poetry, and the two empty glasses. Her purse was on the table. She looked for a bra, then remembered she hadn't worn one. Her underwear she saw crumpled near the entrance like a red stain.

She dressed with clumsy haste, for the sun was rising. She wet her hands in the kitchen sink, attempted to tame her errant locks, walked lightly to the bedroom, and from the doorway stared at the sleeping man. The air smelled of fresh rain and raw mushrooms.

Here the romance ended and the guilt began.

Should she tell him she was departing? Leave a note? *Thank you for last night, you were divine, the music was beautiful, but please don't contact me again.* Or maybe, *The flesh is weak, the wine doesn't help. Let's leave this here, please* . . . No. Notes could betray. She knew this from experience. She would let him sleep, and hope that the man would only awaken many hours later, perhaps thinking it all a dream.

Before she left, Cloé rummaged through her purse, retrieved a pamphlet entitled *Seven Reasons Why You Should Accept Jesus Now*, and placed it beside his head. That way, at least, some good would come from this prurient vice of her body's; after all, she thought, what does it matter how a shepherd finds his sheep? She shut the door softly and hurried out, racing against the sun, for by the time its rays brightened Miami's sleepy streets, Brother Milton, her husband, would be arriving home.

Cloé's history with men began as a child of six, in her homeland of Bahia, Brazil, where she faithfully watched, along with Maria José, her nanny, Friday-night episodes of *The Incredible Hulk*, dubbed in perfect Portuguese.

He was her first love—that peaceful, charming scientist who struggled with his inner demon. She fantasized about Dr. David Banner night after night, during the purgatorial stage between awareness and sleep. She imagined herself entangled in some great danger when he appeared, calm, smooth, hands in his pockets, to help her out of her predicament. Sometimes it was *she* who saved Dr. Banner, right before his alter ego emerged: the good doctor cornered by thugs, she coincidentally walking by, displaying an impressive knowledge of jujitsu and *capoeira*, and the robbers, afraid, dropping his wallet as they fled. Then came the climactic embrace, the scientist's promise of undying gratitude and remembrance.

But after some time, just like the meek scientist, those fantasies underwent a dark metamorphosis. They became distorted, insidiously taking on a life of their own. No matter how hard she tried, little Cloé could no longer control the direction or the characters in her fantasies, and instead of Dr. Banner, it was Hulk, the ultra macho; Hulk, the brutish incarnation of male essence, whom she loved; and now the love itself had warped into something else. She lost the lead role in her fantasies to another—a strange woman, voluptuous, seductive, always in a white dress, who did things to Hulk, acts Cloé witnessed mutely from the corner of the small room where these lurid scenes unfolded. The sequence of events was monotonously repetitive; nothing really befell the monster or the woman except that which they did to themselves. Sometimes, after they both collapsed on top of each other, or rather, after the woman collapsed over Hulk, for she was always on top, they talked:

Hulk, my little safado, you're too much!
Hulk no safado.
Yes Hulk, you are, you nasty boy. You delicious little animal.
Hulk no animal. Hulk crush puny human.
Yes, my baby, I know, I know. Come here. Crush me, my boy.

And the two would resume their rolling and rubbing about until sleep delivered Cloé to more innocent dreams, of dolls and trees and deep blue waters.

Those fantasies changed Cloé. Something roused within her, afflicted her with new sensations. They surged up everywhere, in bed, in the classroom, in the chapel during mass, in friends' houses, at the table while she ate. A warmth would spread from her feet to her thighs, from her thighs to her loins. She made use of pillows, chairs, the ceramic donkey in the living room, whatever aided her in achieving that intense relief, that release that made earth and sky nonexistent, always careful that no one saw her, for a tiny, grim voice imbued with all the authority of her grandmother's church, of the nuns at school, told her that what she did was fundamentally wrong.

After a few months of this, she decided to confess to her mother. "Before I sleep I think about men, and I rub on things, and it feels good."

The woman fell silent. When she finally spoke, she stammered something vague about absent fathers that left the little girl wondering if she had understood her. The next day she presented Cloé with a book about puberty, reluctantly surrendering it into the little seven-year old hands. In the book Cloé read that what she did had a name, *masturbation*, but it did not reveal its cause or how to stop it. Ultimately dissatisfied, the child regretted having ever revealed her secret.

As she also regretted, two years later, telling her mother about kissing Angelica, the neighbor, on the mouth: "With tongue and everything, like in the *novelas*."

"Women's mouths are cold, Cloé" her mother replied. Cloé never kissed Angelica or any other girl again. But she did wonder what cold-mouthed woman her mother had based her advice on.

Inevitably her fantasies of Hulk and his Brazilian lover were preempted by ones featuring real boys. Cloé loved every single one of them, those boys of her everyday life. She had no affection for dolls or her hair, which she butchered on a regular basis, for dresses, makeup, or the Menudo kids (actually she did like them, but in secret). She excelled at their own games: soccer, *bafo*, chess, marbles, and in school, trounced them in math and science. For their part the boys generally despised her. Some called her the worst names they could find: *man, mulher-macho, sapatão*.

She took refuge from her classmates in a newly discovered passion for chemistry, a discipline that made sense of a chaotic universe. Her enthusiasm was encouraged by Dona Pegueiro, her chemistry teacher and beacon of sanity, who never tired of telling Cloé what an amazing natural talent she possessed for the science.

At the age of nine she had her first boyfriend, Mauro—a tall, quiet boy with curly red hair and acute acne. They met after school, in the subterranean garage of Lido da Bahia, the apartment building where both lived, she on the tenth floor, he on the fourth. There they kissed all afternoon, breaking for dinner, then meeting again behind some chosen car, a black Volkswagen Beetle, an orange Chevette. When too much vehicular activity disturbed their privacy, Cloé dragged Mauro to the service elevator, stopped it between floors by rocking it from side to side, a trick she had proudly mastered, and kissed him until someone complained to the security guard that the elevator was stuck.

She liked nothing better in the world than kissing Mauro, perhaps because those kisses had no promise, and deep down she knew that promiseless kisses were the best kisses of all.

But she soon found out that she liked kissing others just as much as she did Mauro. Two brothers, Rodrigo and Ricardo, who lived on the twelfth (and highest), floor and whom all the girls liked because they were blond, made her feel the exact same way. At first she chose Ricardo, the older one. She kissed him a whole Saturday morning in his room, his brother and father out at the beach, only the maid singing along to her radio in the kitchen. Then she tried Rodrigo, younger and shorter than she. She liked him also, but preferred Ricardo, and imprudently admitted this fact to his younger brother, who turned out to be vengeful and masterful in his use of drama. He chose a day when all the kids in the building had gathered for a game of soccer and proclaimed, for everyone to hear, that "Cloé has kissed so many mouths her own has no taste left. She is a *puta.*"

Cloé felt a sudden blow, an ache in the chest, a sting in the eyes. She ran home, where she could still hear their jeers floating up through her bedroom window, and at night, when her mother returned from work, Cloé told her, in tears, that Rodrigo had called her a whore. Her mother slapped her across the face and said, "Have you no respect for yourself?" To Cloé this was an unforgiving act that only deepened the chasm between the two.

Besides boys, Cloé had another obsession: a love of the occult, of other dimensions, of supernatural beings and things unexplainable, subjects that abounded in the stories told by Maria José and her five sisters; by *Seu* Elias, the security guard; by the maids who worked for other families that lived in her building; by Ceça, the school's Angolan librarian. All she had to do was ask, and listen. They spoke of ghosts, monsters, beasts from the sea, of Cumade Florzinha, devourer of children's belly buttons; of Saci Pererê, the witchy one-legged boy who roamed the forests at night; of miraculous fish in the desert; of phantoms and apparitions who haunted the world of people in one way or another. Some, they said, approached men in the guise of lovely women, seduced them, and at the moment of utmost ecstasy, vanished from their lover's arms, while others came to women in the form of abandoned babies, twisting into snakes the moment the women offered them their breasts. One of her favorite stories was that of the Bôto, a salacious dolphin who, during the feast of Saint John, transformed into a man, concealing his blowhole under a straw hat, roaming the celebration in search of young virgins to deflower and impregnate.

Her grandmother's conversion from Catholicism to Spiritism, a religion based on the teachings of unseen intelligences channeled by the French medium Alain Kardec, inflamed her obsession even further.

As with her nanny, Cloé felt closer to Lourdes, her maternal grandmother, than she did to her own mother, Vanessa. And although the two women did not get along, Vanessa left Cloé in Lourdes's care during her frequent travels to Rio, New York,

Barcelona. The old woman, who seemed much younger than her seventy-odd years, lived with her sad sister, Cloé's great-aunt Nelza. Lourdes had once been rich, but had donated practically everything she owned to a charity for homeless elders after her marriage to Cloé's grandfather crumbled. She had declared that being rich when so many around her died of thirst and hunger was the greatest sin of all.

The house was large, haunted by the ghost of aunt Nelza's late husband. On many nights, his footsteps echoed off the marble floors, in the living room, in the kitchen, and Lourdes would say, "Poor man, he doesn't know he's dead, and is wondering why dinner is never served for him." When the closet doors in his old room opened and closed mysteriously, she said, "He probably wants to go gambling, but can't find his white suit."

"Really, grandma?"

"Yes, Cló. Sometimes people die and don't realize they're dead. It is up to us to pray for them, talk to them, so that they can accept the other world a bit more easily."

On Tuesday nights, Lourdes brought Cloé to the Espirita's congregation, which met in a building shaped like a pyramid, eight blocks away from the house. The two walked alone through the dark streets, each carrying a jug of water to be "energized" by the healing powers of the central pyramid, a shrine Cloé was forbidden to enter. She stayed in the main atrium, surrounded by people reading passages from *The Spirit's Book*, its pages dictated to Mr. Alain Kardec by spirits of higher order—the man only provided the paper, the pen, the hand, and the spirit did the rest.

One Tuesday night as they returned home, each carrying a jug, Cloé, who accepted the strange doctrine with curious fascination, made a joke about the energized water. The jug in her grandmother's hand shattered, to the stupefied astonishment of the two. Cloé never joked about such things again.

She did not know then that her grandmother was sick with cancer and would die three years later. A month before her death, Lourdes, almost unrecognizable from the ravages of the disease, told Cloé from her hospital bed that her greatest wish was to see her only granddaughter get married.

And so when Cloé married for the first time, in Miami, at the age of twenty-five, she felt her grandmother's spirit with her. It was also there four years later, forlorn and disapproving, when Cloé got divorced.

Being unfaithful proved quite easy, especially after the first few times. Her husband, Jeremy, led the dual life of the struggling artist, waiting tables by day and drumming in various bars by night, and so was hardly ever home, especially on weekends. She had met him at a tiny jazz club that she frequented during the slow weeknights, a pleasant spot for a relaxing nightcap after a long day of work. Although the attraction was obviously mutual, on their first date, the timid, nervous man confessed to her, reluctantly, that he had very little experience in the matters of love. Cloé had no problem playing the role of navigator in their relationship, a position she especially savored during their carnal encounters, where she could steer her pliant lover into perverse and, for him, hitherto uncharted areas. But after the wedding, the game lost its charm for her, and she became irritated at her husband's passivity, his seeming inability to reach out spontaneously and cast his lust upon her, always meekly awaiting her initiative. She stopped meeting him for lunch and going to his gigs, filling her time alone by putting in long hours at Ferminisch, the small perfume laboratory where she worked as a fragrance technician.

One evening, after finishing a project she had been laboring over single-mindedly for five months, an intricate musky blend, Cloé asked a coworker to try it on for her, on the basis that she needed to smell it on a man's skin. The jolly, bald chemist with an oversize head, whom Cloé knew only casually, rubbed two small drops behind his ears, saying, "I want you to know that this, for me, is an honor." She approached him, stood on the tips of her toes, her nose beside his earlobe, feeling a hand rest upon her shoulder. She moved closer. His other hand cradled her hip.

"Ummm . . . that's good," she murmured, and then he kissed her neck. Her body stiffened, almost staggering, but she didn't pull back. She wanted to resist, but the old tidal surge welled within her. A second kiss on the lips, and Cloé felt all the blood drain to her stomach. A third, a fourth, and the kissing no longer sufficed, lips needed more than lips, and the rising hunger compelled her to obey that first commandment, to be fruitful and multiply—although multiplication played no part in this dance—a crescendo of need that had no end. The two spent the rest of the evening in the laboratory, coupling on the floor, on tables, chairs, against walls, smearing themselves with expensive fragrances, colorful extracts, honeysuckle for his chest, rose for her breasts, jasmine for his stomach, lavender for her thighs, sandalwood for his groin.

In the morning, when she got home, Cloé, still in a daze, ran straight to the bathroom, carefully skirting the black drum cases scattered all over the living room floor. But as soon as she locked the door Jeremy called her, and from the shower she told him that she had fallen asleep in the lab.

"I'm sorry, baby. I don't know what happened. The herbal extracts, they must have had an effect on me." She prayed that her tone sounded convincing.

"Oh. I see."

"It could have been the valerian. Or the chamomile."

"I tried to call the lab, but no one answered."

"What?"

"I tried to call, but—"

"Can't hear you, baby. How was your gig?"

Despite the guilt that wrenched her heart, Cloé was unstoppable. That first act of adultery released something within her, and once she crossed that threshold, nothing could make her turn back.

She saw a man and her body burned.

Not any man. There had to be something particular about him, a subtle element: his voice, the way he pronounced certain words. It could be his laugh, or the scent on his breath after sipping a beer, a glass of wine. Sometimes the way he used his hands for simple things did it: opening a napkin, holding a pen, touching his lips, chin, hair. But in almost all of them, a specific darkness, a precise perversion churned beneath the surface, calling out to the kindred shadow that stirred inside her.

The affairs, dalliances, and one-night stands continued year after year until her husband opened a lover's letter. She saw it when she got home from work, nailed to the door of the bedroom like a murder weapon, a bloody knife. From the end of the corridor her clinician's olfactory sense detected the tawdry cologne oozing off the paper, and immediately knew the author.

> *Cloé:*
>
> *A day has not gone by since last I saw you that you haven't been in my thoughts.*
>
> *I wish you would call or at least write. I miss you constantly.*
>
> *After you, how will I ever be able to love, or even make love, to another?*
>
> *I wonder how you are, and hope all is well. I am doing my best to accept your absence, but this is not an easy or happy task. Your silence is a painful enigma to bear.*
>
> *With love always,*
> *Jorge*

And on the same paper, in a different handwriting:
I didn't want to open this, but I had to.
Expect the divorce papers.

Jorge. She had told him never to write, never to call.
"It's over, Jorge. This has to stop."
"But I love you, Cloé."
"I'm sorry you do. What can I say? I'm married!"
"Do you love him?" he had asked, naked, holding her panties hostage so she would not leave.
"Yes, I do, very much, and I have no intention of leaving him."
"Then why? Why do you do this?"
Why. She asked herself that same question night after sleepless night as she paced the small apartment in agony while Jeremy slept, swearing to her grandmother, the water, God, the spirits, that the last lover had indeed been the last. Jeremy was a good man. No, wonderful. Intelligent, talented, sensitive, hardworking, neither possessive nor jealous. And forgiving. Even after the dreadful letter, after Cloé's confession to almost every liaison, he had given her another chance, a gift she eventually squandered. That final time she had not dared ask him for another chance; in spite of her adulteries she still had respect for her hapless husband, feeling that he should retain a shred of dignity. Even if she'd had the courage, or the audacity, to ask, Cloé was convinced that Jeremy had no chances left to give. The neighbor's pants to his knees, her legs encircling the man's waist, her ass on the kitchen counter and her husband's early return from a canceled gig—she felt scalded by shame. Jeremy just stood there with a bereft, bewildered stare. "Why, Cloé," he had asked. "Why?"

Cloé's introduction to the *pomba gira*, the whirling dove, was at age thirteen through a soap opera, broadcast at midnight due to its uncensored, unabashed sexual content: *Carmen*, a Brazilian rendition of the classic, with Regina Duarte as the sensuous protagonist. Her mother was in New York for an indefinite period—one month, two, perhaps three or four—and had entrusted her to Aunt Nelza, ever more brittle and withdrawn after the death of her sister, Lourdes. Cloé waited for the inevitable snores of her great-aunt, who fell asleep in front of the television after the eleven-o'clock news, and surreptitiously changed the channel from thirteen to six. She watched with delight as Carmen, laughing and dancing, a red rose in her hair, seduced and enchanted one man after another, using the flesh of various women as the vehicles to pacify her desires. The whirling dove, as she was commonly known, entered these innocent victims when they least expected and prowled the night in search of her ancient husband and lover, Exú, who would in turn possess an equally oblivious mortal man. Once incarnated, the spirits would rejoice in human pleasures, smoking, drinking, cavorting in a bed, an alley, or a deserted vehicle. In the morning, abandoned by the gods, the two strangers stared at each other in chagrin and wondered, dumbfounded, what had passed between them.

One scene in particular stoked Cloé: In it, the whirling dove smeared a thick, white lotion from a small flask onto Exú's body, whichever body he had chosen for that night, and then licked it off his belly, his chest, his neck, the whole time whispering tender obscenities in his ears. Cloé wanted more than anything to know what that lotion was, but knew better than to ask her aunt. That scene, however new, seemed familiar to the young girl. She searched her mind, trying to remember where, in her short years, she had seen these two people before. And in a flash Hulk appeared, green as ever, and beside him, the woman in her long white dress, dancing and twirling in that small room of Cloé's childhood.

So when Cloé attended her first *candomblé* ceremony at the age of fourteen, she was not surprised or shocked. In fact she felt oddly at home. She sat in the circle of women and men who chanted and clapped to the rhythm of the various *atabaque* drums, a different chant and rhythm for each deity summoned. Curious faces scanned her when she entered the dim room guided by Mãe Joana, the mother-of-saints, master of ceremonies. But no one asked her anything. She did not even have to hand Mãe Joana the note Ceça, the school librarian, had written, asking her: "Please welcome this young soul. And moreover, "I know her well and she brings no harm, Mãe Joana, I am sorry that I couldn't come today, the nuns at the school need help to prepare the chapel for Saint Mary's procession, you know how those nuns are, can't do anything on their own. Please give the girl your blessing."

Ceça was the one person whom Cloé confided in, whom she could ask about anything. She introduced Cloé to the joys of reading, knowing just what books to reveal at the right times in order to feed the girl's growing hunger for knowledge. The latest, *Dona Flor and Her Two Husbands*, had been handed to Cloé with a cautionary warning: "Don't let the nuns catch you reading this," she said, in her Portuguese imbued with a rich, lyrical African accent, "if they realize we have this in here it will turn crispy, you hear?" And of course, it was Ceça who told Cloé about the *pomba gira*, her role in *candomblé*, her likes and dislikes, her fickle nature, her cravings for sex, her love for Exú, her boredom with death. She even unveiled the mystery of the white lotion, and explained to Cloé that a part of the *pomba* lived in every woman, although more in some than others.

"Like in *Carmen*?"

"Ai, Cloé, why are you still watching those soap operas? If you really want to experience Candomblé, you should go to a *gira*."

"Yes! I would love to!"

"Oh no, don't come with ideas; I meant when you're older."

"Older? Oh, Ceça. Take me to one, please, please, *pleeease!*"

"I was joking, Cloé. Forget it."

"No, Ceça, you don't understand how much I want this. Take me to one, come on!"

"Hush child! You want me to lose my job? I'll think about it. Now go. I don't want to be blamed again if you're late for class."

Cloé badgered Ceça non-stop that entire week. She stopped by the library in the morning, between classes, on fabricated bathroom trips, at lunch, after school. "Do you have an answer yet?" She tried to assuage any doubt she could think of from the woman's mind: "I swear, Ceça, by Jesus on that cross, that I won't tell anyone—If it's my mother you're worried about, don't, she's in the Estados Unidos, and my aunt, she sleeps all day—it will be our secret, I promise— think of it as a field trip, an educational experience for me."

"I'm sorry, Cloé, but it's turned out I have to work this Saturday, and can't attend the *gira* anyway."

"Then just give me the address. Please. I *have* to go, Ceça. I have to! I'll take the bus. I've been taking it to and from school for the past four months. Trust me."

Finally, on Friday afternoon, Ceça consented to the girl's pleas, but not without a cautionary speech: "When you enter the *terreiro*, Cloé, remember at all times that you are walking on sacred ground, a place full of energies. The first thing you should practice is silence and meditation. Don't ever cross your hands or feet. Don't look into the eyes of anyone. Here." From her purse she pulled out a long leather string. "Tie this to your arm, underneath your shirtsleeve when you go, and throw it in the river when you leave. It imprisons bad energies. That way no low spirit will follow you home."

Cloé hid the string in a safe pocket of her backpack and thanked Ceça with a suffocating hug.

"Come in, my girl, come in," said the petite black woman, much younger than Cloé had imagined, her head crowned by a golden turban that matched her flowing dress.

"You must be Mãe Joana."

"And you must be she whom my shells warned me about." She laughed, a laughter at once gentle and mischievous, and opened her arms to Cloé. "Don't be scared, brave one, you're exactly where you're supposed to be. Come with me. The ceremony is about to start."

The room was lit by long candles, populated by images of various saints, some that Cloé recognized, *São Jorge, São Sebastião*, for identical replicas adorned the numerous Catholic churches and households she had visited, but others she had never seen before. These were black or red, naked except for the beads wrapped around their bodies, their faces fierce, lustful, debauched. One had two heads: the head on the right that of Jesus, blond hair, blond beard, sad blue eyes; the head on the left had horns, a bony jaw, a sharp, triangular beard, a wild grin. The female figures were round, their breasts ample, their hips and buttocks wide, hair that touched their feet. In front of each, an offering—a smoldering cigar or stick of incense, a plate of fruit, a coconut shell filled with liquid. For a moment Cloé enjoyed the thought of the nuns' outraged faces had they seen the Immaculate Virgin next to that muscular brown icon with the colossal erection. A dense aroma of tobacco and coffee saturated the air, so thick that Cloé could massage it between her fingers.

She sat in a circle surrounding a chair, empty except for a red candle on its surface. Beside her a young man rocked slightly back and forth, his eyes closed and spine erect, a picture held tightly between his fingers. She wanted to lean over and look at it, but the woman on her left tapped her arm and handed her a green bottle. "Lavender water," she said, patting her own neck. "Rub some on yourself, and pass it on."

Mãe Joana walked into the center and introduced the solemn, lanky man who was to be the night's medium. "This will be a very special *gira*, my friends," she announced, her hand on his sharp shoulder, "for it is Brother Epaminondas's initiation. He has been studying with me for almost a year, he is very talented and ready to receive our guides, so that they can help us with our sufferings, our difficulties. But please remember, the first few incorporations can be a bit . . . violent; the spirits are somewhat tough to control when one has little experience. If this happens, don't be afraid, stay in place, I'm here to curb any rowdiness on the part of our beloved Orixás." People laughed, some expressing quiet words of encouragement to the serious man who removed the red candle from the chair and placed it before his bare feet. Cloé squeezed her right arm. Ceça's leather string was still there.

"Thank you, brothers, sisters," he said slowly, then sat down, both palms upturned on his lap, and closed his eyes. Mãe Joana walked away and squatted in front of Cloé. The girl stood up, offering her chair, but Mãe Joana, with a gentle yet firm wave of her hand, gestured for her to remain seated.

Three men outside the circle began playing their *atabaques*. First, a low drum initiated a slow pulse, a resonant heartbeat that vibrated within her chest. The second drum joined in with a higher voice, weaving a syncopated rhythm that fell between the deep tones of the first. Finally, the third, the highest voice, chattered in a complex, jagged language simultaneously loose and locked into the cadence of the other two, a message she could almost understand. Voices rose in a chant, forming a single voice that reverberated throughout the walls, the ground, the ceiling, as if the small room were suddenly filled by all the voices that had ever sung those words. After a couple of repetitions, Cloé added hers:

Vamos abrir a nossa gira
Com licença de Oxalá
Salve Xangô
Salve Iemanjá
Mamãe Oxum, Nanã Buroquê
Salve Cosme e Damião
Oxóssi, Ogum
Oxumaré

All at once the drums halted, the voices silenced. Everyone knelt. Mãe Joana spoke again, asking that the spirits bless the *gira*, for them to come in goodwill and aid the needy souls gathered therein. "Now, let us pray," she said, and together they intoned an Our Father followed by a Hail Mary. Then Epaminondas placed some incense kneaded with rose petals onto the lighted coals of an earthenware censer and walked from person to person, dousing their heads with the aromatic smoke. At the center once again, he touched his forehead to the ground, and retrieving the red candle before him, lit a cigar the size of a banana. The room was silent except for his deep breaths, growing heavier with each puff, until his whole body shook. He stood, so suddenly that the chair fell behind him. "Where is my drink?" he demanded, his shoulders broad, his chest inflated, his voice like that of a general returning from war.

"Just a moment, dear Ogum. We weren't expecting you first." Mãe Joana raised her arms and a pale girl darted from somewhere inside the house with a bottle in her hands. She handed it to the man, whom Cloé, stunned, realized was no longer the self-effacing Epaminondas of a minute ago. She had heard of this before. It was impossible to grow up in Bahia, or anywhere in Brazil, without hearing of such stories. But her awe proved overwhelming.

He drank the entire bottle in one gulp. Then he asked the drummers to play his song, and as he danced—a fierce, heavy stomp—three people entered the circle and sat on the ground by his feet. When the song finished, Epaminondas, or Ogum, picked up the fallen chair and took his post. One by one he talked to the people who sat before him, hearing their pleas, whispering in their ears things that Cloé could only guess were *simpatias*—formulas to win a battle, conquer an enemy, a soccer match. He moved his hands emphatically, pointed to the ceiling, stomped his feet, and when he finished giving all his advice, Ogum danced once more, said farewell, and left the novice, who sank into the chair like an empty sack.

Mãe Joana asked Epaminondas how he felt. Despite his pallor and weakened voice, he said that he felt well. Mãe Joana returned to her position in the circle and said, "Now, let us summon Iemanjá." The same pale girl brought out a bowl filled with a clear liquid, and handed it to the mother-of-saints. She released the water over Epaminondas's feet, and from the deep pockets of her dress, scattered white and blue flower petals around him. The *atabaques* started once again, and soon a melancholy wail issued from the lips of Epaminondas, a song that resembled the long, sad cry of a seagull. His hands undulated forward and upward, dispersing drops of water from his fingers.

"Welcome, mother-of-the-seas," said Mãe Joana with a curtsey. The man smiled beatifically and asked, in an almost feminine tone, "Which of my dear sons and daughters needs me today?"

Five people, the young man on Cloé's right among them, stepped inside the circle. Cloé peeked and saw that the picture he carried was of a woman, and she guessed that the nature of his plea, and of the other four who formed a line in front of her, each carrying an item—a shirt, a necklace, a braid of hair—was love. The goddess advised each supplicant in turn, gently addressing their troubles of the heart.

Only one person remained for Iemanjá to counsel, when suddenly a livid shriek escaped Epaminondas, who collapsed to the floor and writhed as if in deep pain. Mãe Joana stood nervously. "Who's there?"

"Shut up, you fucking bitch," he rumbled in dissonant speech. A ripple of consternation passed through the group. The drums faltered and ceased.

"Exú! This is my house, and you are not welcome here. Leave now!" she commanded, standing before him imperiously. He looked up, eyes baleful, his face contorted. Then he rose deliberately, with coiled menace.

"Stay out of this, Joana. I come to claim what's mine."

For the first time that night Cloé was afraid, her back glued to the chair.

"And what is that?" Mãe Joana asked him.

Exú did not bother to answer; he looked over at the petrified girl and grinned wickedly. Cloé remembered Ceça's advice, "Don't look into anyone's eyes," but now it was too late. She wanted to scream, to flee, but instead she could only passively witness her body rising from its seat and calmly walking over to the roaring man, gigantic now, who grabbed her by the shoulders and rent her shirt—no, not a shirt, a white dress that reached her ankles. The room twisted around her. What remained of Cloé escaped altogether, and the last thing she saw before losing consciousness were his fiery yellow eyes; his green, grotesque feet; and inside her head, a familiar voice that said, "Hulk come long way for you."

After Jeremy left and the divorce was finalized, Cloé fell into an inconsolable state of grief, which her mother quickly diagnosed as depression. Due to excessive absences and a steady decrease in production, she lost her job at Ferminisch, where she had recently been promoted to the post of senior perfumist, and moved into a smaller apartment in one of the oldest districts of Miami, a servant's quarter behind a large pink house inhabited during the winter by a quiet Canadian couple. Vanessa, in the throes of her third marriage, offered the extra room in her house, but Cloé politely declined. She didn't want to hear sermons about therapy: "The only way," her mother would say, "of resolving your father issues," for it was her firm and vocal belief that the absence of a father in Cloé's life lay at the root of the young woman's problems. Cloé knew she had inner conflicts, but found the idea of divulging her adulterous misadventures to a stranger, even a so-called professional, mortifying. So she stopped returning her mother's (whom she now addressed simply as Viví) incessant calls.

She ate little and slept much. She took refuge in her dreams, where the sun shone in all its warmth over the dusty streets of her Brazilian childhood—a time upon which she dwelled continuously, coloring it with a bittersweet nostalgia. Her somber state lasted the entire summer and fall, until her savings ran out and she had to find work.

She took the first job offered. Florida Travel Network, a travel agency with questionable marketing ethics, but in need of Portuguese and Spanish speakers. She spent eight hours of her weekdays fielding phone calls from angry South American customers whose vacations had been spoiled by a smelly hotel room, a hidden tax, a nonexistent car rental office, a steam room without steam, a pool without water, too much sun, too much rain, too much pollution, too much poverty: "If I wanted to see homeless people, I wouldn't have traveled half the world, I'd just step outside my door. You guys promised a luxurious, deluxe trip, it says right here in your certificate, Have-the-Time-of-Your-Life-in-Commodities-Fit-for-a-King. This is false advertisement; the hotel was a dump, there were *mujeres libres*, yes, *prostitutas* and God-knew-what-else in those rooms. Imagine! I even saw a cockroach under the bed, *una cu-ca-ra-cha!* I'm calling the *Betta Beehness Byooro* right now, *hony*. Oh yes, you thought I was just another ignorant Boricua, but I know my rights. I'm getting my money back!"

At lunchtime she would sit in her car and, once certain of her privacy, would cry, sobs of regret and self-loathing.

That was how she met Damaris, a kindly Dominican coworker whom Cloé saw every day, but whom she had only addressed with the occasional "Hello, how are you?" The woman knocked on the car window, startling Cloé, and asked to come in. Cloé opened the passenger door, embarrassed that a stranger had witnessed her tears, mumbled that she was all right, "Menstrual cramps, you see," but Damaris insisted.

"I see you crying here every day," she said.

Cloé could say nothing, could only stare at this woman who somehow reminded her of her beloved Maria José.

"You're too young to be carrying so much sadness around," Damaris said in her heavily accented English.

"I'm not as young as you think."

Damaris sat beside her and shut the door. "Tell me about it, *querida*."

And perhaps because she hadn't spoken to anyone in a long time, something yielded within Cloé. Amid a fresh flood of tears, she gave Damaris a brief but complete summary of everything that had transpired during the last four years of her life. Damaris listened with soft eyes, clutching Cloé's hands, drying her face with a handkerchief, and whispering, "Don't worry, *joven. Todo pasará.*"

"How do you know?" Cloé asked.

Damaris sighed and adopted a serious tone. "Because Jesus," she pointed her finger upward, "doesn't give us any more than we can bear. *He* sent me here, you know."

"Oh . . . I'm, I'm sorry. I'm not interested in that just now," she replied.

"That's fine, *joven*, fine. But here, read this." She handed Cloé a thin pamphlet. "And when you feel your heart is ready, know that He is waiting for you."

That night, and for the next three nights, Cloé had a dream. In this dream a dusky man with dark eyes, a long white beard, and a white turban appeared at the end of her bed. A black mole adorned his left cheek, and his expression overflowed with something she could only interpret as infinite tenderness. He would smile, bend forward, and kiss her feet. When she told this to Damaris, the woman widened her eyes and said, "*Ay, Dios mio, és Jesus!*"

"Jesus? I don't know, Damaris. He didn't look like the Jesus I'm familiar with. From Catholic school, you know? This one was way more—what's the word—"

"*Pero mi hija*," she said, clutching Cloé's arm, "that's the *Jesus Católico*! Our Jesus, *el Jesus Pentecostal*, he's different, you see. More personal. He can appear in many ways; he comes in dreams all the time. He sent you a sign! Now you must accept him. He will remove all your hurt, my child."

Goaded by Damaris's pleas, Cloé attended the following Sunday's service. She returned the next week, and the week after that, until slowly it seemed that the dark void in her heart was being filled. At exactly the twelfth hour of her fourth Sunday in the Iglesia Pentecostal de La Santa Resurección, during a passionate sermon about the three servants and their talents, while the man beside her loaned his body to the Holy Spirit and spoke in garbled tongues, Cloé rose from her bench, walked to the front of the congregation, and with the pastor's permission, took the microphone from his hands and proclaimed, for all to hear, in her Spanish laced with Portuguese, that she was ready to accept Jesus Christ into her heart, to renounce the devil, and to lead a life of service and goodness in the name of the Lord. As the pastor and his deacons laid their hands on her head, and the whole church clamored with joy that a new lamb had joined their flock, Cloé murmured to herself: "And please, most importantly, Lord, deliver me from the influence of Maria Padilha."

The first time she had heard that name was in Mãe Joana's house, on the night she could never exorcise from her daily thoughts, when that wanton spirit took control of her body, grinding her hips against Epaminondas like a drunk *mulata* in plain Carnaval, shrieking, howling insults, laughing crudely, demanding expensive drinks and imported cigarettes, increasingly debauched, until several strong men forcibly pried them apart to prevent them from copulating, or, as Mãe Joana put it, "to preserve your virginity, my girl." She recounted all of it when Cloé regained consciousness, sitting up on the edge of the woman's bed, frightened, still drenched in sweat, looking around the dim bedroom.

"I did what?" she asked, a sudden cramp knotting her stomach. A swirling confusion of images from the ceremony returned to her like disjointed fragments from a film she had watched long ago. Mãe Joana repeated the entire story, her voice trembling as if she herself could hardly believe what she said, but Cloé could barely hear anything over the pounding of her blood inside her temples. She gazed down at the too-small dress she wore, and then, from the pile of clothes beside the bed, lifted, with two fingers, a ripped, wet shirt that smelled of alcohol, the shirt she had been wearing at the beginning of the night. She tried to stand but her legs failed. She touched her knees and felt the tender, scraped skin. Mãe Joana, sensing the young girl's terror, said, "I'm sorry, this was my fault, I should have known; my shells warned me and I didn't pay heed."

"I don't understand," Cloé muttered, and out of pure nervous exhaustion, she began to sob. Mãe Joana hugged her, as much to be comforted as to comfort, and after the tears subsided, she asked Cloé what she remembered last, so that she could recount all that had happened once again. Cloé told her about the Hulk, his green feet, his yellow eyes.

"*Hulk?*" Mãe Joana laughed, and quickly added in a bitter tone: "No, my dear, that's how your young mind interpreted what it couldn't fathom, but it was Exú. Of that I'm certain."

She explained who Exú was, how he lights up the night and darkens the day; "God and devil who can save or kill," she said, "sometimes both at once." She told her of his three wives and of Maria Padilha, his favorite, the most whorish of *pomba giras*, with whom Exú loved to roll in the bonfires. "Apparently . . . " she began, stroking Cloé's arm lovingly, but then, as if she had reconsidered what she was about to say, Mãe Joana fell silent, and looked out the window.

"No, you don't have to spare me. Please, tell me everything, Mãe."

"Oh, my poor girl . . . but you're so young."

"I have the right to know. If this thing lives inside me, I have to know who, what it is."

The woman sighed wearily. "Yes, you're right. You're wise beyond your years, Cloé. That's why Maria Padilha chose you. Strange, though..."

"What?"

"She usually only manifests through women, street-smart women who make a living by selling their bodies for small change, but—"

"You mean whores?" she asked, widening her eyes.

"Yes, exactly."

Cloé rubbed her cheek as if the word brought back the sting of her mother's hand on her face. She wanted to retrace her steps back to that afternoon; instead of attending Mãe Joana's, she would have made a different decision, read a book, visited a friend, watched the news with her aunt Nelza. She had no idea how she could return to her life, to her usual gestures and thoughts, seeing what she had seen, knowing what she now knew.

"Cloé!" Mãe Joana was shaking her thigh. "Are you listening?"

But as she continued speaking, of past lives—of the possibility that maybe Maria Padilha was a remnant of a previous incarnation—Cloé thought of Hulk and the woman in the white dress, of the twisted fantasies she had enjoyed as a child, of the nuns, her grandmother, of the fever she felt when she kissed a boy; and every thought brought new pain, lacerating her insides as it passed through. Suddenly it dawned on her that her aunt did not know her whereabouts, that buses were scarce at this hour. She interrupted Mãe Joana and asked about the time, and without waiting for an answer, asked if she had seen a thin leather band she had been wearing on her arm. "It was given to me by Ceça—"

"Cloé, listen," she ordered.

"—to protect me from bad spirits."

"I'll call you a cab in a minute. But please, this is important. If you are to remember anything of what happened here, let it be what I'm about to tell you." She urged the girl to sit still, holding her hands. "This is a man's world, my girl. They run the nations and the corporations—but in their shadows, almost always stands a strong woman. Having a *pomba gira* with you, even if that one is Maria Padilha, isn't necessarily bad. It will all depend on you." She squeezed Cloé's hands, demanding her attention. "If you learn how to control her, she can give you power, strength, and you can have anything you want in this world. Anything. But, if you let her control you—" she let go of the girl's hands, walked to the window, and continued, looking out at the moon, "—she'll use your body, turn you into the biggest harlot the world has ever seen, looking for Exú in every man, drinking, smoking, until you're run down, wasted, incapable of constructing anything for yourself." Outside it started to rain.

On the ride home Cloé was in such a state of disorientation that for several panicky minutes every street looked the same, and she nearly led the cabby astray. Her head hurt, but the ache was nothing compared to the tumult inside her. She asked him the time, and he answered, "One thirty-five." She felt relieved, it was ear-

lier than she had thought; lately she had come home quite fre-
quently at this hour, from a movie or a party, and besides, her aunt
was probably asleep in front of the television. She remained silent
despite the driver's attempts at conversation, thinking about what
she would do from now on, how she would carry this night with
her. Amazing, she thought, how a few hours can change a person
forever.

By the time she arrived at the gate to her aunt's house, Cloé
had decided she would never reveal her experience to anyone.
Instead she would apply herself to the study of *candomblé* and its
gods, approach it like a science, discover the rules of the system,
devise an experiment to excise this aberration that lurked within
her.

For the next six months she dedicated all her free time to
extensive research. Her mother's calls diminished to once every
two weeks, and her letters grew scarcer than ever, but Cloé didn't
complain. More than a year had passed since her mother's departure. She was warming up to her aunt. She appreciated Nelza's
silence, her discretion, her deference to Cloé, almost as an adult,
seldom prying into her whereabouts, her eating habits, her choice
of clothes or friends. It was during this time that she first got
drunk, experimented with mushrooms, marijuana, and lost her
virginity to a Polish boy she met at a reggae concert.

In the middle of Christmas dinner her mother called,
announcing her marriage to an American pilot. She had decided
to live in the United States, Miami, and would be sending for Cloé
at the end of the next month. That night, sharing the bed with
her aunt—the summer had grown unbearably hot, and her aunt's
room was the only one with an air conditioner—Cloé buried her
face in the pillow and cried. And in her misery she had the
impression that Nelza, lying beside her, the lights in her room
always on to dispel her late husband's ghost, cried too.

By the age of twenty-eight, Cloé was done with tears.

Now she only had eyes, or rather, heart, for one man. His name was Jesus. With a new convert's zeal Cloé plunged into the deep end of La Iglesia Pentecostal. She followed the strict dress code for women: no pants; no skirts above the knee; no immodest shirts, shoes, jewelry, or makeup. She threw away her television, the devil's box, and all her worldly music; several crates' worth of samba, bossa nova, jazz, funk, rock, anything that was danceable and did not speak of Jesus. These she replaced with recordings of *coritos*—simple, upbeat sing-alongs that praised Our Lord. She learned the lyrics both in English and Spanish, she attended church on Sundays, Prayer Meeting on Tuesday nights, Youth Service on Wednesday nights, Women's Service on Thursday nights, Singles' Service on Friday nights, Revival on Saturday mornings, and on Monday nights she read passages from the Bible in bed.

She became an active witness, bringing new sheep into the flock. On Saturday afternoons, along with her brothers and sisters in Jesus, Cloé pounded the pavements of South Beach, North Beach, Liberty City, Hialeah, any place frequented by souls in need of salvation, handing out tracts: *Beat the Devil Right Out of Your Life, Smoking or Nonsmoking, Which Would You Prefer in the Afterlife? Five Ways to Recognize Satan,* and the most popular one, *Seven Reasons Why You Should Accept Jesus Now.* On Sundays, before the night service, she studied for baptism, since her childhood baptism in the Catholic Church was not recognized by the Pentecostal faith. This was her favorite class, where she could ask all the questions that kept her awake at night, questions about God's plan for mankind, contradictory biblical passages, about heaven, and, particularly, about hell. The teacher, Brother Milton, always quick to address her questions, impressed her with his deep knowledge of the Good Book, even staying with her for a few minutes after each session to ensure that her unending queries were fully answered. But they never were, the time was never enough, and so he offered to meet with her on Monday afternoons at the public library.

On their first meeting he surprised her with a small, white leather-bound Bible, its edges gilded, the words of Jesus highlighted in red. "A baptismal gift for my favorite student," he said. She immediately recognized the cologne he was wearing, Eau Sauvage, a sweet florid scent with a hint of musk. He had never worn it to church. She tried to refuse the expensive gift, but he insisted. They talked until the library closed, but it was not until their third meeting that the conversation shifted a bit and they exchanged a modicum of information about their personal lives: She learned that his parents were Cuban but that he had grown up in Puerto Rico, that he was a network analyst, that his mother had died the previous year, that he had never been married, and that in four months he would turn forty-two. She in turn told him about Jeremy and her divorce.

"The Lord works in mysterious ways," he said. "Maybe you wouldn't have been saved had you still been married."

Soon after that, their meetings began taking place not only on Monday afternoons at the library, but on Saturday evenings at La Teresita, a tiny Cuban café. From there they started meeting whenever they could, stealing time from their busy secular and ecclesiastic schedules. They agreed to skip a Wednesday Youth Service and meet at her apartment, with the intention of studying the story of Nicodemus, in the third chapter of the book of John. She had recently been baptized, but her questions hadn't subsided.

She cooked him a Bahian delicacy, shrimp *bobó*, since his birthday fell on the next day, and with each bite he repeated how his mouth had never experienced an explosion of taste such as this. After the meal they sat side by side on the sofa, where she read: "There was a man of the Pharisees . . ." She couldn't help noticing, out of the corner of her eyes, that Brother Milton seemed distracted, fidgeting impatiently, crossing and uncrossing his legs, tapping his fingers on his knees. She had just finished the passage that read, "and as Moses lifted up the serpent in the wilderness, even so must the Son of man be lifted up," when Brother Milton pulled out a ring from the pocket of his pants, knelt before her, and asked Cloé if she would do him the honor of being his wife.

"But . . . but Brother Milton, I . . . you barely know me, and . . . are you sure?"

"Forty-two years, Cloé, and I have never been so sure about a woman as I am now. I'll give you time, if that's what you need. But your yes would be the greatest birthday gift of my entire life."

She mulled it over for two weeks. Her suitor was the polar opposite of Jeremy, who had been three years younger than she, a handsome, artistic Libra with a full head of luxurious hair, a muscular build, and a deep, sexy voice. Brother Milton, on the other hand, was twelve years her senior, a stoop-shouldered, balding Capricorn, his voice nasal, his hands feminine, his lips thin. She found him physically unattractive. He was pragmatic, analytical, conservative, without her previous lovers' dark abandon and recklessness. It was precisely for these reasons that Cloé decided to accept his proposal.

They were united in holy matrimony with the full and solemn blessing of the Pentecostal Church. Immediately after the small ceremony, the newlyweds flew to Puerto Rico so she could meet her new father-in-law, who, due to poor health, had not attended the wedding. For one week they slept in Brother Milton's childhood room. It took them three nights to engage in intimate caresses. "After all," she would whisper in his ear, pushing away his clumsy, probing hands, "there's no hurry, we have an entire life to learn each other." On the fourth night he succeeded in removing her clothes, and, finally, on the fifth night, silently so as not to awaken the old man in the bedroom next to theirs, she allowed Brother Milton to enter her, and thanks to Jesus, whom she focused on for the full five minutes it lasted, he fell asleep promptly after the deed was consummated. If it had lasted any longer, Cloé was afraid she would have fantasized Brother Milton as another, and had not Jesus said, on the Mount, "Whosoever looketh or thinketh of a woman to lust after her hath committed adultery with her already in his heart"? That surely applies to women too, she thought. Yes it does.

Back in Florida, the two moved out of their respective apartments into a modest house in the suburbs, and fell into domestic routine. On weekdays both got up at seven, he used the bathroom while she made breakfast, they sat at the kitchen table and ate, left separately for work, met at five in church, dined after service, slept, she on the right, he on the left, and on Friday and Saturday nights, Cloé fulfilled her conjugal duties, all the while looking at the picture of Jesus on the night table. They also had a routine for weekends, a little less strict, but regular nonetheless.

Cloé felt good about herself. Anyone could say she was an exemplary wife. Every day her tainted past slipped away a little more, until it only surfaced in scattered dreams that evaporated once she awoke.

One evening during prayer service, she had the God-given realization that her traumatic adolescent incident had simply been the product of a young, susceptible mind influenced by its fantastic and frightening surroundings. She'd fallen into what her mother would have called a hysterical fugue state, nothing more. Her tears of joy and relief splashed onto the pew as she thanked the Almighty for providing a clear-cut answer to her secret pain.

On occasion Brother Milton had to travel, setting up wireless networks in different states for companies that contracted him. He preferred not to leave, but the commissions were too generous to refuse. Sometimes a whole month's wages could be made in one weekend. Cloé encouraged him to go, stating that it would do him good to see other places, to get out of his routine. She would have liked to accompany him on some of those trips, but it was bad enough that one of them should miss so many services, and, since she wrote well in English, and they were among the few in the congregation who owned a computer, Cloé had accepted the job of building a Web site for the church.

The pastor allowed her to miss services in order to complete the project. "The favor you're granting the church is a great blessing in itself," he said; "now, through a medium that is, for the most part, *diabólico*, a vehicle of Lucifer, full of filth, vice, wickedness, full of *porrr-no-gra-fi-a*—his eyes rolled in their sockets, as they always did when he spoke of the devil—"Our Lord will spread his message all over the world, and everyone will know that we, my dear sister, exist in the name of Our Savior, that the Pentecostal Church is not only unthreatened by, but can take advantage of the most advanced technologies." He lowered his voice, stroked his long chin. "Now, make us look good. And whenever you're ready to put my picture in there, let me know, so Brother Francisco can take a recent one."

That weekend Brother Milton received an offer of a month's work in New York City. The pay, plus the bonus, would allow her to stop working and open the perfumery she once told him she would like to own.

"Oh, Milton, I was just daydreaming. . . . I'm happy with things as they are," she replied. However, at the mention of his one-month absence, Cloé felt a sudden fluttering, a rush of adrenaline.

I committed myself already." He hugged her, kissed her forehead. "You deserve it. I can tell you're tired of the travel agency."

That was true, she was burned out with busy telephone lines, whining customers, and the more she thought about his leaving, the more her heart beat with excitement, an enthusiasm inappropriate for Cloé the wife, Cloé the Christian. She told him to go ahead, to try to enjoy himself, not to worry about her. He promised to call every night at ten.

Once he left, Cloé would sit in front of the computer after arriving home from work and labor until the time came for his telephone call. After they hung up she would bathe, ready herself for bed, and attend to her nightly prayers. She missed all services that week, periodically calling the pastor to deliver progress reports on the web site. "I'm sorry for the delay, Pastor, I'm learning as I go." She did attend Sunday service, however. After almost one year of daily proximity, Cloé was surprised by how little she had thought of her husband during their first week apart.

By her third week alone, the project was not even halfway completed. She encountered more complications than ever, the programming language confounded her, and the manual she used no longer seemed to help. She realized that it would take a lot more work than she had estimated, and that the timetable she had given the pastor, one month, had been unrealistic; Cloé wondered whether she would finish it by Christmas, three months away. She was now torn by her sense of duty to the congregation and the frustration of not fulfilling the promised task. She inflated her progress reports, not knowing how to inform the pastor that he would have to wait longer than he thought to deliver his cybersermons to the world. The more obstacles she encountered, the more patience she lost. She could easily have consulted an outside expert, but it wasn't her nature to admit defeat.

She filled her time surfing the Internet, visiting other religious sites, furious every time a beautiful page, complete with animated images and music, unscrolled before her. She prayed for a miracle, for inspiration, for God to grant her a sudden knowledge of web design, asking him to use her body as those spirits had used

Alain Kardec's for the writing of books. Nothing happened, so she resigned herself to asking for courage. Courage to tell the pastor the truth. One night she lost her sense of time and missed her husband's call as she played and won all five games of chess on the Web, with someone who called himself Merantus. At the end of the last game, a message appeared at the bottom of the screen. It was obvious from its inverted syntax that the writer was not an English speaker, but she deciphered that she was the best opponent Merantus had ever played against, and that this person wanted to know her real name. At first she hesitated, but then thought, "What harm could it do?" and typed, complete with accent, "Cloé."

"Encantado, Cloé. Claudio. Chileno. You are Brasileira?"

"Yes. How did you know?"

"Is intuition . . . and the way you spell your name."

Here Cloé felt an urge to sign off, find a different opponent, but another question appeared at the bottom of her screen: "Where you live in Brazil?"

"I'm not in Brazil." And before he could ask, she added, "I'm in the United States."

"Are you near to Miami?" He quickly added, "Sorry I ask very much. And sorry about my English."

"It's OK. If you prefer, you can write in Spanish."

"No, I need practice. I will be in Miami for work, in few days. That is why I ask."

She felt a little ashamed at her evasiveness, and at the same time, ridiculous for the feeling—what did it matter how she treated this man? She confessed that she lived in Miami. The exchange continued, he divulging much and she divulging little, but gradually, she found herself enjoying their banter, and after another fifty lines or so, wrote to him as if he were an old friend. As he wrote, she conjured an imaginary, musical voice to accompany the words.

They talked of art: books, music, of Hermeto Pascoal, the Brazilian pianist whom he loved; she told him that she had met him personally, a long time ago, at a concert—of Pablo Neruda, her favorite poet, Chilean or otherwise; he told her that he dabbled in poetry himself, and asked if it would be an imposition on his part if he were to send her one of his poems.

They did not speak of Jesus.

Before she knew it, the living room grew light—morning had arrived. She would have to work eight hours after a nightlong vigil, but that didn't bother her. She said good-bye to her correspondent, and only then did he reveal that in six days he would star as a guest pianist with the Miami Philharmonic, that he would be staying at the Hotel Buena Vista, and that he would put her name on the guest list, adding that he would very much like to meet her—maybe she could show him the city, for this was his first visit, and maybe they could play a live game of chess. Only then did she reveal, reluctantly, that she was married.

"Well, bring your husband, too."

"He's out of town."

Now it was he who hesitated. "OK, Cloé. Just in case, I will put your name, right? Will you give me your last name?"

She thought for a moment, then gave him her maiden name rather than her married name.

Before signing off, he asked for her email address, so that he could send her the exact time and location of the concert. She complied.

> *Two lovers dove into each other's mouths*
> *and became fire*
> *in the night of their bodies.*
> *Everything was bathed red...*

She stopped reading, her eyes burning from no sleep, turned off the computer, walked to the bedroom, removed her work clothes, set some water to boil for tea, and sat with the Bible in her lap, praying for guidance. She shut her eyes and opened the book to the middle: "Honey and milk are under thy tongue . . ." She closed it, for the Song of Solomon was the last thing she'd had in mind, but when she reopened the book, the Song persisted: "And the roof of thy mouth, like the best wine . . . For my beloved, that goeth down sweetly, causing the lips of those who are asleep to break."

She put the book down, rebooted the computer, and read more of the message from Claudio Arriagada, entitled, simply, *Buenos Días, Poesía.*

> *. . .When morning entered the room,*
> *only one of them lay there, breathless, wet,*
> *smelling of opened flower . . .*

Once again she stopped—she did not like how the words made her breathe—and skipped to the end of the message. Like the poem, it was also written in Spanish:

> *I know it is light years from Neruda, but thank you for reading it.*
> *You will probably think it strange, I find it strange myself, but after our conversation last night, your name has been on my mind all day; I now feel like my trip would be a waste if I don't get to meet you. The concert is on September seventeenth, at The Rubalcaba Arts Center, eight o'clock. I will be in town until the twenty-first, at the Hotel Buena Vista. Your name will be on the guest list.*
> *Please come see me, Cloé. I would be very honored if you did.*
>
> *Con cariño, Alberto*

The message ended with a postscript:

How full of surprises life is, no?

What a tired old cliché, thought Cloé, unaware that the water she had put on the stove was already boiling.

She awoke with the music of the previous evening resonating in her mind. She spent more time than usual in the shower, meticulously washing her hair, shaving, dallying on parts that usually received perfunctory attention. She stepped out, anointed her neck with rose oil, plucked an abandoned silk dress from the back of her closet, a dusty book of poetry from a box in the garage, and, for the first time in her employment with Florida Travel Network, called in sick.

Cloé sat in the lobby of the Hotel Buena Vista and waited. Although she had only seen him from afar, and never, before or after the concert, made her presence known to him, she recognized the dark, angular man the moment he stepped out of the elevator. He saw her and froze in midstep, his face caught in an expression that wavered between uncertainty and familiarity. He approached her, and in a low, cautious voice—yes, identical to the one she had heard in her mind—uttered, "Cloé?"

She smiled.

"I can't explain how, but I knew you were there last night. I could feel you as I played." Like a gentleman from another age, he took her hand and raised it to his lips.

"Alberto, I'm sorry I didn't speak to you, but I was—"

"No need to explain. I'm just happy that you came, and that you are here now."

"The music . . . it was beautiful."

"Would you like to hear more?"

"I would love to."

"There's a piano in my suite. "

Once again she smiled, and said, "What about a chess set?"

"Of course, that too."

She arose, picked up her book, took his arm, and together they entered the elevator. Tomorrow Brother Milton would arrive, but today he did not exist.

As soon as her husband, exhausted from his long, tiring trip, began to snore, Cloé knelt by the bedside with the contrition of the damned. She considered self-flagellation, but only briefly, for the noise might awaken Brother Milton, who would demand to know what sin merited such punishment. She then remembered a story of her grandmother's, about her childhood in school, in which the nuns would scatter corn on the ground and order rowdy kids to kneel on the kernels until their knees bled. But Cloé had no corn in the house, only rice and beans, which probably wouldn't have the same effect. Besides, she wouldn't know what to say if her husband awoke in the middle of the night and saw her sweeping the consequent mess. Words were all she had to offer God. At this point Cloé knew that her words amounted to nothing.

She had neither the heart to beg forgiveness nor the nerve to promise she'd never do it again. She prayed only for punishment; "Please Jesus, please Jesus," she repeated silently, a mantra, "burn this weakness from my flesh." She thought of all the times she had asked him to manifest himself, all the times she'd lain down with his image in her mind, hoping that he would appear, even if in a dream, and all the times in church when she had offered herself to the Holy Spirit, waiting for it to dance and speak its angelic tongue through her. She opened her eyes and saw her husband lying on his back, his hands crossed upon his belly, his snores growing louder as his breathing grew more labored. She reached over and nudged him gently. He rolled to his side, the snoring subsided, and she returned to her prayer, trying to pick up her Ariadne's thread. But the words had vanished from her head; all that remained were images from the previous night. She had done it again, and now, she thought, anything could happen, a door had been opened; or, it had never been locked. She stood up, leaning against the bed. She stumbled as if she couldn't bear the weight her body. The room was dark, but she knew the exact position of things. She lay down, looked at the picture of Jesus beside her, and whispered, "I don't know how else to ask you, Jesus, but if I don't see you tonight . . ." She refrained from uttering the rest of the sentence, of confessing that her faith wavered, that if she didn't see him, then he might just as well not exist. She was powerless to suppress pornographic memories of last night's encounter; a snake in her holy garden moaning, biting, kissing, slithering between her legs, flicking its tongue into her ear, obscuring her vision of Jesus.

A flutter of wings startled her from prayer. She reached for the bedside lamp and, to her utter astonishment, saw that a white dove had entered the bedroom, despite the fact that the wall unit, running full throttle against the Miami heat, blocked most of the window. "The Holy Spirit!" she whispered in awe, only to doubt her judgment the very next second, when the bird began to whistle a simple three-note melody, a favorite of drunks and revelers everywhere in Brazil.

She turned off the lamp and hugged her husband, burying her face in the arc of his back, and shutting her eyes until she could no longer hear anything but his snores, which lulled her to sleep. The next day she dismissed the incident as the product of her desperation. But as the weeks passed she noticed the birds everywhere she looked, on park benches, in trees, on power lines. During prayer service, when the church got quiet, she could hear that little three-note melody insinuating itself. The meaning of the dove and its song did not come in a flash of understanding but rather blossomed into its meaning as clear as the red words of Jesus in her white Bible: carnality and virtue, flesh and spirit,

Maria and the Holy Spirit, a singular vessel that embodied two polar opposites in divine unity.

In December, the hottest month of the year, a woman stepped out onto the terminal of Bahia's main airport, Aeroporto Nacional de São Salvador, and instantly merged with the colors, smells, loud voices, and pulse of the place. Her path was marked by a wake of turning heads, craning necks, and avid looks.

At the luggage terminal, a shameless young man, after insisting that he retrieve her suitcase, wound up his courage and asked for her phone number. She rummaged through her purse, and his face lit up with joy. Handing him a slip of paper, she walked away, leaving him to stare in rapt fascination at the play of her buttocks beneath the thin fabric of her long white dress until she stepped out into the blinding sunlight and he could no longer see her. He examined his prize, turning it over and over, searching for the precious digits in increasing bewilderment; but the only digits he found were those cataloging the *Seven Reasons Why You Should Accept Jesus Now.*